D1116361

AN AREA OF DARKNESS

Complete & Unabridged

V. S. NAIPAUL

AN AREA OF DARKNESS

With an introduction by
PAUL THEROUX

MACMILLAN COLLECTOR'S LIBRARY

First published 1964 by André Deutsch

This edition first published by Macmillan Collector's Library 2020
an imprint of Pan Macmillan
The Smithson, 6 Briset Street, London EC1M 5NR
Associated companies throughout the world
www.panmacmillan.com

ISBN 978-1-5290-3210-9

1 3 5 7 9 8 6 4 2

A CIP catalogue record for this book is available from the British Library.

Casing design and endpaper pattern by Andrew Davidson
Typeset in Plantin by Jouve (UK), Milton Keynes
Printed and bound in China by Imago

INTRODUCTION

Naipaul's India

In a spirit of inquiry, V. S. Naipaul sailed in 1962 to India, a country he had never seen, but a place that had been on his mind since childhood. He was twenty-nine years old. His work was praised in England, but his great literary reputation was yet to be made. He spent a year in India and on his return, after a period of muddle ('overwhelmed by the distress I saw'), he wrote *An Area of Darkness* (1964). The book was acclaimed. He returned to India in 1975, in a period of national anxiety during the Emergency declared by the authoritarian government of Prime Minister Indira Gandhi. He travelled widely and wrote a series of essays on the situation he experienced, and these became *India: A Wounded Civilization* (1977). Fifteen years later he went back, with a particular strategy in mind, that in order to understand India better he would need to spend more time with individuals and know their stories in depth. The result was *India: A Million Mutinies Now* (1990), more ambitious than his first two books, both in the complexity of its themes and the ways in which he tackled them, through portraiture and an extensive series of encounters, lengthy interviews that might better be described as interrogations.

That last book contains one of Naipaul's wisest observations: 'I believe that the present, accurately seized, foretells the future.'

Three books, one thousand pages of text, written over thirty years, a work that could be described as *India: A Chronicle*. But still he was not done. He travelled a number of times to India after that, always inquisitive, often writing, sometimes speaking, now an honoured and garlanded guest rather than an anonymous traveller. His last visit in January 2015 was to Rajasthan to speak at the Jaipur Literary Festival. He was then eighty-two, in a wheelchair because of ill-health, but the wheelchair propelled by his wife Nadira was less like a medical expedient than a portable throne. In his public presentations Naipaul was funny, friendly, benign, reflective – hardly the fierce young man of a half-century earlier who reported in *An Area of Darkness* on the times he'd lost his temper, or denounced 'the fat, impertinent Anglo-Indian girl and the rat-faced Anglo-Indian manager' at his Bombay hotel – a litany of his exasperations. People said he was much mellower.

Then, after one of his talks, a woman in the Jaipur audience hectored him in an aggrieved tone, asking him why he did not regard India as a singular place of piety, its problems of poverty and social justice receiving insufficient sympathy from the wider world. There came a flash of the old Naipaul, bristling in his chair: 'What makes you think' – and he rose slightly from his seat in temper – 'what makes you think India deserves more compassion than other countries?'

Later that same week, being driven to Amber Fort, Naipaul looked out the side window as the car was delayed in traffic at a crowded intersection. I was beside him, our friendship had been restored a few years ear-r. A small boy, no more than four or five, was seated triangular section of broken pavement between two busy roads. The boy was neatly dressed, in a shirt and shorts, cross-legged on a folded square of cloth, at risk amid the confusion of traffic and pedestrians, sadhus, box-wallahs, beggars, hawkers with baskets on their head, school children, bus fumes, pushcarts, and motorbikes and honking horns. The child was animated by the scene, yet he was alone – no adult near him, no one attending to him. Very odd, symbolic and unlikely.

Naipaul stared sadly at him and the scene for a long moment, and as our car began to move on he said to me, 'I see myself in that child.'

★

He had been raised in a traditional Indian household in Trinidad. He wrote, 'I had no belief; I disliked religious ritual; and I had a sense of the ridiculous. I refused to go through the *janaywa*, or thread ceremony ... A pleasing piece of theatre. But I knew we were in Trinidad, an island separated by only ten miles from the South American coast'.

Still, he has stayed true to the world he knows. Indians have populated nearly all his fiction – his heroes, his central characters, from Pundit Ganesh in his earliest novel, through Mr Biswas and the mimic man Ralph Singh, and Salim in *A Bend in the River*, to Willie Chandran of his last two novels, *Half a Life* and *Magic Seeds*. But India remained a mystery. He explains in *An Area of Darkness* that 'The India ... which was the background to my childhood was an area of the imagination' – stimulated by books, films, conjecture, and religious rituals. 'I was without belief or interest in belief; I was incapable of worship, of God or holy men; and so one whole side of India was closed to me.'

Later, in *India: A Wounded Civilization*, he wrote: 'India, which I visited for the first time in 1962, turned out to be a very strange land', adding: 'India is for me a difficult country. It isn't my home and cannot be my home; and yet I cannot reject it or be indifferent to it; I cannot travel only for the sights ... It has taken me much time to come to terms with the strangeness of India'.

Deepening his intention, he speaks of his sense of alienation and 'neurosis' on his previous journeys and wrote in *India: A Million Mutinies Now*, that in order to fulfil himself as a writer, to understand the currents of history and his place in the world, he had to create a new way of seeing, and, 'In the practising of this new way I had to deal first of all with my ancestral land, India. I was not an insider, even after many months of travel; nor could I consider myself an outsider: India and the idea of India had always been important to me. So I was always divided about India, and found it hard to say a final word.'

'Travel in itself for a book about a journey doesn't interest me,' he told me once, long ago. 'My intention has always been to travel with a theme in mind.' Naipaul says the three books are non-fiction 'but they are as personal and varied and deeply felt as any work of fiction could be'.

You could say that India has been Naipaul's obsessive, almost life-long subject, a way of evaluating the world, a way of understanding his origins; and it is clear from his first experiences that India is maddening. Many would admit that it would take at least a lifetime to understand India. Naipaul persisted, and this per-s accounts for the fact that though the books are nt in form, and in structure, and set years apart, they overlap in subject matter, always going deeper, distrusting appearances. Naipaul notices the physical world, the stinks, the sewers, the slums, but nowhere in these books are the mock ordeals of the conventional travel books; mentions of meals and hotels are made in passing, and there is no sightseeing, no account of ruins or temples unless they are related to his argument. The dinner parties are often occasions for combat. A thousand pages about India with no mention of the Taj Mahal, tiger hunts, or chicken biryani.

The Harijans ('Children of God') – or untouchables – figure, though, and so do the Naxalite rebels, the paradoxes of the caste system and the conflicts in Indian marriages. The long shadow of Indian history with the legacies of empire is a theme throughout, Gandhi a recurring personage, the failures of government, urban life and architecture, the disclosures in Indian novels, the notion of cleanliness, the implications of ruins, the imperatives of Hinduism (but without any recitation of the attributes of gods or goddesses), the plight of the poor, the oppression of poverty, the intrusions of outsiders, Indian vision and the Indian sense of self.

Naipaul said that his difficulty in writing *An Area of Darkness* was that he had been bewildered or enraged by much of what he saw on his first experience of India. He was not a prodigal son but a foreigner, who looked Indian ('one of the crowd') but who did not speak the language or have the support of any local relatives. He was on his own, with limited resources, staying in the more modest hotels and as a paying guest with Indian families (Mrs Mahindra's stands out, with her chant that she is 'craze, just craze for foreign'). Intent on making the most of his year, he spent a good part of the time in a small hotel in Srinagar, writing his London novel, *Mr Stone and the Knights Companion*. He says he did not keep a diary, and had only scraps of notes.

But his memory served him – and it is important to point out that none of the thousand pages of this India trilogy were written with the aid of a tape-recorder. Naipaul has maintained that, in all his non-fiction, he practised the mental discipline of remembering in detail what someone had said to him. He has also said that, wishing to verify what someone told him, he might revisit the person and ask him or her to repeat the story.

An Area of Darkness is closer to what we think of as a traditional travel book, although unlike most others it is personal and passionate. The traveller arrives, is bewildered, battles bureaucracy, begins to make finer distinctions, discovers contradictions and the repetition of certain national habits, compares appearance with reality, and is subjected to a certain amount of harassing detail, and at last finds an oasis of peace in which to work (the hotel in Srinagar). In the end, he makes a sentimental visit to the village of his ancestors – and is appalled, and sums up his experience. In the beginning, India was a darkness. For a period of his travel he felt the shadows lift. And then with his departure the darkness closes in again.

What makes this book unusual (and this is true of the two which follow) is the unsparing eye of the traveller, the originality of his thought, the vividness of his physical description – of people and places; and the vitality of the dialogue. Naipaul is first a novelist, and he brings to his non-fiction a power to recreate a person's physical presence, a manner of speech, or the look of a landscape. Indians generally were upset by the book when it appeared.

Naipaul had expected this, because one of its repeated themes was that Indians had lived so long with contradictions and received wisdom that they had lost the ability to see things as they are.

'Indians defecate everywhere. They defecate, mostly, beside the railway tracks. But they also defecate on the beaches; they defecate on the hills; they defecate on the river banks; they defecate on the streets; they never look for cover.'

These three sentences, with their Churchillian rhythms, drove Indian reviewers mad. And there is more, a whole closely printed page, in which Naipaul offers the quaint image of 'These squatting figures – to the visitor, as eternal and emblematic as Rodin's Thinker', and he makes his point: they are never spoken of, written about, or mentioned, because he says with the emphasis of italics *'Indians do not see these squatters.'*

Naipaul uses this as an example of a fundamental Indian deficiency, the inability or unwillingness to see things as they are. 'There is little subtlety to India. The poor are thin; the rich are fat.' Naipaul's India of 1962 was moribund, characterized by decay and dereliction, and the confinement of the caste system. 'Class is a system of rewards. Caste imprisons a man in his function.' There is a sweeper caste, but sweepers are not required to clean, only to *be* sweepers. In a powerful paragraph that begins 'Study these four men washing down the steps of this unpalatable Bombay hotel', Naipaul presents the reader with a ritualized instance of caste.

Gandhi 'saw India so clearly because he was in part a colonial', returning to India having spent twenty years in South Africa. And the implication is that Naipaul himself, with his colonial childhood, brought this clear-sightedness to India and to his book, which is much more than a condemnation of Indian faults. It is a series of discoveries and examinations, but here the traveller is on the move in a spirited way – confronting obstinacy or fraudulence, weighing Indian explanations. There is more landscape in this book than the others, and (though it ends in futility) Naipaul recounts the bittersweet experience of a pilgrimage he took. Naipaul is physically more present and opinionated in this book than in any other – losing his temper, arguing, being happy and humorous, as well as exhausted and dispirited. In the end, he sees that it is no homecoming; he has no place in this static and self-deluded country. You assume he won't go back. But new events, and dramatic changes, brought him again to India years later to re-examine the 'difficult country', and to reassess his memories.

Paul Theroux
2016

PREFACE

The travel for *An Area of Darkness* followed immediately on the writing of *The Middle Passage*. I was living at the time, very happily, in South London, and the complicated arrangements for the travel out to India – by train and by ship – were made by the Streatham branch of a travel agency. The dates were not easy to rearrange, and I hurried through *The Middle Passage* not to lose the bookings for the later book. The idea of doing a book like *An Area of Darkness* had come to me during the writing of *A House for Mr Biswas*. That was a two-year labour, and at that period when things moved more slowly for me it began to seem that I had been engaged for too long in fiction. The idea of the other form, non-fiction, began to seem like a liberation, and I arranged with André Deutsch to do a book on India – although at this time I had done very little non-fiction and couldn't be said to know my way around the special difficulties of the form.

At last I was ready to go. I remember a winter journey across France by rail and I remember the achingly romantic sight of a big white horse ploughing. The rest of that journey to India is recorded in these pages. I had tried before leaving England to place a piece or two with an English paper. I had no success; I had no reputation. I remember only a letter from a newspaper telling me that India was 'inexhaustible', and that they would be happy in due course to see what I could come up with.

India was inexhaustible perhaps, but my India was not like an English or British India. My India was full of pain. Sixty years or so before, my ancestors had made the very long journey to the Caribbean from India, six weeks at least, and though this was hardly spoken about when I was a child, it worried me more and more as I got older. So, writer though I was, I wasn't travelling to Forster's India or Kipling's. I was travelling to an India which existed only in my head. The India I found in those early days was sad and simple and repetitive, too repetitive for a book, and I began to feel that André Deutsch wasn't going to get his book. I was saved by the deeper anxiety that had been with me throughout the journey to India. This anxiety was that after *A House for Mr Biswas* I had run out of fictional material and that life was going to be very hard for me in the future; perhaps the writing career would have to stop. This anxiety took various forms, some mental, some physical, some a combination of the two. The most debilitating anxiety was that I was losing the gift of speech. It was at the back of everything I did, at the back of everything that is recorded in the early pages of *An Area of Darkness*. India was physically like a blow. I exaggerated the heat, the squalor, everything that might make me unhappy. I wondered how I was going to last the year which I had thought of spending in the country. And all the time, as I have said, was the pressing need to get started on a novel – not that I had a subject, but merely to do something to reassure myself that I still had a career.

I went to Kashmir. I found a rough but friendly hotel ⟨on⟩ the Dal Lake in Srinagar. It was cooler; I could think ⟨more⟩ rationally; the reader of these pages will find out ⟨how I⟩ changed my life there. And then I had some luck.

An idea for a novel came to me and for three months I settled down to write that novel. That bit of work was a blessing. It gave me a point of rest; it enabled the life of India to flow slowly around me, giving me material for an Indian narrative, which developed even as the matter in my typewriter grew. Without that piece of work, that point of rest, I would not have been able to last in India; I would have been too unhappy; I might even have had to go back to England – a failure in every way. And it is strange to recall that it was that small fiction, that little piece of luck, which made the rest of my time in India possible, and led to the fruitfulness and growth of the next two or three years.

After that piece of good fortune *An Area of Darkness* wrote itself. I could be as flexible as I wished. I could go back to the beginnings of the journey itself or into my own family story. The travel I did after Kashmir was like a filling in, and an addition to a country already half known. I could deal with the large or the small; everything could be made to fit; it was a dazzling experience; and though a new fiction didn't come easily afterwards, yet the memory of this writing ease stayed with me, gave a measure of possible things, and made later essays or projects manageable.

An idea for a novel came to me and for three months I settled down to write that novel. That bit of work was a blessing. It gave me a point of rest; it enabled the life of India to flow slowly around me, giving me material for an Indian narrative, which developed even as the matter in my typewriter grew. Without that piece of work, that point of rest, I would not have been able to last in India; I would have been too unhappy; I might even have had to go back to England – a failure in every way. And it is strange to recall that it was that small fiction, that little piece of luck, which made the rest of my time in India possible, and led to the fruitfulness and growth of the next two or three years.

After that piece of good fortune *An Area of Darkness* wrote itself. I could be as flexible as I wished. I could go back to the beginnings of the journey itself or into my own family story. The travel I did after Kashmir was like a filling in, and an addition to a country already half known. I could deal with the large or the small; everything could be made to fit; it was a dazzling experience; and though a new fiction didn't come easily afterwards, yet the memory of this writing ease stayed with me, gave a measure of possible things, and made later essays or projects manageable.

AN AREA OF DARKNESS

To Francis Wyndham

Contents

Contents

TRAVELLER'S PRELUDE:
A LITTLE PAPERWORK

As soon as our quarantine flag came down and the last of the barefooted, blue-uniformed policemen of the Bombay Port Health Authority had left the ship, Coelho the Goan came aboard and, luring me with a long beckoning finger into the saloon, whispered, 'You have any cheej?'

Coelho had been sent by the travel agency to help me through the customs. He was tall and thin and shabby and nervous, and I imagined he was speaking of some type of contraband. He was. He required cheese. It was a delicacy in India. Imports were restricted, and the Indians had not yet learned how to make cheese, just as they had not yet learned how to bleach newsprint. But I couldn't help Coelho. The cheese on this Greek freighter was not good. Throughout the three-week journey from Alexandria I had been complaining about it to the impassive chief steward, and I didn't feel I could ask him now for some to take ashore.

'All right, all right,' Coelho said, not believing me and not willing to waste time listening to excuses. He left the saloon and began prowling light-footedly down a corridor, assessing the names above doors.

I went down to my cabin. I opened a new bottle of Scotch and took a sip. Then I opened a bottle of Metaxas and took a sip of that. These were the two

I

bottles of spirits I was hoping to take into prohibition-dry Bombay, and this was the precaution my friend in the Indian Tourist Department had advised: full bottles would be confiscated.

Coelho and I met later in the dining-room. He had lost a little of his nervousness. He was carrying a very large Greek doll, its folk costume gaudy against his own shabby trousers and shirt, its rosy cheeks and unblinking blue eyes serene beside the restless melancholy of his long thin face. He saw my opened bottles and nervousness returned to him.

'Open. But why?'

'Isn't that the law?'

'Hide them.'

'The Metaxas is too tall to hide.'

'Put it flat.'

'I don't trust the cork. But don't they allow you to take in two bottles?'

'I don't know, I don't know. Just hold this dolly for me. Carry it in your hand. Say souvenir. You have your Tourist Introduction Card? Good. Very valuable document. With a document like that they wouldn't search you. Why don't you hide the bottles?'

He clapped his hands and at once a barefooted man, stunted and bony, appeared and began to take our suitcases away. He had been waiting, unseen, unheard, ever since Coelho came aboard. Carrying only the doll and the bag containing the bottles, we climbed down into the launch. Coelho's man stowed away the suitcases. Then he squatted on the floor, as though to squeeze himself into the smallest possible space, as though to apologize for his presence, even at the exposed stern, in the launch in which his master was travelling. The master, only occasionally glancing at the doll in my lap, stared ahead, his face full of foreboding.

For me the East had begun weeks before. Even in Greece I had felt Europe falling away. There was the East in the food, the emphasis on sweets, some of which I knew from my childhood; in the posters for Indian films with the actress Nargis, a favourite, I was told, of Greek audiences; in the instantaneous friendships, the invitations to meals and homes. Greece was a preparation for Egypt: Alexandria at sunset, a wide shining arc in the winter sea; beyond the breakwaters, a glimpse through fine rain of the ex-king's white yacht; the ship's engine cut off; then abruptly, as at a signal, a roar from the quay, shouting and quarrelling and jabbering from men in grubby jibbahs who in an instant overran the already crowded ship and kept on running through it. And it was clear that here, and not in Greece, the East began: in this chaos of uneconomical movement, the self-stimulated din, the sudden feeling of insecurity, the conviction that all men were not brothers and that luggage was in danger.

Here was to be learned the importance of the guide, the man who knew local customs, the fixer to whom badly printed illiterate forms held no mysteries. 'Write here,' my guide said in the customs house, aswirl with porters and guides and officials and idlers and policemen and travellers and a Greek refugee whispering in my ear, 'Let me warn you. They are stealing tonight.' 'Write here. One Kodak.' He, the guide, indicated the dotted line marked *date*. 'And here,' pointing to *signature*, 'write no gold, ornaments or precious stones.' I objected. He said, 'Write.' He pronounced it like an Arabic word. He was tall, grave, Hollywood-sinister; he wore a fez and lightly tapped his thigh with a cane. I wrote. And it worked. 'And now,' he said, exchanging the fez marked *Travel Agent* for one marked *Hotel X*, 'let us go to the hotel.'

Thereafter, feature by feature, the East, known only from books, continued to reveal itself; and each recognition was a discovery, as much as it had been a revelation to see the jibbah, a garment made almost mythical by countless photographs and descriptions, on the backs of real people. In the faded hotel, full, one felt, of memories of the Raj, there was a foreshadowing of the caste system. The old French waiter only served; he had his runners, sad-eyed silent Negroes in fezzes and cummerbunds, who fetched and cleared away. In the lobby there were innumerable Negro pages, picturesquely attired. And in the streets there was the East one had expected: the children, the dirt, the disease, the undernourishment, the cries of *bakshish*, the hawkers, the touts, the glimpses of minarets. There were the reminders of imperialisms that had withdrawn in the dark, glass-cased European-style shops, wilting for lack of patronage; in the sad whispering of the French hairdresser that French perfumes could no longer be obtained and that one had to make do with heavy Egyptian scents; in the disparaging references of the Lebanese businessman to 'natives', all of whom he distrusted except for his assistant, who, quietly to me, spoke of the day when all the Lebanese and Europeans would be driven out of the country.

Feature by feature, the East one had read about. On the train to Cairo the man across the aisle hawked twice, with an expert tongue rolled the phlegm into a ball, plucked the ball out of his mouth with thumb and forefinger, considered it, and then rubbed it away between

4

his palms. He was wearing a three-piece suit, and his transistor played loudly. Cairo revealed the meaning of the bazaar: narrow streets encrusted with filth, stinking even on this winter's day; tiny shops full of shoddy goods; crowds; the din, already barely supportable, made worse by the steady blaring of motor-car horns; medieval buildings partly collapsed, others rising on old rubble, with here and there sections of tiles, turquoise and royal blue, hinting at a past of order and beauty, crystal fountains and amorous adventures, as perhaps in the no less disordered past they always had done.

And in this bazaar, a cobbler. With white skullcap, lined face, steel-rimmed spectacles and white beard, he might have posed for a photograph in the *National Geographic Magazine*: the skilled and patient Oriental craftsman. My sole was flapping. Could he repair it? Sitting almost flat on the pavement, bowed over his work, he squinted at my shoes, my trousers, my rain-coat. 'Fifty piastres.' I said: 'Four.' He nodded, pulled the shoe off my foot and with a carpenter's hammer began hammering in a one-inch nail. I grabbed the shoe; he, smiling, hammer raised, held on to it. I pulled; he let go.

The Pyramids, whose function as a public latrine no guide book mentions, were made impossible by guides, 'watchmen', camel-drivers and by boys whose donkeys were all called Whisky-and-soda. *Bakshish! Bakshish!* 'Come and have a cup of coffee. I don't want you to buy anything. I just want to have a little intelligent con-versation. Mr Nehru is a great man. Let us exchange ideas. I am a graduate of the university.' I took the des-ert bus back to Alexandria and, two days before the appointed time, retreated to the Greek freighter.

Then came the tedium of the African ports. Little

clearings, one felt them, at the edge of a vast continent; and here one knew that Egypt, for all its Negroes, was not Africa, and for all its minarets and jibbahs, not the East: it was the last of Europe. At Jeddah the jibbahs were cleaner, the American automobiles new and numerous and driven with great style. We were not permitted to land and could see only the life of the port. Camels and goats were being unloaded by cranes and slings from dingy tramp steamers on to the piers; they were to be slaughtered for the ritual feast that marks the end of Ramadan. Swung aloft, the camels splayed out their suddenly useless legs; touching earth, lightly or with a bump, they crouched; then they ran to their fellows and rubbed against them. A fire broke out in a launch; our freighter sounded the alarm and within minutes the fire engines arrived. 'Autocracy has its charms,' the young Pakistani student said.

We had touched Africa, and four of the passengers had not been inoculated against yellow fever. A Pakistan-fed smallpox epidemic was raging in Britain and we feared stringency in Karachi. The Pakistani officials came aboard, drank a good deal, and our quarantine was waived. At Bombay, though, the Indian officials refused alcohol and didn't even finish the Coca-Cola they were offered. They were sorry, but the four passengers would have to go to the isolation hospital at Santa Cruz; either that or the ship would have to stay out in the stream. Two of the passengers without inoculations were the captain's parents. We stayed out in the stream.

It had been a slow journey, its impressions varied and superficial. But it had been a preparation for the East. After the bazaar of Cairo the bazaar of Karachi was no surprise; and *bakshish* was the same in both

6

languages. The change from the Mediterranean winter to the sticky high summer of the Red Sea had been swift. But other changes had been slower. From Athens to Bombay another idea of man had defined itself by degrees, a new type of authority and subservience. The physique of Europe had melted away first into that of Africa and then, through Semitic Arabia, into Aryan Asia. Men had been diminished and deformed; they begged and whined. Hysteria had been my reaction, and a brutality dictated by a new awareness of myself as a whole human being and a determination, touched with fear, to remain what I was. It mattered little through whose eyes I was seeing the East; there had as yet been no time for this type of self-assessment.

Superficial impressions, intemperate reactions. But one memory had stayed with me, and I had tried to hold it close during that day out in the stream at Bombay, when I had seen the sun set behind the Taj Mahal Hotel and had wished that Bombay was only another port such as those we had touched on the journey, a port that the freighter passenger might explore or reject.

It was at Alexandria. Here we had been pestered most by horsecabs. The horses were ribby, the coachwork as tattered as the garments of the drivers. The drivers hailed you; they drove their cabs beside you and left you only when another likely fare appeared. It had been good to get away from them, and from the security of the ship to watch them make their assault on others. It was like watching a silent film: the victim sighted, the racing cab, the victim engaged, gesticulations, the cab moving beside the victim and matching his pace, at first brisk, then exaggerated slow, then steady.

Then one morning the desert vastness of the dock was quickened with activity, and it was as if the silent film had become a silent epic. Long rows of two-toned taxicabs were drawn up outside the terminal building; scattered all over the dock area, as though awaiting a director's call to action, were black little clusters of horsecabs; and steadily, through the dock gates, far to the right, more taxis and cabs came rolling in. The horses galloped, the drivers' whip hands worked. It was a brief exaltation. Soon enough for each cab came repose, at the edge of a cab-cluster. The cause of the excitement was presently seen: a large white liner, possibly carrying tourists, possibly carrying ten-pound immigrants to Australia. Slowly, silently, she idled in. And more taxis came pelting through the gates, and more cabs, racing in feverishly to an anti-climax of nosebags and grass.

The liner docked early in the morning. It was not until noon that the first passengers came out of the terminal building into the wasteland of the dock area. This was like the director's call. Grass was snatched from the asphalt and thrust into boxes below the drivers' seats; and every passenger became the target of several converging attacks. Pink, inexperienced, timid and vulnerable these passengers appeared to us. They carried baskets and cameras; they wore straw hats and bright cotton shirts for the Egyptian winter (a bitter wind was blowing from the sea). But our sympathies had shifted; we were on the side of the Alexandrians. They had waited all morning; they had arrived with high panache and zeal; we wanted them to engage, conquer and drive away with their victims through the dock gates.

But this was not to be. Just when the passengers had

been penned by cabs and taxis, and gestures of remonstrance had given way to stillness, so that it seemed escape was impossible and capture certain, two shiny motor-coaches came through the dock gates. From the ship they looked like expensive toys. They cleared a way through taxis and cabs, which closed in again and then opened out to permit the coaches to make a slow, wide turn; and where before there had been tourists in gay cottons there was now only asphalt. The cabs, as though unwilling to accept the finality of this disappearance, backed and moved forward as if in pursuit. Then without haste they made their way back to their respective stations, where the horses retrieved from the asphalt what grass had escaped the hurried snatch of the drivers.

All through the afternoon the cabs and taxis remained, waiting for passengers who had not gone on the coaches. These passengers were few; they came out in ones and twos; and they appeared to prefer the taxis. But the enthusiasm of the horsecabs did not wane. Still, when a passenger appeared, the drivers jumped on to their seats, lashed their thin horses into action and rattled away to engage, transformed from idlers in old overcoats and scarves into figures of skill and purpose. Sometimes they engaged; often then there were disputes between drivers and the passengers withdrew. Sometimes a cab accompanied a passenger to the very gates. Sometimes at that point we saw the tiny walker halt; and then, with triumph and relief, we saw him climb into the cab. But this was rare.

The light faded. The cabs no longer galloped to engage. They wheeled and went at walking pace. The wind became keener; the dock grew dark; lights appeared. But the cabs remained. It was only later, when the liner blazed with lights, even its smoke-stack illuminated, and hope had been altogether extinguished, that they went away one by one, leaving behind shreds of grass and horse-droppings where they had stood.

Later that night I went up to the deck. Not far away, below a lamp standard, stood a lone cab. It had been there since the late afternoon; it had withdrawn early from the turmoil around the terminal. It had had no fares, and there could be no fares for it now. The cab-lamp burned low; the horse was eating grass from a shallow pile on the road. The driver, wrapped against the wind, was polishing the dully gleaming hood of his cab with a large rag. The polishing over, he dusted; then he gave the horse a brief, brisk rub down. Less than a minute later he was out of his cab again, polishing, dusting, brushing. He went in; he came out. His actions were compulsive. The animal chewed; his coat shone; the cab gleamed. And there were no fares. And next morning the liner had gone, and the dock was deserted again.

Now, sitting in the launch about to tie up at the Bombay pier where the names on cranes and buildings were, so oddly, English; feeling unease at the thought of the mute animal crouching on the floor at his master's back, and a similar unease at the sight of figures – not of romance, as the first figures seen on a foreign shore ought to be – on the pier, their frailty and raggedness contrasting with the stone buildings and metal cranes; now I tried to remember that in Bombay, as in Alexandria, there could be no pride in power, and that to give way to anger and contempt was to know a later self-disgust.

*

And of course Coelho, guide, fixer, knower of government forms, was right. Bombay was rigorously dry, and my two opened bottles of spirit were seized by the customs officers in white, who summoned a depressed-looking man in blue to seal them 'in my presence'. The man in blue worked at this manual and therefore degrading labour with slow relish; his manner proclaimed him an established civil servant, however degraded. I was given a receipt and told that I could get the bottles back when I got a liquor permit. Coelho wasn't so sure; these seized bottles, he said, had a habit of breaking. But his own worries were over. There had been no general search; his Greek doll had passed without query. He took it and his fee and disappeared into Bombay; I never saw him again.

To be in Bombay was to be exhausted. The moist heat sapped energy and will, and some days passed before I decided to recover my bottles. I decided in the morning; I started in the afternoon. I stood in the shade of Churchgate Station and debated whether I had it in me to cross the exposed street to the Tourist Office. Debate languished into daydream; it was minutes before I made the crossing. A flight of steps remained. I sat below a fan and rested. A lure greater than a liquor permit roused me: the office upstairs was air-conditioned. There India was an ordered, even luxurious country. The design was contemporary; the walls were hung with maps and coloured photographs; and there were little wooden racks of leaflets and booklets. Too soon my turn came; my idleness was over. I filled in my form. The clerk filled in his, three to my one, made entries in various ledgers and presented me with a sheaf of foolscap papers: my liquor permit. He had been prompt and courteous. I thanked him. There was no need, he said; it was only a little paperwork.

One step a day: this was my rule. And it was not until the following afternoon that I took a taxi back to the docks. The customs officers in white and the degraded man in blue were surprised to see me.

'Did you leave something here?'

'I left two bottles of liquor.'

'You didn't. We seized two bottles from you. They were sealed in your presence.'

'That's what I meant. I've come to get them back.'

'But we don't keep seized liquor here. Everything we seize and seal is sent off at once to the New Customs House.'

My taxi was searched on the way out.

The New Customs House was a large, two-storeyed PWD building, governmentally gloomy, and it was as thronged as a court-house. There were people in the drive, in the galleries, on the steps, in the corridors. 'Liquor, liquor,' I said, and was led from office to office, each full of shrunken, bespectacled young men in white shirts sitting at desks shaggily stacked with paper. Someone sent me upstairs. On the landing I came upon a barefooted group seated on the stone floor. At first I thought they were playing cards: it was a popular Bombay pavement pastime. But they were sorting parcels. Their spokesman told me I had been misdirected; I needed the building at the back. This building, from the quantity of ragged clothing seen in one of the lower rooms, appeared to be a tenement; and then, from the number of broken chairs and dusty pieces of useless furniture seen in another room, appeared to be a junk-shop. But it was the place for unclaimed baggage and was therefore the place I wanted. Upstairs I stood in a slow queue, at the end of which I discovered only an accountant.

'You don't want me. You want that officer in the white pants. Over there. He is a nice fellow.'

I went to him.

'You have your liquor permit?'

I showed him the stamped and signed foolscap sheaf.

'You have your transport permit?'

It was the first I had heard of this permit.

'You must have a transport permit.'

I was exhausted, sweating, and when I opened my mouth to speak I found I was on the verge of tears. 'But they *told* me.'

He was sympathetic. 'We have told them many times.'

I thrust all the papers I had at him: my liquor permit, my customs receipt, my passport, my receipt for wharf-age charges, my Tourist Introduction Card.

Dutifully he looked through what I offered. 'No. I would have known at once whether you had a transport permit. By the colour of the paper. A sort of buff.'

'But what is a transport permit? Why didn't they give it to me? Why do I need one?'

'I must have it before I can surrender anything.'

'Please.'

'Sorry.'

'I am going to write to the papers about this.'

'I wish you would. I keep telling them they must tell people about this transport permit. Not only for you. We had an American here yesterday who said he was going to break the bottle as soon as he got it.'

'Help me. Where can I get this transport permit?'

'The people who gave you the receipt should also give you the transport permit.'

'But I've just come from them.'

'I don't know. We keep on telling them.'

'Back to the Old Customs,' I said to the taxi-driver.

This time the police at the gates recognized us and didn't search the car. This dock had been my own gateway to India. Only a few days before everything in it had been new: the sticky black asphalt, the money-changers' booths, the stalls, the people in white, khaki or blue: everything had been studied for what it portended of India beyond the gates. Now already I had ceased to see or care. My stupor, though, was tempered by the thought of the small triumph that awaited me: I had trapped those customs officers in white and that degraded man in blue.

They didn't look trapped.

'Transport permit?' one said. 'Are you sure?'

'Did you tell them you were leaving Bombay?' asked a second.

'*Transport* permit?' said a third and, walking away to a fourth, asked, 'Transport permit, ever hear of *transport* permit?'

He had. 'They've been writing us about it.'

A transport permit was required to transport liquor from the customs to a hotel or house.

'Please give me a transport permit.'

'We don't issue transport permits. You have to go to –' He looked up at me and his manner softened. 'Here, let me write it down for you. And look, I will also give you your code-number. That will help them out at the New Customs.'

The taxi-driver had so far been calm; and it seemed now that my journeys had fallen into a pattern that was familiar to him. I began to read out the address that had been given me. He cut me short and without

14

another word buzzed through the thickening afternoon traffic to a large brick building hung with black-and-white government boards.

'You go,' he said sympathetically. 'I wait.'

Outside every office there was a little crowd.

'Transport permit, transport permit.'

Some Sikhs directed me round to the back to a low shed next to a gate marked *Prohibited Area*, out of which workers came, one after the other, raising their hands while armed soldiers frisked them.

'Transport permit, transport permit.'

I entered a long corridor and found myself among some Sikhs. They were lorry-drivers.

'Liquor permit, liquor permit.'

And at last I reached the office. It was a long low room at ground level, hidden from the scorching sun and as dark as a London basement, but warm and dusty with the smell of old paper, which was everywhere, on shelves rising to the grey ceiling, on desks, on chairs, in the hands of clerks, in the hands of khaki-clad messengers. Folders had grown dog-eared, their edges limp with reverential handling; and to many were attached pink slips, equally faded, equally limp, marked URGENT, VERY URGENT, or IMMEDIATE. Between these mounds and columns and buttresses of paper, clerks were scattered about unimportantly, men and women, mild-featured, Indian-pallid, high-shouldered; paper was their perfect camouflage. An elderly bespectacled man sat at a desk in one corner, his face slightly puffy and dyspeptic. Tremulous control of the paper-filled room was his: at his disappearance the clerks might be altogether overwhelmed.

'Transport permit?'

He looked up slowly. He showed no surprise, no

displeasure at being disturbed. Papers, pink-slipped, were spread all over his desk. A table fan, nicely poised, blew over them without disturbance.

'Transport permit.' He spoke the words mildly, as though they were rare words but words which, after searching for only a second in the files of his mind, he had traced. 'Write an application. Only one is necessary.'

'Do you have the form?'

'No forms have been issued. Write a letter. Here, have a sheet of paper. Sit down and write. To the Collector, Excise and Prohibition, Bombay. Do you have your passport? Put down the number. Oh, and you have a Tourist Introduction Card. Put down that number too. I will expedite matters.'

And while I wrote, noting down the number of my Tourist Introduction Card, TIO (L) 156, he, expediting matters, passed my documents over to a woman clerk, saying, 'Miss Desai, could you start making out a transport permit?' I thought I detected an odd pride in his voice. He was like a man still after many years discovering the richness and variety of his work and subduing an excitement which he nevertheless wished to communicate to his subordinates.

I was finding it hard to spell and to frame simple sentences. I crumpled up the sheet of paper.

The head clerk looked up at me in gentle reproof. 'Only one application is necessary.'

At my back Miss Desai filled in forms with that blunt, indelible, illegible pencil which government offices throughout the former Empire use, less for the sake of what is written than for the sake of the copies required.

I managed to complete my application.

And at this point my companion slumped forward on

16

her chair, hung her head between her knees and fainted.

'Water,' I said to Miss Desai.

She barely paused in her writing and pointed to an empty dusty glass on a shelf.

The head clerk, already frowningly preoccupied with other papers, regarded the figure slumped in front of him.

'Not feeling well?' His voice was as mild and even as before. 'Let her rest.' He turned the table fan away from him.

'Where is the water?'

Giggles came from women clerks, hidden behind paper.

'Water!' I cried to a male clerk.

He rose, saying nothing, walked to the end of the room and vanished.

Miss Desai finished her writing. Giving me a glance as of terror, she brought her tall bloated pad to the head clerk.

'The transport permit is ready,' he said. 'As soon as you are free you can sign for it.'

The male clerk returned, waterless, and sat down at his desk.

'Where is the water?'

His eyes distastefully acknowledged my impatience. He neither shrugged nor spoke; he went on with his papers.

It was worse than impatience. It was ill-breeding and ingratitude. For presently, sporting his uniform as proudly as any officer, a messenger appeared. He carried a tray and on the tray stood a glass of water. I should have known better. A clerk was a clerk; a messenger was a messenger.

The crisis passed.

I signed three times and received my permit.

The head clerk opened another folder.

'Nadkarni,' he called softly to a clerk. 'I don't understand this memo.'

I had been forgotten already.

It was suffocatingly hot in the taxi, the seats scorching. We drove to the flat of a friend and stayed there until it was dark.

A friend of our friend came in.

'What's wrong?'

'We went to get a transport permit and she fainted.' I did not wish to sound critical. I added, 'Perhaps it's the heat.'

'It isn't the heat at all. Always the heat or the water with you people from outside. There's nothing wrong with her. You make up your minds about India before coming to the country. You've been reading the wrong books.'

The officer who had sent me on the track of the transport permit was pleased to see me back. But the transport permit wasn't enough. I had to go to Mr Kulkarni to find out about the warehouse charges. When I had settled what the charges were I was to come back to that clerk over there, with the blue shirt; then I had to go to the cashier, to pay the warehouse charges; then I had to go back to Mr Kulkarni to get my bottles.

I couldn't find Mr Kulkarni. My papers were in my hand. Someone tried to take them. I knew he was expressing only his kindness and curiosity. I pulled the papers back. He looked at me; I looked at him. I yielded. He went through my papers and said with authority that I had come to the wrong building.

I screamed: '*Mr Kulkarni!*'

Everyone around me was startled. Someone came up to me, calmed me down and led me to the adjoining room where Mr Kulkarni had been all along. I rushed to the head of the queue and began to shout at Mr Kulkarni, waving my papers at him. He got hold of them as I waved and began to read. Some Sikhs in the queue complained. Mr Kulkarni replied that I was in a hurry, that I was a person of importance, and that in any case I was younger. Curiously, they were pacified.

Mr Kulkarni called for ledgers. They were brought to him. Turning the crisp pages, not looking up, he made a loose-wristed gesture of indefinable elegance with his yellow pencil. The Sikhs at once separated into two broken lines. Mr Kulkarni put on his spectacles, studied the calendar on the far wall, counted on his fingers, took off his spectacles and returned to his ledgers. He made another abstracted gesture with his pencil and the Sikhs fell into line again, obscuring the calendar.

Upstairs again. The clerk with the blue shirt stamped on Mr Kulkarni's sheet of paper and made entries in two ledgers. The cashier added his own stamp. I paid him and he made entries in two more ledgers.

'It's all right,' the officer said, scanning the twice-stamped and thrice-signed sheet of paper. He added his own signature. 'You're safe now. Go down to Mr Kulkarni. And be quick. They might be closing any minute.'

PART ONE

1

A RESTING-PLACE FOR THE IMAGINATION

These Antipodes call to one's mind old recollections
of childish doubt and wonder. Only the other day
I looked forward to this airy barrier as a definite
point in our journey homewards; but now I find it,
and all such resting-places for the imagination, are
like shadows, which a man moving onwards cannot
catch.

Charles Darwin: *Voyage of the Beagle*

You've been reading the wrong books, the businessman
said. But he did me an injustice. I had read any number
of the books which he would have considered right.
And India had in a special way been the background
of my childhood. It was the country from which my
grandfather came, a country never physically described
and therefore never real, a country out in the void
beyond the dot of Trinidad; and from it our journey
had been final. It was a country suspended in time; it
could not be related to the country, discovered later,
which was the subject of the many correct books issued
by Mr Gollancz and Messrs Allen and Unwin and was
the source of agency dispatches in the *Trinidad Guardian*. It remained a special, isolated area of ground
which had produced my grandfather and others I knew
who had been born in India and had come to Trinidad
as indentured labourers, though that past too had fallen
into the void into which India had fallen, for they

carried no mark of indenture, no mark even of having been labourers.

There was an old lady, a friend of my mother's family. She was jewelled, fair and white-haired; she was very grand. She spoke only Hindi. The elegance of her manner and the grave handsomeness of her husband, with his thick white moustache, his spotless Indian dress and his silence, which compensated for his wife's bustling authority, impressed them early upon me as a couple who, though so friendly and close – they ran a tiny shop not far from my grandmother's establishment – as to be considered almost relations, were already foreign. They came from India; this gave them glamour, but the glamour was itself a barrier. They not so much ignored Trinidad as denied it; they made no attempt even to learn English, which was what the children spoke. The lady had two or three gold teeth and was called by everyone Gold Teeth Nanee, Gold Teeth Grandmother, the mixture of English and Hindi revealing to what extent the world to which she belonged was receding. Gold Teeth was childless. This probably accounted for her briskness and her desire to share my grandmother's authority over the children. It did not make her better liked. But she had a flaw. She was as greedy as a child; she was a great uninvited eater, whom it was easy to trap with a square of laxative chocolate. One day she noticed a tumbler of what looked like coconut milk. She tasted, she drank to the end, and fell ill; and in her distress made a confession which was like a reproach. She had drunk a tumbler of blanco fluid. It was astonishing that she should have drunk to the end; but in matters of food she was, unusually for an Indian, experimental and pertinacious. She was to carry the disgrace till her death. So one India crashed; and as we grew older, living now in the town, Gold Teeth dwindled to a rustic oddity with whom there could be no converse. So remote her world seemed then, so dead; yet how little time separated her from us!

Then there was Babu. Moustached, as grave and silent as Gold Teeth's husband, he occupied a curious position in my grandmother's household. He too was born in India; and why he should have lived alone in one room at the back of the kitchen I never understood. It is an indication of the narrowness of the world in which we lived as children that all I knew about Babu was that he was a *kshatriya*, one of the warrior caste: this solitary man who, squatting in his dark-room at the end of the day, prepared his own simple food, kneading flour, cutting vegetables and doing other things which I had always thought of as woman's work. Could this man from the warrior caste have been a labourer? Inconceivable then; but later, alas, when such disillusionment meant little, to be proved true. We had moved. My grandmother required someone to dig a well. It was Babu who came, from that back room where he had continued to live. The well deepened; Babu was let down in a hammock, which presently brought up the earth he had excavated. One day no more earth came up. Babu had struck rock. He came up on the hammock for the last time and went away back into that void from which he had come. I never saw him again and had of him as a reminder only that deep hole at the edge of the cricket ground. The hole was planked over, but it remained in my imagination a standing nightmare peril to energetic fielders chasing a boundary hit.

More than in people, India lay about us in things: in a string bed or two, grimy, tattered, no longer serving any function, never repaired because there was no one with this caste skill in Trinidad, yet still permitted to take up room; in plaited straw mats; in innumerable brass vessels; in wooden printing blocks, never used because printed cotton was abundant and cheap and because the secret of the dyes had been forgotten, no dyer being at hand; in books, the sheets large, coarse and brittle, the ink thick and oily; in drums and one ruined harmonium; in brightly coloured pictures of deities on pink lotus or radiant against Himalayan snow; and in all the paraphernalia of the prayer-room: the brass bells and gongs and camphor-burners like Roman lamps, the slender-handled spoon for the doling out of the consecrated 'nectar' (peasant's nectar: on ordinary days brown sugar and water, with some shreds of the tulsi leaf, sweetened milk on high days), the images, the smooth pebbles, the stick of sandalwood.

The journey had been final. And it was only on this trip to India that I was to see how complete a transference had been made from eastern Uttar Pradesh to Trinidad, and that in days when the village was some hours' walk from the nearest branch-line railway station, the station more than a day's journey from the port, and that anything up to three months' sailing from Trinidad. In its artefacts India existed whole in Trinidad. But our community, though seemingly self-contained, was imperfect. Sweepers we had quickly learned to do without. Others supplied the skills of carpenters, masons and cobblers. But we were also without weavers and dyers, workers in brass and makers of string beds. Many of the things in my grandmother's house were therefore irreplaceable. They were cherished because they came from India, but they continued to be used and no regret attached to their disintegration. It was an Indian attitude, as I was to recognize. Customs are to be maintained because they are felt to be ancient. This is continuity enough; it does not need to be supported by a cultivation of the past, and the old, however hallowed, be it a Gupta image or a string bed, is to be used until it can be used no more.

To me as a child the India that had produced so many of the persons and things around me was featureless, and I thought of the time when the transference was made as a period of darkness, darkness which also extended to the land, as darkness surrounds a hut at evening, though for a little way around the hut there is still light. The light was the area of my experience, in time and place. And even now, though time has widened, though space has contracted and I have travelled lucidly over that area which was to me the area of darkness, something of darkness remains, in those attitudes, those ways of thinking and seeing, which are no longer mine. My grandfather had made a difficult and courageous journey. It must have brought him into collision with startling sights, even like the sea, several hundred miles from his village; yet I cannot help feeling that as soon as he had left his village he ceased to see. When he went back to India it was to return with more things of India. When he built his house he ignored every colonial style he might have found in Trinidad and put up a heavy, flat-roofed oddity, whose image I was to see again and again in the small ramshackle towns of Uttar Pradesh. He had abandoned India; and, like Gold Teeth, he denied Trinidad. Yet he walked on solid earth. Nothing beyond his village had stirred him; nothing had forced him out of himself; he carried his village with him. A few reassuring relationships, a strip of land, and he could satisfyingly re-create an eastern Uttar

Pradesh village in central Trinidad as if in the vastness of India.

We who came after could not deny Trinidad. The house we lived in was distinctive, but not more distinctive than many. It was easy to accept that we lived on an island where there were all sorts of people and all sorts of houses. Doubtless they too had their own things. We ate certain food, performed certain ceremonies and had certain taboos; we expected others to have their own. We did not wish to share theirs; we did not expect them to share ours. They were what they were; we were what we were. We were never instructed in this. To our condition as Indians in a multi-racial society we gave no thought. Criticism from others there was, as I now realize, but it never penetrated the walls of our house, and I cannot as a child remember hearing any discussion about race. Though permeated with the sense of difference, in racial matters, oddly, I remained an innocent for long. At school I was puzzled by the kinky hair of a teacher I liked; I came to the conclusion that he was still, like me, growing, and that when he had grown a little more his hair would grow straighter and longer. Race was never discussed; but at an early age I understood that Muslims were somewhat more different than others. They were not to be trusted; they would always do you down; and point was given to this by the presence close to my grandmother's house of a Muslim, in whose cap and grey beard, avowals of his especial difference, lay every sort of threat. For the difference we saw as the attribute of every group outside our own was more easily discernible in other Indians and more discernible yet in other Hindus. Racial awareness was to come; in the meantime – and until how recently – for the social antagonisms that give savour to life we relied on the old, Indian divisions, meaningless though these had become.

Everything beyond our family had this quality of difference. This was to be accepted when we went abroad and perhaps even forgotten, as for instance at school. But the moment any intercourse threatened, we scented violation and withdrew. I remember – and this was later, after this family life had broken up – being taken to visit one family. They were not related. This made the visit unusual; and because it became fixed in my mind, no doubt from something that had been said, that they were Muslims, everything about them had a heightened difference. I saw it in their appearance, their house, their dress and presently, as I had been fearing, in their food. We were offered some vermicelli done in milk. I believed it to be associated with some unknown and distasteful ritual; I could not eat it. They were in fact Hindus; our families were later joined by marriage.

Inevitably this family life shrank, and the process was accelerated by our removal to the capital, where there were few Indians. The outside world intruded more. We became secretive. But once we made an open assault on the city. My grandmother wished to have a *kattha* said, and she wished to have it said under a pipal tree. There was only one pipal tree in the island; it was in the Botanical Gardens. Permission was applied for. To my amazement it was given; and one Sunday morning we all sat under the pipal tree, botanically labelled, and the pundit read. The crackling sacrificial fire was scented with pitch-pine, brown sugar and ghee; bells were rung, gongs struck, conch-shells blown. We attracted the silent interest of a small mixed crowd of morning strollers and the proselytizing attentions of a Seventh Day

Adventist. It was a scene of pure pastoral: aryan ritual, of another continent and age, a few hundred yards from the governor's house. But this is a later appreciation. For those of us at school at the time the public ceremony had been a strain. We were becoming self-conscious, self-assessing: our secret world was shrinking fast. Still, very occasionally, some devout Hindu of the few in Port of Spain might wish to feed some brahmins. We were at hand. We went; we were fed; we received gifts of cloth and money. We never questioned our luck. Luck indeed it seemed, for immediately afterwards, walking back home in trousers and shirt, we became ordinary boys again.

To me this luck was touched with fraudulence. I came of a family that abounded with pundits. But I had been born an unbeliever. I took no pleasure in religious ceremonies. They were too long, and the food came only at the end. I did not understand the language – it was as if our elders expected that our understanding would be instinctive – and no one explained the prayers or the ritual. One ceremony was like another. The images didn't interest me; I never sought to learn their significance. With my lack of belief and distaste for ritual there also went a metaphysical incapacity, this again a betrayal of heredity, for my father's appetite for Hindu speculation was great. So it happened that, though growing up in an orthodox family, I remained almost totally ignorant of Hinduism. What, then, survived of Hinduism in me? Perhaps I had received a certain supporting philosophy. I cannot say; my uncle often put it to me that my denial was an admissible type of Hinduism. Examining myself, I found only that sense of the difference of people, which I have tried to explain, a vaguer sense of caste, and a horror of the unclean.

It still horrifies me that people should put out food for animals on plates that they themselves use; as it horrified me at school to see boys sharing Popsicles and Palates, local iced lollies; as it horrifies me to see women sipping from ladles with which they stir their pots. This was more than difference; this was the uncleanliness we had to guard against. From all food restrictions sweets were, curiously, exempt. We bought cassava pone from street stalls; but black pudding and souse, favourite street-corner and sports-ground dishes of the Negro proletariat, were regarded by us with fascinated horror. This might suggest that our food remained what it always had been. But this was not so. It is not easy to understand just how communication occurred, but we were steadily adopting the food styles of others: the Portuguese stew of tomato and onions, in which almost anything might be done, the Negro way with yams, plantains, breadfruit and bananas. Everything we adopted became our own; the outside was still to be dreaded, and my prejudices were so strong that when I left Trinidad, shortly before my eighteenth birthday, I had eaten in restaurants only three times. The day of my swift transportation to New York was a day of misery. I spent a frightened, hungry day in that city; and on the ship to Southampton I ate mainly the sweets, which encouraged the steward to say when I tipped him, 'The others made pigs of themselves. But you sure do like ice-cream.'

Food was one thing. Caste was another. Though I had quickly grown to see it as only part of our private play, it was capable on occasion of influencing my attitude to others. A distant relation was married; it was rumoured that her husband was of the *chamar*, or leather-worker, caste. The man was rich and travelled;

he was successful in his profession and was later to hold a position of some responsibility. But he was a *chamar*. The rumour was perhaps unfounded – few marriages are not attended by disparagement of this sort – but the thought still occurs whenever we meet and that initial sniffing for difference is now involuntary. He is the only person thus coloured for me; the marriage took place when I was very young. In India people were also to be tainted by their caste, especially when this was announced beforehand, approvingly or disapprovingly. But caste in India was not what it had been to me in Trinidad. In Trinidad caste had no meaning in our day-to-day life; the caste we occasionally played at was no more than an acknowledgement of latent qualities; the assurance it offered was such as might have been offered by a palmist or a reader of handwriting. In India it implied a brutal division of labour; and at its centre, as I had never realized, lay the degradation of the latrine-cleaner. In India caste was unpleasant; I never wished to know what a man's caste was.

I had no belief; I disliked religious ritual; and I had a sense of the ridiculous. I refused to go through the *janaywa*, or thread ceremony of the newborn, with some of my cousins. The ceremony ends with the initiate, his head shaved, his thread new and obvious, taking up his staff and bundle – as he might have done in an Indian village two thousand years ago – and announcing his intention of going to Kasi-Banaras to study. His mother weeps and begs him not to go; the initiate insists that he must; a senior member of the family is summoned to plead with the initiate, who at length yields and lays down his staff and bundle. It was a pleasing piece of theatre. But I knew that we were in Trinidad, an island separated by only ten miles from the South American coast, and that the appearance in a Port of Spain street of my cousin, perhaps of no great academic attainment, in the garb of a Hindu mendicant-scholar bound for Banaras, would have attracted unwelcome attention. So I refused; though now this ancient drama, absurdly surviving in a Trinidad yard, seems to me touching and attractive.

I had contracted out. Yet there is a balancing memory. In the science class at school one day we were doing an experiment with siphons, to an end which I have now forgotten. At one stage a beaker and a length of tube were passed from boy to boy, so that we might suck and observe the effects. I let the beaker pass me. I thought I hadn't been seen, but an Indian boy in the row behind, a Port of Spain boy, a recognized class tough, whispered, 'Real brahmin.' His tone was approving. I was surprised at his knowledge, having assumed him, a Port of Spain boy, to be ignorant of these things; at the unexpected tenderness of his voice; and also at the bringing out into public of that other, secret life. But I was also pleased. And with this pleasure there came a new tenderness for that boy, and a sadness for our common loss: mine, which he did not suspect, the result of my own decision or temperament, his, which by his behaviour he openly acknowledged, the result of history and environment: a feeling which was to come to me again more strongly and much later, in entirely different circumstances, when the loss was complete, in London.

I have been rebuked by writers from the West Indies, and notably George Lamming, for not paying sufficient attention in my books to non-Indian groups. The confrontation of different communities, he said, was the fundamental West Indian experience. So indeed it is, and increasingly. But to see the attenuation of the culture of my childhood as the result of a dramatic confrontation of opposed worlds would be to distort the reality. To me the worlds were juxtaposed and mutually exclusive. One gradually contracted. It had to; it fed only on memories and its completeness was only apparent. It was yielding not to attack but to a type of seepage from the other. I can speak only out of my own experience. The family life I have been describing began to dissolve when I was six or seven; when I was fourteen it had ceased to exist. Between my brother, twelve years younger than myself, and me there is more than a generation of difference. He can have no memory of that private world which survived with such apparent solidity up to only twenty-five years ago, a world which had lengthened out, its energy of inertia steadily weakening, from the featureless area of darkness which was India.

That this world should have existed at all, even in the consciousness of a child, is to me a marvel; as it is a marvel that we should have accepted the separateness of our two worlds and seen no incongruity in their juxtaposition. In one world we existed as if in blinkers, as if seeing no more than my grandfather's village; outside, we were totally self-aware. And in India I was to see that so many of the things which the newer and now perhaps truer side of my nature kicked against – the smugness, as it seemed to me, the imperviousness to criticism, the refusal to *see*, the double-talk and double-think – had an answer in that side of myself which I had thought buried and which India revived as a faint memory. I understood better than I admitted. And to me it is an additional marvel that an upbringing of the kind I have described, cut short and rendered invalid so soon, should have left so deep an impression. Indians are an old people, and it might be that they continue to belong to the old world. That Indian reverence for the established and ancient, however awkward, however indefensible, however little understood: it is part of the serious buffoonery of Ancient Rome, an aspect of the Roman *pietas*. I had rejected tradition; yet how can I explain my feeling of outrage when I heard that in Bombay they used candles and electric bulbs for the Diwali festival, and not the rustic clay lamps, of immemorial design, which in Trinidad we still used? I had been born an unbeliever. Yet the thought of the decay of the old customs and reverences saddened me when the boy whispered 'Real brahmin', and when, many years later, in London, I heard that Ramon was dead.

He was perhaps twenty-four. He died in a car crash. It was fitting. Motor-cars were all that mattered to him, and it was to continue to handle them that he came to London, abandoning mother and father, wife and children. I met him almost as soon as he had arrived. It was in a dingy Chelsea boarding-house whose façade was like all the other façades in that respectable, rising street: white, the area railings black, the door an oblong of vivid colour. Only milk bottles and a quality of curtaining betrayed the house where, in a passageway, below the diffused, misty glow of a forty-watt bulb, I first saw Ramon. He was short, his hair thick and curling at the ends, his features blunt, like his strong stubby fingers. He wore a moustache and was unshaved; and in his pullover, which I could see had belonged to someone else who had made the pilgrimage to London from Trinidad and had taken back the pull-over as a mark of the voyager to temperate climes, he looked shabby and unwashed.

He was of a piece with the setting, the green grown dingy of the walls, the linoleum, the circles of dirt around door handles, the faded upholstery of cheap chairs, the stained wallpaper; the indications of the passage of numberless transients to whom these rooms had never been meant for the arranging of their things; the rim of soot below the windowsill, the smoked ceiling, the empty fireplace bearing the marks of a brief, ancient fire and suggesting a camping ground; the carpets smelly and torn. He was of a piece, yet he was alien. He belonged to unfenced backyards and lean-tos, where, pullover-less and shirtless, he might wander in the cool of the evening, about him the unfading bright green of Trinidad foliage, chickens settling down for the night, while in a neighbouring yard a coalpot sent up a thin line of blue smoke. Now, at a similar time of day, he sat choked in someone else's pullover on a low bed, how often used, how little cleaned, in the dim light of a furnished room in Chelsea, the electric fire, its dull reflector seemingly spat upon and sanded, making little impression on the dampness and cold. His fellow voyagers had gone out. He was not bright, as they were; he cared little about dress; he could not support or share their high spirits.

He was shy, and spoke only when spoken to, responding to questions like a man who had nothing to hide, a man to whom the future, never considered, held no threat and possibly no purpose. He had left Trinidad because he had lost his driving licence. His career of crime had begun when, scarcely a boy, he was arrested for driving without a licence; later he was arrested for driving while still banned. One offence led to another, until Trinidad had ceased to be a place where he could live; he needed to be in motor-cars. His parents had scraped together some money to send him to England. They had done it because they loved him, their son; yet when he spoke of their sacrifice it was without emotion.

He was incapable of assessing the morality of actions; he was a person to whom things merely happened. He had left his wife behind; she had two children. 'And I believe I have something else boiling up for me.' The words were spoken without the Trinidad back-street pride. They recorded a fact; they passed judgement neither on his desertion nor his virility.

His name was Spanish because his mother was part Venezuelan; and he had spent some time in Venezuela until the police had hustled him out. But he was a Hindu and had been married according to Hindu rites. These rites must have meant as little to him as they did to me, and perhaps even less, for he had grown up as an individual, had never had the protection of a family life like mine, and had at an early age been transferred to a civilization which remained as puzzling to him as this new transference to Chelsea.

He was an innocent, a lost soul, rescued from animality only by his ruling passion. That section of the mind, if such a section exists, which judges and feels was in him a blank, on which others could write. He wished to drive; he drove. He liked a car; he applied his skill to it and drove it away. He would be eventually caught; that he never struggled against or seemed to doubt. You told him, 'I need a hubcap for my car. Can you get me one?' He went out and took the first suitable hubcap he saw. He was caught; he blamed no one. Things happened to him. His innocence, which was not mere simpleness, was frightening. He was as innocent as a complicated machine. He could be animated by his wish to please. There was an unmarried mother in the house; to her and her child he was unfailingly tender, and protective, whenever that was required of him.

But there was his ruling passion. And with motorcars he was a genius. The word quickly got around; and it was not unusual some weeks later to see him in grease-stained clothes working on a run-down motorcar, while a cavalry-twilled man spoke to him of money. He might have made money. But all his profits went on fresh cars and on the fines he had already begun to pay to the courts for stealing this lamp and that part which he had needed to complete a job. It was not necessary for him to steal; but he stole. Still, the news of his skill went round, and he was busy.

Then I heard that he was in serious trouble. A friend in the boarding-house had asked him to burn a scooter. In Trinidad if you wished to burn a motor-car you set it alight on the bank of the muddy Caroni River and rolled it in. London, too, had a river. Ramon put the scooter into the van which he owned at the time and drove down one evening to the Embankment. Before he could set the scooter alight a policeman appeared, as policemen had always appeared in Ramon's life.

I thought that, as the scooter hadn't been burnt, the case couldn't be serious.

'But no,' one man in the boarding-house said. 'This is conspiracy.' He spoke the word with awe; he too had been booked as a conspirator.

So Ramon went up to the assizes, and I went to see how the case would go. I had some trouble finding the correct court – 'Have you come to answer a summons yourself, sir?' a policeman asked, his courtesy as bewildering as his question – and when I did find the court, I might have been back in St Vincent Street in Port of Spain. The conspirators were all there, looking like frightened students. They wore suits, as though all about to be interviewed. They, so boisterous, so anxious to antagonize their neighbours in the Chelsea street – they had taken to clipping one another's hair on the pavement of a Sunday morning (the locals washing their cars the while), as they might have done in Port of Spain – now succeeded in giving an opposed picture of themselves.

Ramon stood apart from them, he too wearing a suit, but with nothing in his face or in his greeting to show that we were meeting in circumstances slightly different from those in the boarding-house. A girl was attached to him, a simple creature, dressed as for a dance. Not anxious they seemed, but blank; she too was a person to whom things difficult or puzzling kept happening. More worried than either of them was Ramon's employer, a garage-owner. He had come to give evidence about Ramon's 'character', and he again was in a suit, of stiff brown tweed. His face was flushed and puffy, hinting at some type of heart disorder; his eyes blinked continually behind his pink-rimmed spectacles. He stood beside Ramon.

'A good boy, a good boy,' the garage-owner said, tears coming to his eyes. 'It's only his company.' It was strange that this simple view of the relationships of the simple could hold so much force and be so moving.

The trial was an anti-climax. It began sombrely enough, with police evidence and cross-examinations. (Ramon was quoted as saying at the moment of arrest: 'Yes, copper, you got me now, sah.' This I rejected.) Ramon was being defended by a young court-supplied

39

lawyer. He was very brisk and stylish, and beside himself with enthusiasm. He showed more concern than Ramon, whom he had needlessly encouraged to cheer up. Once he caught the judge out on some point of legal etiquette and in an instant was on his feet, administering a shocked, stern rebuke. The judge listened with pure pleasure and apologized. We might have been in a nursery for lawyers: Ramon's lawyer the star pupil, the judge the principal, and we in the gallery proud parents. When the judge began his summing up, speaking slowly, in a voice courthouse rich, sombreness altogether disappeared. It was clear he was not used to the ways of Trinidad. He said he found it hard to regard an attempt to burn a scooter on the Embankment as more than a foolish student's prank; however, an intention to defraud the insurance company was serious . . . There was an Indian lady in the gallery, of great beauty, who smiled and had to suppress her laughter at every witticism and every elegant phrase. The judge was aware of her, and the summing up was like a dialogue between the two, between the elderly man, confident of his gifts, and the beautiful, appreciative woman. The tenseness of the jury – a bespectacled, hatted woman sat forward, clutching the rail as if in distress – was irrelevant; and no one, not even the police, seemed surprised at the verdict of not guilty. Ramon's lawyer was exultant. Ramon was as serene as before; his fellow conspirators suddenly appeared utterly exhausted.

Soon enough, however, Ramon was in trouble again, and this time there was no garage-owner to speak for him. He had, I believe, stolen a car or had pillaged its engine beyond economic repair; and he was sent to prison for some time. When he came out he said he had spent a few weeks in Brixton. 'Then I went down to a place in Kent.' I heard this from his former co-accused in the boarding-house. There Ramon had become a figure of fun. And when I next heard of him he was dead, in a car crash.

He was a child, an innocent, a maker; someone for whom the world had never held either glory or pathos; someone for whom there had been no place. 'Then I went down to a place in Kent.' He was guiltless of humour or posturing. One place was like another; the world was full of such places in which, unseeing, one passed one's days. He was dead now, and I wished to offer him recognition. He was of the religion of my family; we were debased members of that religion, and this very debasement I felt as a bond. We were a tiny, special part of that featureless, unknown country, meaningful to us, if we thought about it, only in that we were its remote descendants. I wished his body to be handled with reverence, and I wished it to be handled according to the old rites. This alone would spare him final nonentity. So perhaps the Roman felt in Cappadocia or Britain; and London was now as remote from the centre of our world as, among the ruins of some Roman villa in Gloucestershire, Britain still feels far from home and can be seen as a country which in an emblematic map, curling at the corners, is partly obscured by the clouds blown by a cherub, a country of mist and rain and forest, from which the traveller is soon to hurry back to a warm, familiar land. For us no such land existed.

I missed Ramon's funeral. He was not cremated but buried, and a student from Trinidad conducted the rites which his caste entitled him to perform. He had read my books and did not want me to be there. Denied a presence I so much wished, I had to imagine the scene: a man in a white dhoti speaking gibberish over the corpse of Ramon, making up rites among the tombstones and crosses of a more recent religion, the mean buildings of a London suburb low in the distance, against an industrial sky.

But how could the mood be supported? Ramon died fittingly and was buried fittingly. In addition to everything else, he was buried free, by a funeral agency whose stalled hearse, encountered by chance on the road only a few days before his death, he had set going again.

The India, then, which was the background to my childhood was an area of the imagination. It was not the real country I presently began to read about and whose map I committed to memory. I became a nationalist; even a book like Beverley Nichols's *Verdict on India* could anger me. But this came almost at the end. The next year India became independent; and I found that my interest was failing. I now had almost no Hindi. But it was more than language which divided me from what I knew of India. Indian films were both tedious and disquieting; they delighted in decay, agony and death; a funeral dirge or a blind man's lament could become a hit. And there was religion, with which, as one of Mr Gollancz's writers had noted with approval, the people of India were intoxicated. I was without belief or interest in belief; I was incapable of worship, of God or holy men; and so one whole side of India was closed to me.

Then there came people from India, not the India of Gold Teeth and Babu, but this other India; and I saw that to this country I was not at all linked. The Gujerati and Sindhi merchants were as foreign as the Syrians. They lived enclosed lives of a narrowness which I considered asphyxiating. They were devoted to their work, the making of money; they seldom went out; their pallid women were secluded; and all day their houses screeched with morbid Indian film songs. They contributed nothing to the society, nothing even to the Indian community. They were reputed among us to be sharp businessmen. In so many ways, as I now see, they were to us what we were to other communities. But their journey had not been final; their private world was not shrinking. They made regular trips to India, to buy and sell, to marry, to bring out recruits; the gap between us widened.

I came to London. It had become the centre of my world and I had worked hard to come to it. And I was lost. London was not the centre of my world. I had been misled; but there was nowhere else to go. It was a good place for getting lost in, a city no one ever knew, a city explored from the neutral heart outwards until, after years, it defined itself into a jumble of clearings separated by stretches of the unknown, through which the narrowest of paths had been cut. Here I became no more than an inhabitant of a big city, robbed of loyalties, time passing, taking me away from what I was, thrown more and more into myself, fighting to keep my balance and to keep alive the thought of the clear world beyond the brick and asphalt and the chaos of railway lines. All mythical lands faded, and in the big city I was confined to a smaller world than I had ever known. I became my flat, my desk, my name.

As India had drawn near, I had felt more than the usual fear of arrival. In spite of myself, in spite of lucidity and London and my years, and over and above every other fear, and the memory of the Alexandrian cab-driver, some little feeling for India as the mythical land of my childhood was awakened. I knew it to be foolish. The launch was solid enough and dingy enough; there was a tariff for fair weather and foul weather; the heat was real and disagreeable; the city we could see beyond the heat-mist was big and busy; and its inhabitants, seen in other vessels, were of small physique, betokening all the fearful things that had soon to be faced. The buildings grew larger. The figures on the docks became clearer. The buildings spoke of London and industrial England; and how, in spite of knowledge, this seemed ordinary and inappropriate! Perhaps all lands of myth were like this: dazzling with light, familiar to drabness, the margin of the sea unremarkably littered, until the moment of departure.

And for the first time in my life I was one of the crowd. There was nothing in my appearance or dress to distinguish me from the crowd eternally hurrying into Churchgate Station. In Trinidad to be an Indian was to be distinctive. To be anything there was distinctive; difference was each man's attribute. To be an Indian in England was distinctive; in Egypt it was more so. Now in Bombay I entered a shop or a restaurant and awaited a special quality of response. And there was nothing. It was like being denied part of my reality. Again and again I was caught. I was faceless. I might sink without a trace into that Indian crowd. I had been made by Trinidad and England; recognition of my difference was necessary to me. I felt the need to impose myself, and didn't know how.

'You require dark glasses? From your accent, sir, I perceive that you are perhaps a student, returned from Europe. You will understand therefore what I am about to say. Observe how these lenses soften glare and heighten colour. With the manufacture of these lenses I assure you that a new chapter has been written in the history of optics.'

So I was a student, perhaps returned from Europe. The patter was better than I had expected. But I didn't buy the lenses the man offered. I bought Crookes, hideously expensive, in a clip-on Indian frame which broke almost as soon as I left the shop. I was too tired to go back, to talk in a voice whose absurdity I felt whenever I opened my mouth. Feeling less real than before behind my dark glasses, which rattled in their broken frame, the Bombay street splintering into dazzle with every step I took, I walked, unnoticed, back to the hotel, past the fat, impertinent Anglo-Indian girl and the rat-faced Anglo-Indian manager in a silky fawn-coloured suit, and lay down on my bed below the electric ceiling fan.

2

DEGREE

They tell the story of the Sikh who, returning to India after many years, sat down among his suitcases on the Bombay docks and wept. He had forgotten what Indian poverty was like. It is an Indian story, in its arrangement of figure and properties, its melodrama, its pathos. It is Indian above all in its attitude to poverty as something which, thought about from time to time in the midst of other preoccupations, releases the sweetest of emotions. This is poverty, our especial poverty, and how sad it is! Poverty not as an urge to anger or improving action, but poverty as an inexhaustible source of tears, an exercise of the purest sensibility. 'They became so poor that year,' the beloved Hindi novelist Premchand writes, 'that even beggars left their door empty-handed.' That, indeed, is our poverty: not the fact of beggary, but that beggars should have to go from our doors empty-handed. This is our poverty, which in a hundred Indian short stories in all the Indian languages drives the pretty girl to prostitution to pay the family's medical bills.

India is the poorest country in the world. Therefore, to see its poverty is to make an observation of no value; a thousand newcomers to the country before you have seen and said as you. And not only newcomers. Our own sons and daughters, when they return from Europe and America, have spoken in your very words. Do not think that your anger and contempt are marks of your sensitivity. You might have seen more: the smiles on the faces of the begging children, that domestic group among the pavement sleepers waking in the cool Bombay morning, father, mother and baby in a trinity of love, so self-contained that they are as private as if walls had separated them from you: it is your gaze that violates them, your sense of outrage that outrages them. You might have seen the boy sweeping his area of pavement, spreading his mat, lying down; exhaustion and undernourishment are in his tiny body and shrunken face, but lying flat on his back, oblivious of you and the thousands who walk past in the lane between sleepers' mats and house walls bright with advertisements and election slogans, oblivious of the warm, overbreathed air, he plays with fatigued concentration with a tiny pistol in blue plastic. It is your surprise, your anger that denies him humanity. But wait. Stay six months. The winter will bring fresh visitors. Their talk will also be of poverty; they too will show their anger. You will agree; but deep down there will be annoyance; it will seem to you then, too, that they are seeing only the obvious; and it will not please you to find your sensibility so accurately parodied.

Ten months later I was to revisit Bombay and to wonder at my hysteria. It was cooler, and in the crowded courtyards of Colaba there were Christmas decorations, illuminated stars hanging out of windows against the black sky. It was my eye that had changed. I had seen Indian villages: the narrow, broken lanes with green slime in the gutters, the choked back-to-back mud houses, the jumble of filth and food and animals and people, the baby in the dust, swollen-bellied, black with flies, but wearing its good-luck amulet. I had seen the starved child defecating at the roadside while the mangy dog waited to eat the excrement. I had seen the physique of the people of Andhra, which had suggested the possibility of an evolution downwards, wasted body to wasted body, Nature mocking herself, incapable of remission. Compassion and pity did not answer; they were refinements of hope. Fear was what I felt. Contempt was what I had to fight against; to give way to that was to abandon the self I had known. Perhaps in the end it was fatigue that overcame me. For abruptly, in the midst of hysteria, there occurred periods of calm, in which I found that I had grown to separate myself from what I saw, to separate the pleasant from the unpleasant, the whole circular sky ablaze at sunset from the peasants diminished by its glory, the beauty of brassware and silk from the thin wrists that held them up for display, the ruins from the child defecating among them, to separate things from men. I had learned too that escape was always possible, that in every Indian town there was a corner of comparative order and cleanliness in which one could recover and cherish one's self-respect. In India the easiest and most necessary thing to ignore was the most obvious. Which no doubt was why, in spite of all that I had read about the country, nothing had prepared me for it.

But in the beginning the obvious was overwhelming, and there was the knowledge that there was no ship to run back to, as there had been at Alexandria, Port Sudan, Djibouti, Karachi. It was new to me then that the obvious could be separated from the pleasant, from the areas of self-respect and self-love. Marine Drive, Malabar Hill, the lights of the city at night from Kamala Nehru Park, the Parsi Towers of Silence: these are what the tourist brochures put forward as Bombay, and these were the things we were taken to see on three successive days by three kind persons. They built up a dread of what was not shown, that other city where lived the hundreds of thousands who poured in a white stream in and out of Churchgate Station as though hurrying to and from an endless football match. This was the city that presently revealed itself, in the broad, choked and endless main roads of suburbs, a chaos of shops, tall tenements, decaying balconies, electric wires and advertisements, the film posters that seemed to derive from a cooler and more luscious world, cooler and more luscious than the film posters of England and America, promising a greater gaiety, an ampler breast and hip, a more fruitful womb. And the courtyards behind the main streets: the heat heightened, at night the sense of outdoors destroyed, the air holding on its stillness the odours of mingled filth, the windows not showing as oblongs of light but revealing lines, clothes, furniture, boxes and suggesting an occupation of more than floor space. On the roads northwards, the cool redbrick factories set in gardens: Middlesex it might have been, but not attached to these factories any semi-detached or terrace houses, but that shanty town, that rubbish dump. And, inevitably, the prostitutes, the 'gay girls' of the Indian newspapers. But where, in these warrens where three brothels might be in one building and not all the sandal-oil perfumes of Lucknow could hide the stench of gutters and latrines, was the gaiety? Lust, like compassion, was a refinement of hope. Before this one felt only the fragility of one's own sexual impulses. One hesitated to probe, to imagine; one concentrated on one's own revulsion. Men with clubs stood guard at the entrances. Protecting whom from what? In the dim, stinking corridors sat expressionless women, very old, very dirty, shrivelled almost to futility; and already one had the feeling that people were negligible: these were the sweepers, the servants of the gay girls of the Bombay poor, doubtless lucky because employed: a frightening glimpse of India's ever receding degrees of degradation.

Degrees of degradation, because gradually one discovers that in spite of its appearance of chaos, in spite of all the bustling white-clad crowds which by their number would appear to defy or to make worthless any attempt at categorization, this degradation is charted, as the Indian landscape itself which, from the train no more than a jumble of tiny irregularly shaped fields, private follies of which no official organization would take cognizance, has yet been measured and surveyed and sketched and remains recorded in all its absurdity in the various collectorates, where the title deeds, wrapped in red cloth or yellow cloth, rise in bundles from floor to ceiling. This is the result of an English endeavour answering the Indian need: definition, distinction. To define is to begin to separate oneself, to assure oneself of one's position, to be withdrawn from the chaos that India always threatens, the abyss at whose edge the sweeper of the gay girl sits. A special type of hat or turban, a way of cutting the beard or a way of not cutting the beard, the Western-style suit or the unreliable politicians' khadi, the caste mark of the Kashmiri Hindu or Madras brahmin: this gives proof of one's community, one's worth as a man, one's function, as the title deed in the collectorate gives proof of one's ownership of part of the earth.

The prompting is universal, but the Indian practice is purely of India. 'And do thy duty, even if it be humble, rather than another's, even if it be great. To die in one's duty is life: to live in another's is death.' This is the Gita, preaching degree fifteen hundred years before Shakespeare's Ulysses, preaching it today. And the man who makes the dingy bed in the hotel room will be affronted if he is asked to sweep the gritty floor. The clerk will not bring you a glass of water even if you faint. The architecture student will consider it a degradation to make drawings, to be a mere draughts-man. And Ramnath, the stenographer, so designated on the triangular block of wood that stands on his desk, will refuse to type out what he has taken down in shorthand.

Ramnath was a clerk in a government department. He earned 110 rupees a month and was happy until Malhotra, a 600-rupee-a-month officer, came to his department. Malhotra was an Indian from East Africa; he had been educated at an English university, and had just returned from a European posting. Ramnath and his 110-rupee colleagues secretly scoffed at Europe-returned Indians, but they were all a little frightened of Malhotra, whose reputation was terrify-ing. He was supposed to know every paragraph of the Civil Service code; he knew his privileges as well as his responsibilities.

Soon enough Ramnath was summoned to Mal-hotra's office, and there a letter was dictated to him at speed. Ramnath was happily able to catch it all and he returned to the desk marked 'Steno' with a feeling of satisfaction. No further summons came that day; but one came early next morning and when Ramnath went in he found Malhotra quite pale with anger. His neatly trimmed moustache bristled; his eyes were hard. He was freshly bathed and shaved, and Ramnath could feel the difference between his own loose white trousers and open-necked, long-tailed blue shirt and Malhotra's European-tailored grey suit set off by the university tie. Ramnath remained composed. The anger of a superior, for whatever reason, was as natural as Ramnath's own abuse of the sweeper who twice daily cleaned out his tenement privy in Mahim. In such relationships anger and abuse were almost without meaning; they merely marked proper distinctions.

'That letter you took yesterday,' Malhotra said. 'Why wasn't it returned for signature yesterday afternoon?'

'It wasn't? I am sorry, sir. I will see about it now.' Ramnath took his leave and presently returned. 'I have spoken about it to the typist, sir. But Hiralal has had quite a lot of work these last few days.'

'Hiralal? Typist? Don't you type?'

'Oh no, sir. I am a steno.'

'And what do you think a steno is? In future you type out the letters I give you, do you hear?'

Ramnath's face went blank.

'Do you hear?'

'That is not my job, sir.'

'We'll see about that. Take another letter now. And I want this one back before lunch.'

Malhotra dictated. Ramnath made his squiggles with a dancing pen, bowed when the dictating was over, and left the room. In the afternoon Malhotra buzzed for him.

'Where is that letter you took this morning?'

'It is with Hiralal, sir.'

'And yesterday's letter is still with Hiralal. Didn't I tell you that you must type out the letters I give you?'

Silence.

'Where is my letter?'

'It is not my job, sir.'

Malhotra banged the table. 'But we went through all that this morning.'

This was what Ramnath also felt. 'I am a steno, sir. I am not a typist.'

'I am going to report you, Ramnath, for insubordination.'

'That is your right, sir.'

'Don't *talk* to me like that! You won't type my letters. Let me have it from you like that. Say, "I won't type your letters".'

'I am a steno, sir.'

Malhotra dismissed Ramnath and went to see the head of his department. He was made to wait a little in the ante-room before he was called in. The head was tired, tolerant. He understood the impatience of a man like Malhotra, fresh from Europe. But no one before had required a steno to type. Of course, a steno's duties might be said to include typing. But that would be extending the definition of the word. Besides, this was India, and in India it was necessary to take people's feelings into consideration.

'If that is your attitude, sir, then I am sorry to say that you leave me with no alternative but to take the matter to the Union Public Service Commission. I shall report Ramnath for insubordination to you. And through you I shall ask for a full-scale inquiry into the duties of stenos.'

The head sighed. Malhotra wasn't going to get far in the service. That was clear; but he had his rights, and a demand for an inquiry would at some time, though not immediately, create a good deal of trouble: papers, questions, reports.

'Try a little persuasion, Malhotra.'

'I take it, sir, that this is your last word on the subject?'

'Last word?' The head was vague. 'My last word . . .'

The telephone rang: the head seized it, smiling at Malhotra. Malhotra rose and withdrew.

There was no letter awaiting signature on Malhotra's desk. He buzzed for Ramnath and very promptly Ramnath appeared. His triumph could scarcely be concealed by his excessive gravity, his bowed shoulders, his pad pressed to his blue-shirted breast, his gaze fixed on his shoes. He knew that Malhotra had been to see the head, and that not even a rebuke had resulted.

'A letter, Ramnath.'

Pad fell open; pen squiggled above and below ruled lines. But as he squiggled, Ramnath's assurance gave way to terror. What he was taking down was Malhotra's request for his sacking, for insubordination, for inefficiency as a stenographer, and for insolence. This committing of a thing to paper was threatening enough. What was worse was that the letter would have to be typed out by Hiralal. For Ramnath now there seemed only a choice of humiliations. Controlling his terror, he took the letter down, waited with bowed head to be dismissed, and when dismissal came, fled to the office of the head of the department. He waited a long time in the ante-room; he went in; and in no time he came out again.

At five that afternoon Ramnath tapped at Malhotra's door and stood in the doorway. In a trembling hand he held some typewritten sheets; and as soon as Malhotra looked up, Ramnath's eyes filled with tears.

'Ah,' Malhotra said. 'Hiralal has been catching up with his work, I see.'

Saying nothing, Ramnath shot to the side of Malhotra's desk, placed the typewritten sheets on the green blotting pad and, in a continuation of this downward action, dropped to the floor and touched Malhotra's polished shoes with his clasped palms.

'Get up! Get up! Did Hiralal type this?'

'I did! I did!' Ramnath was sobbing on the worn floor mat.

'Treat you people like people, and the net result is that you get insubordinate. Treat you like animals, and then you behave like this.'

Sobbing, embracing the shoes, polishing them with his palms, Ramnath agreed.

'You will type my letters from now on?'

Ramnath struck his forehead on Malhotra's shoes.

'All right. We'll tear this letter up. This is how we get through our work in this department.'

Sobbing, banging his forehead on Malhotra's shoes, Ramnath waited until the interleaved scraps of top copy and carbon fell into the wastepaper basket. Then he rose, his eyes dry, and ran out of the room. The day's work was over; now, with the great jostling crowds, home to Mahim. He had yet to accustom himself to the humiliations of the new world. He had been violated in the tenderest area of his self-esteem, and fear of the abyss alone had given him the strength to endure such a violation. It was a little tragedy. He had learned to obey; he would survive.

Countless such tragedies are marked on the hearts of those whom one sees in those brisk white-clad crowds, hurrying to and from their homes like city-workers in every city of the world, people for whom all the advertisements are meant, all the electric trains run, to whom the film posters are directed, all the extravagantly coloured women with big breasts and big hips, descendants of those figures of old Indian sculpture which, until separated from the people who created them, are like a tragic folk longing.

For Malhotra, too, with his Italian-styled suit and English university tie, the society and its violations were new. East Africa, the English university and the years in Europe had made him just enough of a colonial to be out of place in India. He had no family to speak of. He was only a 600-rupee-a-month man, and his place was therefore with 600-rupee-a-month men. But at that level there were no outsiders, no one who, like Malhotra, had rejected the badges of food and caste and dress. He wished to marry; it was also what his parents wished for him. But his colonial eye made him aspire too high. 'Don't call us. We will call you.' 'We thank you for your interest, and we will let you know as soon as the numerous applications have been gone through.' 'We don't appreciate 600 rupees a month.' This was what the son of one family said. And below that there was, in Malhotra's view, little more than village society. No marriage, then, for him; and the years were going by, and his parents were breaking their hearts. He could only share his bitterness with his friends.

Malik was one of these. He too was a 'new man'. He and Malhotra were bound only by their common bitterness, for Malik was an engineer and earned 1,200 rupees a month. He lived in a well-appointed flat in one of the finer areas of Bombay. By the standards of London he was well off. By the standards of Bombay he was overprivileged. But he was miserable. European engineers less qualified than himself earned three times as much for their services as experts and advisers; the mere fact that they were Europeans commended them to Indian firms. This was his story. A new man, he remained a stranger in Bombay, more of an outsider than any visiting European technician, to whom many doors were open. Malik's qualifications for the young business executive or 'box-wallah' society seemed high, but at our first meeting he told me of the probing by which he was continually rejected. He was an engineer; that was good. That he was Scandinavia-returned was impressive. That he worked for an established firm with European connexions made him more than promising. Then: 'Do you own a car?' Malik didn't. The probing was abandoned; no one was even interested in his parentage.

He spoke sadly in his passé modernistic flat, which he was beginning to let go: the irregular bookshelves, the irregular ceramics, the irregular coffee table. For all this there was no audience, and it was like the scrupulous preparation for going out of a girl whom no one will notice. It is with contemporary furniture as with contemporary clothes: sad unless there is someone who notices and cares. On the irregular coffee table there was a large photograph in a gilt frame of a pretty white girl with dark hair and high cheekbones. I asked no questions, but Malhotra told me later that the girl had died years before in her Northern land. While we talked and drank the tape-recorder played songs Malik had recorded in his student days in Europe, songs which even I could recognize as old. And in that Bombay flat, surrounded by the dramatic squares of light and darkness of other metropolitan blocks, below us the glittering arc of Marine Drive, in that room with the central photograph of the dead girl and the sour background of dead songs, we looked through the well-thumbed photograph albums: Malik in overcoat, Malik and his friends, Malik and the girl, against snow- or pine-covered mountains, against open-air cafés: Malik and Malhotra sharing the past (Ibsen in the original on the irregular bookshelves), 600-rupee-a-month and 1,200-rupee-a-month men temporarily forgetting their humiliations in memories of a past acceptance, when to be a man and a student was enough, and to be Indian gave glamour.

Jivan was thirteen or fourteen when he left his village to look for work in Bombay. He had no friends in the city and nowhere to go. He slept on the pavements. At last he found a job in a printery in the Fort area. He earned fifty rupees a month. He did not look for lodgings; he continued to sleep on that stretch of pavement which custom had now made his. Jivan could read and write; he was intelligent and anxious to please; and after some months he was chasing advertisements for a magazine his firm printed. His wages steadily rose and it seemed he was set for success and high responsibility in the firm. Then one day, without warning, he went to his employer and gave notice.

'It is my luck,' his employer said. 'I can never keep good people. I train them. Then they leave me. What's this new job you've found?'

'I have none, sir. I was hoping you would find one for me.'

'Oho! It's another rise you're after.'

'No, sir. It isn't money I want. It's this cycling about. It was all right when I was younger. But now I would like an office job. I want a desk of my own. I will even take less money if I can get an office job. I hope you will help me find one.'

Jivan's mind was made up. His employer was a kind-hearted man and he recommended Jivan for a clerkship in another firm. Here, as a clerk, Jivan rose fast. He was as loyal and hard-working as he had been in the print-ery; and he had the magic touch. Soon he was almost running the firm. After some time he had saved eight thousand rupees, slightly more than six hundred pounds. He bought a taxi and hired it out at twenty rupees a day: Malhotra's salary. He still worked for his firm. He still slept on the pavements. He was twenty-five years old.

Vasant grew up in a Bombay slum. He was very young when he left school to look for work. He took to hanging around the stock exchange. His face became familiar and the stockbrokers sent him on little errands. They began to use him as a telegraph-runner. One day a stockbroker gave Vasant a message but no money. 'It's all right,' the stockbroker said. 'They'll bill me at the end of the month.' So Vasant discovered that if you sent telegrams in some number the telegraph office gave you credit for a month. He offered a service to stockbrokers: he would collect all their telegrams from their offices, file them, and he would ask for money only at the end of the month. He charged a small fee; he made a little money; he even managed to rent a little cubby-hole of a 'telegraph office'. He read all the stockbrokers' tele-grams: his knowledge of the market grew. He began to deal himself. He became rich. Now he was old and established. He had a respectably furnished office in a suitable block. He had a receptionist, secretaries, clerks. But this was mainly for show. He continued to do all his important work in his cramped little 'telegraph office'; he could think nowhere else. When he was poor he had never eaten during the day. The habit remained with him. If he ate during the day he became sluggish.

The worker in leather is among the lowest of the low, the most tainted of the tainted, and it was unusual, especially in the far South, where caste distinctions are rigid, to find two brahmin brothers making leather goods. Their establishment was small and self-contained: house, workshops and vegetable gardens on a plot of four acres. One brother, lean, nervous, hunted orders in the town and with his quick eyes observed foreign designs in briefcases, diary bindings, camera cases; the other brother, plump, placid, superintended the work. The greatest praise, which made both of them smirk and squirm with pleasure, was: 'But you didn't make this here. It looks foreign. American, *I* would say.' They both had progressive views about what the lean brother, in khaki shorts and vest on this Sunday morning, referred to as 'labour relations'. 'You've got to keep them happy. I can't do the work. I can't get my children to do it. You've got to keep them happy.' An 'ar-chin', picked off the streets, got one rupee a day; when he was fourteen or fifteen he could get four rupees a day; the 'maistry' got one hundred and twenty rupees a month, with a yearly bonus of about two hundred and forty rupees. 'Yes,' the other brother said. 'You have to keep them happy.' They were proud that everything in their workshops was made by hand, but their ambition was to create an 'industrial estate' which would bear their name. They had come from a poor family. They had begun by making envelopes. They still made envelopes. In one corner of the workshop a boy was standing on a neat stack of envelope sheets; a 'maistry', wielding a broad-bladed chopper, chopped the paper close to the boy's toes; elsewhere boys were folding up the paper that had been cut to the pattern required. The brothers were worth seventy thousand pounds.

Adventure is possible. But a knowledge of degree is in the bones and no Indian is far from his origins. It is like a physical yearning: the tycoon in his cubby-hole, the entrepreneur clerk sleeping on the pavement, the brahmin leather-goods manufacturers anxious to protect their children against caste contamination. However incongruous the imported mechanics of the new world – stockbrokers, telegrams, labour relations, advertisements – might seem, they have been incorporated into the rule of degree. Few Indians are outsiders. Malik and Malhotra are exceptional. They are not interested in the type of adventure the society can provide; their aspirations are alien and disruptive. Rejecting the badges of dress and food and function, rejecting degree, they find themselves rejected. They look for Balzacian adventure in a society which has no room for Rastignacs.

'When unrighteous disorder prevails, the women sin and are impure; and when women are not pure, Krishna, there is disorder of castes, social confusion.' This is the Gita again. And in India there is no social confusion, no disorder of castes, no adventure, in spite of the bingo on Sunday mornings in the old British clubs, in spite of the yellow-covered overseas editions of the *Daily Mirror* which the ladies in their graceful saris seize with eager manicured hands, and the copy of *Woman's Own* which the dainty shopper, basket-carrying servant respectfully in her train, presses to one breast like a badge of caste; in spite of the dance floors of Bombay, Delhi and Calcutta: those sad bands, those sad Anglo-Indian girls at the microphone, and the air full of dated slang. 'Oh, just bung your coat down there.' 'I say, by Jove!' And the names fly: Bunty, Andy, Freddy, Jimmy, Bunny. They are real, the men who answer to these names, and they answer them well: their jackets and ties and collars and accents do make them Bunty and Andy and Freddy. But they are not wholly what they seem. Andy is also Anand, Danny Dhandeva; their marriages have been strictly arranged, their children's marriages will be arranged; the astrologer will be earnestly consulted and horoscopes will be cast. For every man and woman on the dance floor is marked by destiny, on every one Fate has its eye. The Parsis, perhaps Freddy's lesser friends or relations, in their enclosure between decks on the holiday steamer from Goa, might loudly sing, their pleasure heightened by the confusion of the native crowd, *Barbara Allen* and *The Ash Grove* and *I Don't Have a Wooden Heart*. But that little corner of merry England which they have created in Bombay is also Druidical. It worships fire; its ways are narrow and protective, and at the end lie the Towers of Silence and the grim rites behind those walls whose main portals are marked with a symbol from the ancient world.

The outer and inner worlds do not have the physical separateness which they had for us in Trinidad. They coexist; the society only pretends to be colonial; and for this reason its absurdities are at once apparent. Its mimicry is both less and more than a colonial mimicry. It is the special mimicry of an old country which has been without a native aristocracy for a thousand years and has learned to make room for outsiders, but only at the top. The mimicry changes, the inner world remains constant: this is the secret of survival. And so it happens that, to one whole area of India, a late seventeenth-century traveller like Ovington remains in many ways a reliable guide. Yesterday the mimicry was Mogul; tomorrow it might be Russian or American; today it is English.

Mimicry might be too harsh a word for what appears so comprehensive and profound: buildings, railways, a system of administration, the intellectual discipline of the civil servant and the economist. Schizophrenia might better explain the scientist who, before taking up his appointment, consults the astrologer for an auspicious day. But mimicry must be used because so much has been acquired that the schizophrenia is often concealed; because so much of what is seen remains simple mimicry, incongruous and absurd; and because no people, by their varied physical endowments, are as capable of mimicry as the Indians. The Indian Army officer is at a first meeting a complete English army officer. He even manages to look English; his gait and bearing are English; his mannerisms, his tastes in drink are English; his slang is English. In the Indian setting this Indian English mimicry is like fantasy. It is an undiminishing absurdity; and it is only slowly that one formulates what was sensed from the first day: this is a mimicry not of England, a real country, but of the fairy-tale land of Anglo-India, of clubs and sahibs and syces and bearers. It is as if an entire society has fallen for a casual confidence trickster. Casual because the trickster has gone away, losing interest in his joke, but leaving the Anglo-Indians flocking to the churches of Calcutta on a Sunday morning to assert the alien faith, more or less abandoned in its country of origin; leaving Freddy crying, 'Just bung your coat down there, Andy'; leaving the officer exclaiming, 'I say, by Jove! I feel rather bushed.' Leaving 'civil lines', 'cantonments', leaving people 'going off to the hills'; magic words now fully possessed, now spoken as of right, in what is now at last Indian Anglo-India, where smartness can be found in the cosy proletarian trivialities of *Woman's Own* and the *Daily Mirror* and where Mrs Hauksbee, a Millamant of the suburbs, is still the arbiter of elegance.

But room has been left at the top, and out of this mimicry a new aristocracy is being essayed, not of politicians or civil servants, but of the business executives of foreign, mostly British, firms. To them, the box-wallahs, as they are called, have gone the privileges India reserves for the foreign and conquering; and it is to this new commercial caste that both Malik, the engineer 'drawing' twelve hundred rupees a month, and Malhotra, the government servant drawing six hundred, aspire with despair, and, despairing, seek to ridicule. We are now as far above them as they are above Ramnath, with his flapping Indian-style white cotton trousers, boarding the crowded suburban electric train to get to his tenement room in Mahim; as far above them as Ramnath is above the sweeper of the 'gay girl' in Forras Road. We have left even the lower-class Parsis far below; we can hardly hear them singing *Flow Gently, Sweet Afton* on the holiday steamer from Goa.

Bunty the box-wallah. He is envied and ridiculed throughout India. Much is made of the name, and even Bunty, from the security of his aristocracy, sometimes pretends to find its origin in the box of the street pedlar, though it is more likely that the name derives from the Anglo-Indian office box, the burden in the old days of a special servant, of which Kipling speaks so feelingly in *Something of Myself*. Bunty is envied for his luxurious company flat, his inflated salary and his consequent ability, in an India which is now independent, guiltlessly to withdraw from India. For this withdrawal he is also ridiculed. He is an easy target. He is new to the caste, but the caste is old and, though essentially engaged in trade, it has been ennobled by the glamour of the conqueror, the rewards of trade, and now by Bunty himself, whom these two things in conjunction have attracted.

Bunty comes of a 'good' family, Army, ICS; he might even have princely connexions. He is two or three generations removed from purely Indian India; he, possibly like his father, has been to an Indian or English public school and one of the two English universities, whose accent, through all the encircling hazards of Indian intonation, he strenuously maintains. He is a blend of East and West; he is 'broad-minded'. He permits his name to be corrupted into the closest English equivalent, like place names in the mouth of the conqueror. So Firdaus becomes Freddy, Jamshed Jimmy, and Chandrashekhar, which is clearly impossible, becomes the almost universal Bunty or Bunny. Bunty knows it will count in his favour, as a mark of his broadmindedness, though at this level it requires a minimum of heroism, if he makes a mixed marriage; if, say, as a Punjabi Hindu he marries a Bengali Muslim or a Bombay Parsi. Freed of one set of caste rules, he obeys another, and these are as nice: to introduce Jimmy, whose air-conditioned office is shared and has hard furnishings, into the home of Andy, who has an office to himself with soft furnishings, is to commit a blunder.

Bunty's grandfather might have conducted his

business over a hookah or while reclining on bolsters in a dreadfully furnished room. Bunty discusses business over drinks at the club or on the golf course. There is no need for the golf course: the box-wallah circle is tiny. But it is a condition of Bunty's employment that he play golf, in order to make suitable 'contacts', and on the golf courses of clubs all over the country he can be seen with an equally unhappy Andy, who, as he goes out into the drizzle of Bangalore, might remark that it is rather like the rain of England. There are other traditions, which vary from city to city. In Calcutta there is the Friday afternoon revelry at Firpo's restaurant on Chowringhee. In the days of the British this celebrated the departure of the mail boat for England and marked the end of the four-and-a-half-day week. Letters to England now go by air; but Bunty is caste-minded; he maintains the tradition, unembarrassed by its origin.

It is easy for Indians to make fun of Bunty for being called 'daddy' by his English-speaking children; for his imitated manners: he rises when ladies come into a room; for his foreign interest in interior decoration; for the spotless bathroom and adequate towels he provides for his guests (such attentions in India being beneath the notice of all but the latrine-cleaner: the Indian lavatory and the Indian kitchen are the visitor's nightmare). But Bunty is no fool. He has withdrawn from India, but he does not wish to be a European. He sees the glamour of Europe; but, being in almost daily contact with Europeans, he is compelled by his pride to be Indian. He strives too hard perhaps to blend East with West; his patronage of Indian arts and crafts is a little like that of the visitor. In his drawing-room, hung with contemporary Indian fabrics, the odd sketch from Kangra, Basohli or Rajasthan or a piece of the bright bazaar art of Jamini Roy stands beside the Picasso lithograph or the Sisley reproduction. His food is a mixture of Indian and European; his drink is wholly European.

But this mixture of East and West in Bunty's home tells more of the truth about Bunty than either his friends or enemies believe. For Bunty is only pretending to be a colonial. He sees himself as every man's equal and most men's superior; and in him, as in every Indian, the inner world continues whole and untouched. Bunty might relish the light, attractive complexions of his wife and children. He might be at especial pains to draw your attention to the complexions of his children, and he might do so by some flippant denigratory assessment. But their paleness is not a European paleness, which to Bunty is reminiscent of the Indian albino; and indeed about the European, however to be imitated, fawned upon and resented, there still remains some stigma of the *mleccha*, the unclean. Bunty's caste is European; but Bunty carries within himself a strong sense of aryan race and ancientness as exclusive possessions. It is for this reason that the Anglo-Indian half-breed, however pale, however anglicized, can form no respectable part of Bunty's society unless graced by some notable family connexion; for this group there can be no room in India except as outsiders and not at the top. (Nor would they wish there to be room. Their dream is of England; and to England they come – the paler go to Australia, white – and they congregate in sad little colonies in places like Forest Hill, busy churchgoers in short dresses which, in India anti-Indian, in London are un-English and colonial; and they read *Woman's Own* and the *Daily Mirror* on the day of publication: a dream of romance fulfilled.) Towards Europe Bunty is like the puritan seducer: he despises even while he violates.

On Sunday morning Bunty entertains his friends to drinks in his flat. This might be on Malabar Hill if it is in Bombay; if in Calcutta, it will be well hidden from the *bustees* which provide factory labour.

'I had a round of golf yesterday with the Deputy Director . . .' This is from Andy.

'Well, the Director told me . . .'

Bunty and Andy are not discussing business. They are talking of the Chinese invasion. Even now, however, they appear to be taking delight in their new closeness to power. It is not for this reason alone that their gossip is disturbing. It is a unique type of gossip. How can it be described? It is unslanted; it states facts and draws no conclusions. It makes one long to shake them by the shoulder and say, 'Express your prejudices. Say at least, "If I had the power I would do this". Say that you are on the side of this and against that. Don't just go on calmly reporting unrelated little disasters. Get angry. Get excited. Get worried. Try to link all that you have been saying. Make some sort of pattern out of it, however prejudiced. Then at least I will understand. Right now you are behaving as though you are talking of well-known history.'

It is with this gossip that one begins to doubt what Bunty and Andy show of themselves and one begins to feel that they are not what they seem, that there are areas to which they can retreat and where they are hard to get at. The flat now seems to hang in a void. India is a stone's throw away, but in the flat it is denied: the beggars, the gutters, the starved bodies, the weeping swollen-bellied child black with flies in the filth and cowdung and human excrement of a bazaar lane, the dogs, ribby, mangy, cowed and cowardly, reserving their anger, like the human beings around them, for others of their kind. The decoration of the flat is contemporary; many of its ingredients are Indian; but it is based on nothing. On the shelves there are novels that might be found on shelves in a dozen other countries: vulgarity nowadays is international and swift. But novels imply an interest in people. This flat holds a rejection of concern. And did not that educated brahmin read the romances of Denise Robins, which lay on his shelves next to the bulky volumes of ancient astrological prophecies published by the Madras Government? Did not that young man, a student at Punjab University, read the paperbound volumes of the Schoolgirl's Own Library for relaxation? Will not Bunty's wife fall on the *Daily Mirror* and *Woman's Own* in the club? Will she not consult her astrologer?

Somewhere there has been a failure of communication, unrecognized because communication seems to have been established. In the cafés there are earnest groups of the young who talk about 'theatre' and the need for bringing theatre to the 'people'. They are like their counterparts in England, whom, like the army officers, they even manage physically to resemble; and like their counterparts in England, by theatre they mean *Look Back in Anger*, professionally abbreviated to *Look Back*. A willingness to accept, an underlying, unwitting rejection of the values implied: in Bunty's rooms, the irritating gossip going on, the Chinese about to break through into Assam, the mimicry is no longer as funny as the sight on that first day in Bombay, after the exhaustion and hysteria, of the banner hung across the hot, squalid street advertising the Oxford and

Cambridge Players' production of *The Importance of Being Earnest*.

Withdrawal, denial, confusion of values: these are vague words. We need more direct evidence; and a little, I feel, is provided by a recent Indian novel, *The Princes*, by Manohar Malgonkar, published in London by Hamish Hamilton in 1963. *The Princes* is the medieval tragedy of a medieval Indian petty prince who loses power with Independence and feels the humiliation of his fall so deeply that he goes out unarmed after a wounded tiger and is killed. It is an honest book, and the writing is not without skill. Malgonkar has a feeling for outdoor life and his descriptions of hunting and shooting can convey the enchantment of these pastimes even to those who do not practise them.

The Prince is descended from casteless Deccani bandits who, when they acquired political power, surrendered a lakh of rupees to the pundits in exchange for caste privileges. The treasures they amassed remain in the state treasury, objects of almost religious awe, guarded by a special group of retainers. For the ruling house these treasures are a private delectation, a reminder of the past; it is unthinkable that they should be used to improve the impoverished state. The Prince is opposed to progress. He states the view quite bluntly; and when the British decide to build a dam in territory adjacent to the state, he persuades his aboriginal subjects who live in the area to be affected to vote against the scheme. The Prince gives five annual scholarships, each worth £70, to deserving boys. On himself he is more lavish. He has two palaces, thirty motor-cars and annual pocket money of £70,000. To spend £1,500 to bring down a courtesan from Simla is as nothing. He has much time to devote to his hobbies. He is an excellent shot and a fearless tracker of wounded tigers. 'I am rich and well-born,' he says, quoting the Gita. 'Who else is equal to me?' He matches words with action. When the nationalists of the state occupy the administration building in 1947 he goes in alone, ignoring the crowd, and hauls down the Indian flag. He is unable to accommodate himself to the handsome terms of the Home Ministry in Delhi, and when he sees that it is too late to save his state and his powers he is heartbroken. He does not rage or weep. Quoting that line of the Gita, he goes out unarmed after a wounded tiger and is killed. He was rich and high; he has fallen.

It is a medieval concept of tragedy.

> Reduce we all our lessons unto this:
> To rise, sweet Spenser, therefore live we all.
> Spenser, all live to die, and rise to fall.

But what is puzzling is that it should be so presented to us by the Prince's son, who is the narrator. He was born in 1920, educated at an English-style English-staffed public school for the sons of princes, and served as an officer in the army during the war. 'Indeed it seems to me,' he says, 'that with the passing of the years I have come to identify myself more and more with (my father's) values.' After the public school which sought to root out snobbery between princes of big states and princes of little states; after the army; after the love affair with an Anglo-Indian girl, encountered in Simla:

> The British certainly knew all about resisting change. It was spring in the Himalayas, and Simla was exactly as it had been fifty years ago or a

hundred, and Mrs Hauksbee might have been living just around the corner

'I like your perfume, whatever it is.'
'Chanel number five. I had just a scrap left, but I had to wear it – for going out with a prince.'
'Why, thanks! I'll buy some more.'

After the clubs of Delhi:

'Rumpus?' I exclaimed. 'Why not? Of course we can have a rumpus. One is not a father every day, dammit! What sort of a rumpus had you in mind?' I was certainly learning to handle conversation, now that I had been in New Delhi for nearly two years; meaningless, insincere, but light. You had to keep it frothy, that was all that mattered.

This is how far we will appear to move from the Prince and his derelict principality and the local primary school where, at the beginning of the story, the narrator, Abhayraj, and his half-brother Charudutt are pupils. They are kept separate from the untouchables, who sit on the floor at the back. One morning during the break a game of mango-seed football starts in the veranda. The untouchables watch from a distance. One joins in, trips Charudutt. The caste boys, Abhayraj included, abuse the untouchables: 'Cow-eaters, stinkers, cow-skinners.' And they throw the offending untouchable boy and his satchel into the pond. 'Bastard!' the boy shouts from the pond at Charudutt. 'You are no prince. You are a whore's son.'

It is this word, bastard, which interests Abhayraj. He asks his English tutor, Mr Moreton, what the word means. Mr Moreton hesitates. 'I could understand his embarrassment. He was a sensitive man, and he knew about Charudutt and about the numerous *upraja* sons in our family – children born to rulers out of wedlock.' This is the sensitivity of Mr Moreton. Neither tutor nor pupil speaks of the scene in the school grounds.

The untouchable boy, Kanakchand, has no books the next day. He is put out of the class and in the afternoon Abhayraj sees him 'miserable and downcast, still squatting on the wall'. He is still there the following morning. Abhayraj speaks to him and finds out that he cannot stay at home because he will be flogged if his father gets to know that his books have been destroyed; he cannot go into the class because he has no books and no money to buy new ones. Abhayraj gives Kanakchand all the books in his own satchel. Among them, however, is the *Highroads Treasury*, which is not a school book but a gift from Mr Moreton. Mr Moreton, by some chance, asks after the book that day; the truth is told him; he understands. The next morning Kanakchand comes to Abhayraj and returns the *Highroads Treasury*. 'It was a present. Here, I have brought it back.'

It is a brutal but touching episode, rendered with fidelity, from the taunting to the forgetting to the impulse of pity and generosity. Now comes the sentence which distorts it all, which cuts the ground from under our feet. 'He was as sound as a silver rupee when he began,' Abhayraj comments. 'What made him turn so sour and twisted in later life?' Kanakchand sound as a silver rupee! Kanakchand, untouchable, cow-eater, stinker, squatting on the floor at the back of the class, sitting on the fountain wall for two days because he has lost his books! Did his soundness lie in his acceptance of degree? Did it lie in his refusal to steal from someone who had made him a valuable gift?

The friendship develops. One day Kanakchand makes a gift to Abhayraj of enormous bean seeds, good for nothing except looking at and holding in the hands, and Abhayraj is 'vaguely distressed at my first contact with the playthings of the poor, bean seeds found on the floor of the forest'. And more is to come. 'I did not realize it then, but Kanakchand was my first direct contact with the quivering poverty of India.' It is a singular word, this *quivering*. At first it seems unnecessary; then it seems theatrical yet oddly matter-of-fact; then it seems a concession to a convention of feeling.

Kanakchand's poverty is certainly theatrical. His lunch is one black roti, chillis and an onion.

> It seemed that even the onion was something of a treat, and that bajra or millet bread and chilli powder mixed with groundnut oil formed his main meal of the day. I watched with fascination as he ate, hungrily and with relish . . . He wolfed the very last crumb, biting alternately on the charred bajra roti and the onion. And when he finished the very last mouthful, he licked his fingers clean.

It is like a description of the feeding habits of a rare animal. Poverty as occasional spectacle: this is our poverty. Abhayraj offers Kanakchand a chocolate. Kanakchand throws it, wrapper and all, into his mouth. Abhayraj exclaims. Kanakchand spits it out and – sound as a silver rupee, remember – makes this curious statement: 'Oh, I didn't know. I thought Bal-raje was playing some kind of joke on me – making me eat green paper.'

Kanakchand is intelligent but his English is poor. To

win one of the Prince's five scholarships to a high school he has to write an English essay. Abhayraj writes the essay for him; Kanakchand wins the scholarship; and the day arrives for the Prince to make the presentation. Kanakchand's parents are present, 'deliriously happy'. 'Truth, honesty, faith in God and above all, loyalty,' the Prince begins his speech, 'add up to far more than the gaining of worldly rewards.' With this he raises his riding crop and strikes Kanakchand to the floor, strikes him twice again and 'wiped his hands delicately on a handkerchief'. Abhayraj is horrified. He persuades his mother to provide for Kanakchand's education. But Abhayraj notes that Kanakchand never shows any 'gratitude'; and Abhayraj is tormented, not by Kanakchand's humiliation, but by 'the guilt of turning a high-spirited, ambitious boy into a malevolent revolutionary': again that distorting gloss, that cutting of the ground from under our feet.

The years pass. Kanakchand becomes important in the nationalist movement. He wishes to be avenged, and with Independence vengeance is his. He is now presented to us as physically repulsive and contemptible, overbearing at one moment, instinctively cringing at the next. The Prince's little principality disappears. Kanakchand, adding insult to injury, leads a demonstration through the streets, chanting, 'The raj is dead!'

That, I thought, was the one thing I would never forgive Kanakchand. He was hitting at a man who had already fallen but was putting up a brave front. He was humiliating someone who still held that he had no equal among men. That, truly, was the vengeance of sheep, as my father had said.

The stiff upper lip reinforcing a medieval conception of degree, public school fair-play stimulating an opposed passion: the confusion is now apparent. It is with more than public school righteousness, though it might seem that in its name alone action is being taken, that Abhayraj makes a vow. He will avenge his father. He will do so by inflicting an old humiliation – in retrospect how deserved, answering how apt an assessment of degree – on Kanakchand. He will flog him in public; he will flog him with a riding crop. 'He was one of those who would always squeal, one of those unfortunates who had not learned to take their punishment without showing it.' This is the action with which the book ends. This is what is presented for our approval; this is what, after the tragedy of the Prince's fall, restores calm of mind to the narrator and is meant to restore it to us.

The poverty of India is *quivering*. The guilt Abhayraj carries for his father's flogging of Kanakchand, not public school material in the final analysis, is only the guilt of turning a high-spirited boy into a revolutionary. And all the cruelty of India is magicked away in textbook Western phrases which are as empty as that *quivering*: the narrator sees his father denying 'basic rights' to 'the people', he talks of the 'collective wish of the people'. Nowhere do I see the India I know: those poor fields, those three-legged dogs, those sweating redcoated railway porters carrying heavy tin trunks on their heads. 'The mountains were rainwashed, the sky was a bright blue and the air was stiff with the scent of pine and flowers and charged with an almost electric silence broken by the sharp warnings of the rickshaw pullers.' It is so the rickshaw puller appears, beast of burden more degrading than degraded: unseen, the source only of a holiday sound, part of the atmosphere of a Simla romance. This is the Indian withdrawal and denial; this is part of the confusion of Indian Anglo-India.

So too it comes to the traveller. The poor become faceless. Then all the rest, the dance floors, the Western mimicry, might be subjects for gentle satire. But first the background, the obvious, must be ignored.

3

THE COLONIAL

Well, India is a country of nonsense.

M. K. Gandhi

The man moves briskly among the passengers on the crowded suburban train, distributing leaflets. The leaflets are smudged and dog-eared; in three languages they tell of the misfortunes of a refugee family. Some passengers read the leaflets; many more don't. The train comes into a station. The leaflet-distributor goes out through one door and a woman and a boy enter through another. The leaflet didn't promise this. It promised an impoverished Bengali woman and her six starving children, not this small boy, blind, thin, half-naked, scaly with dirt, whining at a low, steady pitch, tears streaming out of raw red eyes, his arms held aloft in supplication. The boy is manoeuvred and propelled through the coach by the woman, who weeps and whines and briskly, without acknowledgement, collects the small coins which the passengers, barely looking up, hand to her. She does not pause to plead with those who don't give. By the time the train stops she and the boy are at the door, ready to change coaches. They go out. Another man comes in. He too is in a rush. He pushes through the coach, retrieving what leaflets he can before the next station.

It has been swift; everyone, passengers included, is well-drilled; there has been little stir. Stencilled notices in three languages on the grimy woodwork warn against alms-giving, as they warn against accepting cigarettes from strangers since 'these may be doped'. But it is good to give to the beggar. He follows a holy calling; he can exercise the pity and virtue of even the poor. Possibly the boy had been blinded to work this suburban route; and the organization was certainly at fault in issuing the wrong leaflets. But this is not important. What matters is the giving to the beggar, the automatic act of charity which is an automatic reverence to God, like the offering of a candle or a spin of the prayer-wheel. The beggar, like the priest, has his function; like the priest, he might need an organization.

But here is an observer who dissents:

> If I had the power, I would stop every *sadavrata* where free meals are given. It has degraded the nation and it has encouraged laziness, idleness, hypocrisy and even crime. Such misplaced charity adds nothing to the wealth of the country, whether material or spiritual . . . I know that it is . . . much more difficult to organize an institution where honest work has to be done before meals are served . . . But I am convinced that it will be cheaper in the long run, if we do not want to increase in geometrical progression the race of loafers which is fast overrunning this land.

It is the attitude of the foreigner who does not understand the function of the beggar in India and is judging India by the standards of Europe. He is too radical to succeed and of course in this matter of beggary he has failed.

*

Shankaracharya Hill, overlooking the Dal Lake, is one of the beauty spots of Srinagar. It has to be climbed with care, for large areas of its lower slopes are used as latrines by Indian tourists. If you surprise a group of three women, companionably defecating, they will giggle: the shame is yours, for exposing yourself to such a scene.

In Madras the bus station near the High Court is one of the more popular latrines. The traveller arrives; to pass the time he raises his dhoti, defecates in the gutter. The bus arrives; he boards it; the woman sweeper cleans up after him. Still in Madras, observe this bespectacled patriarch walking past the University on the Marina. Without warning he raises his dhoti, revealing a backside bare save for what appears to be a rope-like G-string; he squats, pisses on the pavement, leisurely rises; the dhoti still raised, he rearranges his G-string, lets the dhoti fall, and continues on his promenade. It is a popular evening walk, this Marina; but no one looks, no face is averted in embarrassment.

In Goa you might think of taking an early morning walk along the balustraded avenue that runs beside the Mandovi River. Six feet below, on the water's edge, and as far as you can see, there is a line, like a wavering tidewrack, of squatters. For the people of Goa, as for those of imperial Rome, defecating is a social activity; they squat close to one another; they chatter. When they are done they advance, trousers still down, backsides bare, into the water to wash themselves. They climb back on to the avenue, jump on their cycles or get into their cars, and go away. The strand is littered with excrement; amid this excrement fish is being haggled over as it is landed from the boats; and every hundred yards or so there is a blue-and-white enamelled to disturbance from dangling feet or opening doors. In India, however, where the top bunk has the added advantage of being freer of dust, the lower bunk is preferred, not because it is easier to spread one's bedding on it – there are porters and servants to do that – but because climbing to the top bunk involves physical effort, and physical effort is to be avoided as a degradation.

On this express to Delhi my sleeper had been booked by a high railway official and I was naturally given the lower bunk. My travelling companion was about forty. He wore a suit; he might have been a senior clerk or a university teacher. He was not happy about the top bunk. He complained about it first to the porter and then, after the train had started, to himself. I offered to change with him. His sourness vanished. But he simply stood where he was and did nothing. His bedding had been spread for him on the top bunk by the porter, and he was waiting until we got to the next station, two hours distant, so that he might get a porter to take it down for him. I wished to settle down. I began to do the porter's job. He smiled but offered no help. I lost my temper. His face acquired that Indian expressionlessness which indicates that communication has ceased and that the Indian has withdrawn from a situation he cannot understand. Labour is a degradation; only a foreigner would see otherwise:

> Divorce of the intellect from body-labour has made of us the shortest-lived, most resourceless and most exploited nation on earth.

The observer, the failed reformer, is of course Mohandas Gandhi. Mahatma, great-souled, father of the

cover his waste deserves a heavy penalty even if he
lives in a forest.

The observer is seeing what no Indian sees. But he has
now declared his foreign inspiration. The celebrated
Indian daily bath he frequently dismisses as 'a kind of
bath'. He is unwilling to see beyond the ritual act to the
intention, and in the intention to find reality. Sanitation
is one of his obsessions. And just as in London he had
read books on vegetarianism and clothes-washing and
in South Africa books on bookkeeping, so he has read
books on this subject.

> In his book on rural hygiene Dr Poore says that
> excreta should be buried in earth no deeper than
> nine to twelve inches. The author contends that
> superficial earth is charged with minute life,
> which, together with light and air which easily
> penetrate it, turn the excreta into good soft sweet-
> smelling soil within a week. Any villager can test
> this for himself.

It is the characteristic note of this observer. His interest
in sanitation, which is properly the concern of the
latrine-cleaner, is not widely shared. The briefest
glimpse of the lavatories at New Delhi's international
airport is sufficient. Indians defecate everywhere, on
floors, in urinals for men (as a result of yogic contor-
tions that can only be conjectured). Fearing contamination, they squat rather than sit, and every lavatory
cubicle carries marks of their misses. No one notices.

In Europe and elsewhere the favoured bunk in a railway
sleeper is the top bunk. It is more private and less liable

nation, deified, his name given to streets and parks and squares, honoured everywhere by statues and *mandaps* and in Delhi by Rajghat, which the visitor must approach barefooted over scorching sand, his portrait garlanded in every *pan*-shop, hung in hundreds of offices, bare-chested, bespectacled, radiating light and goodness, his likeness so familiar that, simplified to caricature and picked out in electric lights, it is now an accepted part of the decorations of a wedding house, he is nevertheless the least Indian of Indian leaders. He looked at India as no Indian was able to; his vision was direct, and this directness was, and is, revolutionary. He sees exactly what the visitor sees; he does not ignore the obvious. He sees the beggars and the shameless pundits and the filth of Banaras; he sees the atrocious sanitary habits of doctors, lawyers and journalists. He sees the Indian callousness, the Indian refusal to see. No Indian attitude escapes him, no Indian problem; he looks down to the roots of the static, decayed society. And the picture of India which comes out of his writings and exhortations over more than thirty years still holds: this is the measure of his failure.

He saw India so clearly because he was in part a colonial. He settled finally in India when he was forty-six, after spending twenty years in South Africa. There he had seen an Indian community removed from the setting of India; contrast made for clarity, criticism and discrimination for self-analysis. He emerged a colonial blend of East and West, Hindu and Christian. Nehru is more Indian; he has a romantic feeling for the country and its past; he takes it all to his heart, and the India he writes about cannot easily be recognized. Gandhi never loses the critical, comparing South African eye; he never rhapsodizes, except in the vague Indian way, them, and to this they willingly submit. They are dirt; they wish to appear as dirt.

Class is a system of rewards. Caste imprisons a man in his function. From this it follows, since there are no rewards, that duties and responsibilities become irrelevant to position. A man is his proclaimed function. There is little subtlety to India. The poor are thin; the rich are fat. The petty Marwari merchant in Calcutta eats quantities of sweets to develop the layers of fat that will proclaim his prosperity. 'You look fat and fresh today' is a compliment in the Punjab. And in every Uttar Pradesh town you might see the rich and very fat man in cool, clean white sitting in a cycle-rickshaw being pedalled by a poor and very thin man, prematurely aged, in rags. Beggars whine. Holy men give up all. Politicians are grave and unsmiling. And the cadet of the Indian Administrative Service, when asked why he has joined the service, replies after some thought, 'It gives me prestige.' His colleagues, who are present, do not disagree. It is an honest reply; it explains why, when the Chinese invade, the administration in Assam will collapse.

Service is not an Indian concept, and the providing of services has long ceased to be a concept of caste. The function of the businessman is to make money. He might wish to sell shoes to Russia. He therefore sends good samples; the order obtained, he sends a shipload of shoes with cardboard soles. Overcoming foreign distrust of Indian business practices, he gets an order from Malaya for drugs. And sends coloured water. It is not his duty as a merchant to supply genuine drugs or good shoes or any shoes or drugs at all; his duty is, by whatever means, to make money. The shoes are sent back; there are complaints about the coloured water. This is the merchant's luck; these are the trials he has to endure. He hops from enterprise to enterprise, from shoes to drugs to tea. A tea plantation is a delicate organization; he soon works it to ruin. Short-sightedness and dishonesty do not enter into it. The merchant is simply fulfilling his function. Later, fulfilling another aspect of his function, he might give up his money altogether and end his days as a mendicant sadhu.

The tailor in Madras will give you trousers with a false hem. At the first shrinking the trousers are useless. But his label is in the waistband and he begged you to give his name to others. He can make money only if he gets customers; and he will get customers, not by making good trousers, but by getting his name known. And here is a shirtmaker distributing leaflets to announce the opening of his establishment. The Japanese have driven him out of West Africa. 'Their finish was better.' He speaks without rancour; that defeat was just part of his luck. His response to it is not to improve his finish but, abandoning 'the black Negro savages of Africa', to start afresh in this Indian town. The shirt he makes you is atrocious. The cuffs are an inch too narrow, the tail is several inches too short; and after the first wash the whole thing shrinks. He has made a little extra money by saving on material; for this reason he remains warm towards you and whenever he sees you he presses you to have another shirt made. (If you had gone to him with an introduction and had therefore been represented to him as someone capable of doing him harm, it would have been in his interest to be extravagantly generous; the shirt might even have been a little too large.) Every morning he pauses at the door of his shop, bows and touches the dust of the threshold to his forehead. This is how he guards his luck; his enterprise is a contract between God and himself alone.

'After acceptance she should please him; when he is infatuated with her she should suck him dry of his wealth and at last abandon him. This is the duty of a public woman.' The *Kama Sutra*, it might be said, reveals a society in undress; and no Indian manual is so old that it has ceased to be relevant. It is perhaps inevitable that a religion which teaches that life is illusion should encourage a balancing pragmatism in earthly, illusory relationships. The duty of the public woman – and mark that word duty – resembles the duty of the businessman: if you want to find sharp practice and monopolies preached as high virtues you can do no better than read some of the tales of the Indian classical period. The cow is holy. It is to be reverenced by being allowed to live, even if it has to be turned out into grassless city streets; even if it has been knocked down by a lorry on the Delhi-Chandigarh road and lies dying slowly in its blood for a whole afternoon, it remains holy: the villagers will stand by to see that no one attempts to take its life. The black buffalo, on the other hand, creature of darkness, is always fat and sleek and well looked after. It is not holy; it is only more expensive. The *Kama Sutra* lists fifteen situations in which adultery is permissible; the fifth situation is 'when such clandestine relations are safe and a sure method of earning money'; and at the end of the list comes the warning that 'it must be distinctly understood that it (adultery) is permitted for these purposes alone and not for the satisfaction of mere lust'. This moral ambiguity is in keeping with what the *Kama Sutra*, like other Indian manuals, lays down as the duties of the cultured man: 'to engage in activities that do not endanger one's civil service bazaar. Even ancient and holy buildings are disfigured. The eighth-century temple at the top of Shankaracharya Hill in Srinagar is hung at the gateway with a multi-coloured sign which would serve a haberdasher's shop. Set into the ancient stonework of one of the temples at Mahabalipuram near Madras is a plaque commemorating the minister who inaugurated the work of restoration. The Gandhi Mandap in Madras is a small colonnaded structure; carved on it are the names of the members of the committee that put the mandap up; the list is taller than a man.

The machinery of the modern state exists. The buildings exist; they are labelled; they sometimes anticipate need, and such anticipation can often be its own sufficient fulfilment. Consider the credits at the bottom of a Tourist Department leaflet: *Designed and produced by the Directorate of Advertising and Visual Publicity, Ministry of Information and Broadcasting, for the Department of Tourism, Ministry of Transport and Communications.* The structure is too perfect, too well labelled. It is not surprising that sometimes it proclaims no more than good intentions. The copies of *Family Planning News* that I saw contained little news of families that had been planned and many photographs of charming ladies in those wonderful saris, planning family planning. Traffic lights are part of the trappings of the modern city. Lucknow therefore has them; but they are only decorations, and dangerous, because ministers are required by their dignity never to halt at lights; and there are forty-six ministers in this state. The sweetshops of Gorakhpur are required to have glass cases; the cases accordingly stand, quite empty, next to the heaps of exposed sweets. There is that fine new theatre at Chandigarh; but who will write the plays?

When a crisis occurs, as during the Chinese invasion, the symbolic nature of the structure is made plain. Speeches are made and reported at length. Many gestures – the woman Minister of Health giving blood, somebody else giving jewellery – are given publicity. Various services are suspended. Then no one seems to know what to do next. Perhaps a Defence of the Realm Act? Dora, everyone calls it, adding a comforting familiarity to a correct label; and for a few days it is spoken like a magic word. The British proclaimed Dora in 1939. Now the Indian Government does the same. The British dug trenches. So they dig trenches in Delhi, but only symbolically, here and there, and dangerously, in public parks, below trees. The trenches answer the insatiable Indian need for open-air latrines. And, needless to say, supplies for the army, symbolically armed, find their way to the Calcutta open market.

An eastern conception of dignity and function, reposing on symbolic action: this is the dangerous, decayed pragmatism of caste. Symbolic dress, symbolic food, symbolic worship: India deals in symbols, inaction. Inaction arising out of proclaimed function, function out of caste. Untouchability is not the most important effect of the system; a Western conception of dignity alone has made it so. But at the heart of the system lies the degradation of the latrine-cleaner, and that casual defecation in a veranda which Gandhi observed in 1901.

'The moment untouchability goes the caste system will be purified.' It sounds like a piece of Gandhian and Indian double-think. It might even be interpreted as a recognition of the inevitability of caste. But it is a revolutionary assessment. Land reform does not convince the brahmin that he can put his hand to the plough without disgrace. Making awards to children for bravery does not lessen the feeling that it is unpardonable to risk one's life to save another. Reserving government jobs for untouchables helps nobody. It places responsibility in the hands of the unqualified; and the position of untouchable civil servants, whose reputations always go before them, is intolerable. It is the system that has to be regenerated, the psychology of caste that has to be destroyed. So Gandhi comes again and again to the filth and excrement of India, the dignity of latrine-cleaning; the spirit of service; bread-labour. From the West his message looks limited and cranky; but it is only that to a concerned colonial vision of India he is applying Western simplicities.

India undid him. He became a mahatma. He was to be reverenced for what he was; his message was irrelevant. He roused India to all her 'formless spirituality'; he awakened all the Indian passion for self-abasement in the presence of the virtuous, self-abasement of which the *Kama Sutra* would have approved, since it ensured a man's prospects in the other world, did not encourage him to any prolonged and difficult labour, and was withal pleasant. Symbolic action was the curse of India. Yet Gandhi was Indian enough to deal in symbols. So, latrine-cleaning became an occasional ritual, virtuous because sanctioned by the great-souled; the degradation of the latrine-cleaner continued. The spinning-wheel did not dignify labour; it was only absorbed into the great Indian symbolism, its significance rapidly fading. He remains a tragic paradox. Indian nationalism grew out of Hindu revivalism; this revivalism, which he so largely encouraged, made his final failure certain. He succeeded politically because he was reverenced; he failed because he was reverenced. His failure is there, in his writings: he is still the best guide to India. It is as if, in England, Florence Nightingale had become a saint, honoured by statues everywhere, her name on every lip; and the hospitals had remained as she had described them.

His failure is deeper. For nothing so shakes up the Indian in order that he might be made more securely static, nothing so stultifies him and robs him of his habitual grace, as the possession of a holy man.

'Is this the train for Delhi?' I cried to a peasant group, bounding, with seconds to spare, into a compartment at Moradabad station.

'Where on earth do you think you are? Speak Hindi if you want an answer. Hindi alone here.'

This was from the head of the group. He was not a nationalist, propagating the national language. At any other time he would have been civil and even deferential. But now he was the possessor of a saffron-clad holy man, fat and sleek and oily – there is little subtlety to India – before whom the women and children of the group were abasing themselves.

It is so with Indians and Gandhi. He is the latest proof of their spirituality; he strengthens the private contract with God of all who revere him. Nothing remains of Gandhi in India but this: his name and the worship of his image; the seminars about non-violence, as though this was all he taught; prohibition, rich in symbolism and righteousness, proclaimed as a worthy goal even at the height of the China crisis; and the politician's garb.

Observe this village politician, austerely and correctly clad, speaking of the mahatma and the motherland at a country meeting.

'To get elected,' the Indian Administrative Service officer tells me, 'that man had seventeen people murdered.'

There is no inconsistency; the mahatma has been absorbed into the formless spirituality and decayed pragmatism of India. The revolutionary became a god and his message was thereby lost. He failed to communicate to India his way of direct looking. And strange: in twelve months I could find no one among his ordinary worshippers who could tell me exactly what he looked like. It was not a question to put to Indians, who have no descriptive gift, but the replies were astonishing. For some he was tiny; for one man in Madras he was six feet tall. For some he was dark; for some he was exceedingly fair. Yet all remembered him; many even had personal photographs. These did not help: the image was too familiar. So it is when legends are complete. Nothing can add to them or take away from them. The image is fixed, simplified, unalterable; witness is of no account. Nearly every word Gandhi spoke and wrote is recorded; the Gandhi bibliography is immense. But in India he has already receded; he might have lived in the days when scribes wrote on leaves and strips of brass and people travelled on foot.

chose. Arrosez les excellents repos. On the shining concrete
the figures were stretched out, Indian sleepers on an
Indian railway station. The unemployed porters squatted. The beggar woman, whining, even she squatted.
Arrosez les excellent repos. But there were no fountains.
The streets were wide and grand, the roundabouts endless: a city built for giants, built for its vistas, for its
symmetry: a city which remained its plan, unquickened
and unhumanized, built for people who would be protected from its openness, from the whiteness of its light,
to whom the trees were like the trees on an architect's
drawing, decorations, not intended to give shade: a city
built like a monument. And everything labelled, as on
an architect's drawing; every moving thing dwarfed, the
man on his bicycle, with his black, black shadow; an
endless, ever-spreading city which encouraged no repose, which sent people scuttling through its avenues
and malls, as these scooter-rickshaws scuttled noisily in
and out of the traffic, shrunk to less than human size in
the presence of the monumental city.

The house was in one of the New Delhi 'colonies' or
residential settlements, abrupt huddles of fantasy and
riotous modern lines after the exposed austerity of the
centre. It was as though an Indian village had been
transformed into concrete and glass, and magnified.
The houses were not yet coherently numbered; and the
narrow nameless lanes were full of bewildered Sikhs
seeking houses by plot numbers, whose sequence was
chronological, indicating date of purchase. Dust; concrete white and grey; no trees; each Sikh attached to a
brisk, black shadow.

We sat in front of an empty, unsmoked fireplace
below an electric fan and rested with glasses of
Coca-Cola.

'Duffer, that Bihari boy,' Mrs Mahindra said, apologizing for her chauffeur and making conversation.

She was plump, still young, with large staring eyes. She had little English, and when words failed her she gave a giggle and looked away. She said *Mm*, her eyes became vacant, and her right hand went to her chin.

The house was new and on this ground floor smelled of concrete and paint. The rooms were not yet fully decorated; the furnishings were sparse. But there were fans everywhere; and the bathroom fittings, from Germany, were rare and expensive. 'I am craze for foreign,' Mrs Mahindra said. 'Just craze for foreign.'

She marvelled at our suitcases and at what they contained. She fingered with reverence and delight.

'Craze, just craze for foreign.'

Widening her eyes, it might have been in fear, it might have been in admiration, she told us of her husband, the contractor. He had a hard life. He was always travelling about in forests and jungles and living in tents. She had to stay behind and do the housekeeping.

'Three thousand rupees a month allowance. These days cost-of-living that-is-no-joke.'

She was not really boasting. She came from a simple family and she accepted her new wealth as she would have accepted poverty. She was anxious to learn, anxious to do the correct thing, anxious for our foreign approval. Did we like the colours of her curtains? The colours of her walls? Look, that lamp bracket there was foreign, from Japan. There wasn't a thing which was not foreign except, as she confessed when we went up to her dining-room for lunch, for this brass dish-warmer.

She sat with us, not eating, staring at our plates, hand supporting her chin, widening her eyes dreamily

A tall man of about fifty came to the house in the afternoon. He said he was answering an advertisement in the newspaper; he wished to lease the ground floor which we were occupying. He wore a double-breasted grey suit and spoke English with a strained army accent.

'Mm.' Mrs Mahindra looked away.

The man in the grey suit continued to speak in English. He represented a large firm, he said. A firm with foreign connexions.

'Mm.' Her eyes became vacant; her palm went to her chin.

'No one will sleep here.' He was faltering a little; perhaps it had occurred to him that his firm was not as desirable as the 'diplomatic' foreigners so many advertisements solicited. 'We will give you a year's rent in advance and sign a lease for three years.'

'Mm.' She said, replying in Hindustani to his English, that she would have to talk to her husband. And then there were so many other people who were interested.

'We intend to use the premises just as offices.' His dignity was beginning to yield to a certain exasperation. 'And all we would like is for a caretaker to sleep here at night. The house will remain as your home. We will give you twelve thousand rupees right away.'

She stared in her abstracted way, as though sniffing the new paint and thinking about the curtains.

'Duffer,' she said when he had gone. 'Talking English. *Barra sahib*. Duffer.'

The next morning she was glum.

'*Letter*. My husband's *father* is coming. Today. Tomorrow.' The prospect clearly depressed her. 'Talk, talk, that-is-no-joke.'

When we came back to the house that afternoon we found her sitting, sad and dutiful, with a white-haired man in Indian dress. She already seemed to have shrunk a little; she looked chastened, even embarrassed. It was our foreignness she stressed when she introduced us. Then she looked away, became abstracted and took no further part in the conversation.

The white-haired man looked us over suspiciously. But he was, as Mrs Mahindra had hinted, a talker; and he regarded himself and especially his age, which was just over sixty, with wonder. It was not his adventures he spoke of so much as the habits he had formed in those sixty years. He rose at four every morning, he said; he went for a four- or five-mile walk; then he read some chapters of the Gita. He had followed this routine for forty years, and it was a routine he would recommend to any young man.

Mrs Mahindra sighed. I felt she had taken a lot already and I thought I would release her. I tried to get the old man to talk of his past to me. He had no adventures to relate; he just had a list of places he had lived in or worked in. I asked precise questions; I made him describe landscapes. But Mrs Mahindra, not understanding my purpose, not accepting – or perhaps by duty not able to accept – the release I offered, sat and suffered. In the end it was the old man whom I drove away. He went and sat by himself in the small front garden.

'Naughty, naughty,' Mrs Mahindra said, giving me a smile of pure exhaustion.

'Summer is here,' the old man said after dinner. 'I have been sleeping out in the open for a fortnight. I always find that I begin to sleep out in the open a few weeks before other people.'

'Will you be sleeping out in the open tonight?' I asked.

'Of course.'

He slept just outside the door. We could see him, and no doubt he could see us. At four – so it was reasonable to assume – we heard him rise and get ready for his walk: lavatory chain, gargling, clattering, doors. We heard him return. And when we got up we found him reading the Gita.

'I always read a few pages of the Gita after I come back from my walk,' he said.

After that he idled about the house. He had nothing to do. It was difficult to ignore him; he required to be spoken to. He talked, but I began to feel that he also monitored.

We returned in the afternoon to a painful scene: the interviewing of another applicant for the ground floor. The applicant was uneasy; the old man, who was putting the questions, was polite but reproving; and the object of his reproof, I felt, was Mrs Mahindra, whose face was almost hidden in the top end of her sari.

We lost some of Mrs Mahindra's attentions. In no time at all she had dwindled into the Indian daughter-in-law. We heard little now of her craze for foreign. We had become liabilities. And when, attending to her father-in-law's conversation, she caught our eyes, her smile was tired. It held no conspiracy, only dutiful with-drawal. We had found her, on that first day, in a brief moment of sparkle.

We had to go to the country that week-end, and it was with a feeling almost of betrayal that we told her we were going to leave her alone with her father-in-law for a few days. She brightened at the news; she became active. We must just go, she said, and not worry about a thing. We didn't have to pack everything away; she would look after our room. She helped us to get ready. She gave us a meal and stood in the irregularly pointed stone gateway and waved while the Bihari chauffeur, duffer as we remembered, drove us off. Plump, saddened, wide-eyed Mrs Mahindra!

A week-end in the country! The words suggest cool clumps of trees, green fields, streams. Our thoughts were all of water as we left Delhi. But there was no water and little shade. The road was a narrow metal strip between two lanes of pure dust. Dust powdered the roadside trees and the fields. Once we drove for miles over a flat brown wasteland. At the end of the journey lay a town, and a communal killing. The Muslim murderer had fled; the dead Hindu had to be mourned and cremated in swift secrecy before daybreak; and afterwards troublemakers of both sides had to be watched. This occupied our host for almost all the week-end. We remained in the inspection house, grateful for the high ceiling, below the spinning fan. On one wall there was a framed typewritten digest of rules and regulations. Set into another wall was a fireplace. The winters it promised seemed so unlikely now; and it was as though one was forever doomed to be in places at the wrong time, as though one was forever feeling one's way through places where every label was false: the confectionery machine on the railway platform that hadn't worked for years, the advertisement for something that was no longer made, the timetable which was out of date. Above the mantelpiece there was a photograph of a tree standing on eroded earth beside a meagre stream; and in that photograph, in its message of exhaustion and persistence, there was something which already we could recognize as of India.

was unhinging me. I advanced towards the schoolboys, simple murder in my heart. They ran away, nimble in the heat. The Americans looked assessingly at me: the proud young Indian nationalist. Well, it would do. I walked back to the coach, converting exhaustion into anger and shame.

So it had been in Delhi. I was shouting now almost as soon as I entered government offices. At times the sight of rows of young men sitting at long tables, buried among sheaves of paper, young men checking slips of one sort or another, young men counting banknotes and tying them into bundles of a hundred, all India's human futility, was more than I could bear. 'Don't complain to me. Make your complaint through proper channel.' 'Through proper channel! Proper channel!' But it was hopeless; irony, mockery, was impossible in India. And: 'Don't complain to me. Complain to my officer.' 'Which is your bloody officer?' All this with a liberating sense that my violent mood was inviting violence. Yet so often it was met only with a cold, puncturing courtesy; and I was reduced to stillness, shame and exhaustion.

In Lutyens's city I required privacy and protection. Only then was I released from the delirium of seeing certain aspects of myself magnified out of recognition. I could sense the elegance of the city, in those colonnades hidden by signboards and straw blinds, in those vistas: the new tower at one end of the tree-lined avenue, the old dome at the other. I could sense the 'studious' atmosphere of which people had spoken in Bombay. I could sense its excitement as a new capital city, in the gatherings at the Gymkhana Club on a Sunday morning, the proconsular talk about the abominations of the Congo from former United Nations officials, in the announcements in the newspapers of 'cultural' entertainments provided by the embassies of competing governments: a city to which importance had newly come, and all the new toys of the 'diplomatic'. But to me it was a city in which I could only escape from one darkened room to another, separate from the reality of out of doors, of dust and light and low-caste women in gorgeous saris – gorgeousness in saris being emblematic of lowness – working on building sites. A city doubly unreal, rising suddenly out of the plain: acres of seventeenth- and eighteenth-century ruins, then the ultra-contemporary exhibition buildings; a city whose emblematic grandeur spoke of a rich and settled hinterland and not of the poor, parched land through which we had been travelling for twenty-four hours.

Yet that evening, lying in my bunk in the aluminium coach of the Srinagar Express and waiting for the train to leave, I found that I had begun to take a perverse delight in the violence of it all: delight at the thought of the twenty-four-hour journey that had brought me to Delhi, the thirty-six-hour journey still farther north that awaited me, through all the flatness of the Punjab to the mightiest mountain range in the world; delight at the physical area of luxury I had managed to reserve for myself, the separation from the unpleasant which I was yet, through the easily operated rubber-beaded windows, able to see: the red-turbanned porters, the trolleys of books and magazines, the hawkers, the frenzied fans hanging low so that from my bunk the platform appeared to be ceilinged by spinning blades: once hated symbols of discomfort, now answering all my urgency and exaltation which, fraudulent though I knew it to be, I was already fearing to lose, for with a twenty-degree drop in temperature all would subside to ordinariness.

The Punjab, intermittently glanced at during the night, was silent and featureless except for the moving oblongs of light from our train. A still hut, blacker against the flat black fields awaiting the day-long sun: what more had I expected? In the morning we were at Pathankot, the railhead – and how strange again and again to hear this solitary English word, to me so technical, industrial and dramatic, in a whole sentence of Hindustani – the railhead for Kashmir. It was cool at the station in the early morning; there was a hint of bush and, deceptive though it was, of mountains close at hand. And our passengers appeared in woollen shirts, sporty hats, jackets, cardigans, pullovers and even gloves, the woollen garments of the Indian summer holidays, not yet strictly needed, but an anticipation of the holiday that had almost begun.

At first it was only the army of whose presence we were aware on this flat scrub near the Pakistan border: signposted camps, all whitewash and straight lines, the rows of lorries and jeeps, the occasional manoeuvres of light tanks. These men in olive-green battledress and bush-hats might have belonged to another country. They walked differently; they were handsome. We stopped at Jammu for lunch. Thereafter we climbed, entering Kashmir by the road built by the Indian army in 1947 at the time of the Pakistan invasion. It grew cooler; there were hills and gorges and a broken view, hill beyond hill, receding planes of diminishing colour. We drove beside the Chenab River which, as we climbed, fell beneath us into a gorge, littered with logs.

'And where do you come from?'

It was the Indian question. I had been answering it

five times a day. And now again I went through the explanations.

He was sitting across the aisle from me. He was respectably dressed in a suit. He was bald, with a sharp Gujerati nose, and he looked bitter.

'And what do you think of our great country?'

It was another Indian question; and the sarcasm had to be dismissed.

'Be frank. Tell me exactly what you think.'

'It's all right. It's very interesting.'

'Interesting. You are lucky. You should live here. We are trapped here, you know. That's what we are. Trapped.'

Beside him sat his plump, fulfilled wife. She was less interested in our conversation than in me. She studied me whenever I looked away.

'Corruption and nepotism everywhere,' he said. 'Everybody wanting to get out to United Nations jobs. Doctors going abroad. Scientists going to America. The future is totally black. How much, for instance, do you earn in your country?'

'About five thousand rupees a month.'

It was unfair to strike so hard. But he took it well.

'And what do you do for this?' he asked.

'I teach.'

'What do you teach?'

'History.'

He was unimpressed.

I added, 'And a little chemistry.'

'Strange combination. I'm a chemistry teacher myself.'

It happens to every romancer.

I said, 'I teach in a comprehensive school. You have to do a little of everything.'

'I see.' Annoyance was peeping out of his puzzlement; his nose seemed to twitch. 'Strange combination. Chemistry.'

I was worried. Several hours of our journey together still remained. I pretended to be annoyed by a crying child. This couldn't go on. But relief soon came. We stopped among pines in a lay-by above a green wooded valley. We got out to stretch our legs. It was cool. The plains had become like an illness whose exact sensations it is impossible, after recovery, to recall. The woollens were now of service. The holiday had begun to fulfil itself. And when we got back into the bus I found that the chemistry teacher had changed seats with his wife, so that he would not have to continue talking to me.

It was night, clear and cold, when we stopped at Banihal. The rest-house was in darkness; the electric lights had gone. The attendants fussed around with candles; they prepared meals. In the moonlight the terraced rice fields were like leaded panes of old glass. In the morning their character had changed. They were green and muddy. After the Banihal tunnel we began to go down and down, past fairy-tale villages set in willow groves, watered by rivulets with grassy banks, into the Vale of Kashmir.

Kashmir was coolness and colour: the yellow mustard fields, the mountains, snow-capped, the milky blue sky in which we rediscovered the drama of clouds. It was men wrapped in brown blankets against the morning mist, and barefooted shepherd boys with caps and covered ears on steep wet rocky slopes. At Qazigund, where we stopped, it was also dust in sunlight, the disorder of a bazaar, a waiting crowd, and a smell in the

cold air of charcoal, tobacco, cooking oil, months-old
dirt and human excrement. Grass grew on the mud-
packed roofs of cottages – and at last it was clear why,
in that story I had read as a child in the *West Indian
Reader*, the foolish widow had made her cow climb up
to the roof. Buses packed with men with red-dyed
beards were going in the direction from which we had
come. Another bus came in, halted. The crowd broke,
ran forward and pressed in frenzy around a window
through which a man with tired eyes held out his thin
hand in benediction. He, like the others, was going to
Mecca; and among these imprisoning mountains how
far away Jeddah seemed, that Arabian pilgrim port dangerous with reefs over which the blue water grows
turquoise. In smoky kitchen shacks Sikhs with ferocious
beards and light eyes, warriors and rulers of an age not
long past, sat and cooked. Each foodstall carried an
attractive signboard. The heavy white cups were
chipped; the tables, out in the open, were covered with
oil-cloth in checked patterns; below them the ground
had been softened to mud.

The mountains receded. The valley widened into
soft, well-watered fields. The road was lined with poplars and willows drooped on the banks of clear rivulets.
Abruptly, at Awantipur, out of a fairy-tale village of
sagging wood-framed cottages there rose ruins of grey
stone, whose heavy trabeate construction – solid square
pillars on a portico, steep stone pediments on a colon-
nade around a central shrine, massive and clumsy in
ruin – caused the mind to go back centuries to ancient
worship. They were Hindu ruins, of the eighth century,
as we discovered later. But none of the passengers
exclaimed, none pointed. They lived among ruins; the
Indian earth was rich with ancient sculpture. At

as grimy-grey as their weather-beaten faces, men indistinguishable from women.

But we did not take a houseboat. Their relics were still too movingly personal. Their romance was not mine, and it was impossible to separate them from their romance. I would have felt an intruder, as I felt in those district clubs where the billiard rooms were still hung with framed cartoons of the 1930s, where the libraries had gone derelict, the taste of a generation frozen, and where on the smoking-room walls were stained engravings, difficult to see through the reflections on the dusty glass, of tumultuous horsemen labelled 'Afridis' or 'Baluchis'. Indians could walk among these relics with ease; the romance had always been partly theirs and now they had inherited it fully. I was not English or Indian; I was denied the victories of both.

PART TWO

5

A Doll's House on the Dal Lake

HOTEL LIWARD
Prop: FLUSH SYSTEM M. S. Butt

The sign came later, almost at the end of our stay. 'I am honest man,' the owner of the C-class houseboat had said, as we stood before the white bucket in one of the mildewed and tainted rooms of his rotting hulk. 'And flush system, this is not *honest*.' But Mr Butt, showing us his still small sheaf of recommendations in the sitting-room of the Liward Hotel, and pointing to the group of photographs on the pea-green walls, had said with a different emphasis, '*Before* flush.' We looked at the laughing faces. At least a similar betrayal could not be ours. The sign, dispelling conjecture, was placed high on the pitched roof and lit by three bulbs, and could be seen even from Shankaracharya Hill.

It seemed an unlikely amenity. The hotel stood in the lake, at one end of a plot of ground about eighty feet long by thirty wide. It was a rough two-storeyed structure with ochre concrete walls, green and chocolate woodwork, and a roof of unpainted corrugated iron. It had seven rooms altogether, one of which was the dining-room. It was in reality two buildings. One stood squarely in the angle of the plot, two walls flush with the water; it had two rooms up and two rooms down. A narrow wooden gallery went right around the top floor; around two sides of the lower floor, and hanging directly above the water, there was another gallery. The other building had one room down and two up, the second of which was a many-sided semi-circular wooden projection supported on wooden poles. A wooden staircase led to the corridor that linked the two buildings; and the whole structure was capped by a pitched corrugated-iron roof of complex angular design.

It had a rough-and-ready air, which was supported by our first glimpse of Mr Butt, cautiously approaching the landing stage to welcome us. He wore the Kashmiri fur cap, an abbreviation of the Russian. His long-tailed Indian-style shirt hung out of his loose trousers and dangled below his brown jacket. This suggested unreliability; the thick frames of his spectacles suggested abstraction; and he held a hammer in one hand. Beside him was a very small man, bare-footed, with a dingy grey pullover tight above flapping white cotton trousers gathered in at the waist by a string. A touch of quaintness, something of the Shakespearean mechanic, was given him by his sagging woollen nightcap. So misleading can first impressions be: this was Aziz. And flush was not yet finally installed. Pipes and bowls had been laid, but cisterns were yet to be unwrapped.

'One day,' Aziz said in English. 'Two days.'

'I like flush,' Mr Butt said.

We read the recommendations. Two Americans had been exceedingly warm; an Indian lady had praised the hotel for providing the 'secrecy' needed by honeymoon couples.

'*Before* flush,' Mr Butt said.

With this his English was virtually exhausted, and thereafter we dealt with him through Aziz.

We bargained. Fear made me passionate; it also, I

realized later, made me unnaturally convincing. My annoyance was real; when I turned to walk away I was really walking away; when I was prevailed upon to return – easy, since the boatman refused to ferry me back to the road – my fatigue was genuine. So we agreed. I was to take the room next to the semi-circular sitting-room, of which I was also to have exclusive use. And I needed a reading lamp.

'Ten-twelve rupees, what is that?' Aziz said.

And, I would need a writing-table.

He showed me a low stool.

With my hands I sketched out my larger requirements.

He showed me an old weathered table lying out on the lawn.

'We paint,' he said.

I rocked the table with a finger.

Aziz sketched out two timber braces and Mr Butt, understanding and smiling, lifted his hammer.

'We fix,' Aziz said.

It was then that I felt they were playing and that I had become part of their play. We were in the middle of the lake. Beyond the alert kingfishers, the fantastic hoopoes pecking in the garden, beyond the reeds and willows and poplars, our view unbroken by houseboats, there were the snow-capped mountains. Before me a night-capped man, hopping about restlessly, and at the end of the garden a new wooden shed, his home, unpainted and warm against the gloom of low-hanging willows. He was a man skilled in his own way with hammer and other implements, anxious to please, magically improvising, providing everything. The nightcap did not belong to a Shakespearean mechanic; it had a fairy-tale, Rumpelstiltskin, Snow White-and-the-seven-dwarfs air.

the poplars and the willows, past the houseboats, past Nehru Park, to the *ghat* and the lake boulevard, to cycle to the Tourist Reception Centre and stand in the shade of chenars outside the entrance, with the tonga-wallahs, houseboat-owners or their agents, below the hoarding with Mr Nehru's portrait. And there was the *khansamah*, the cook. He was older than Aziz or Ali Mohammed, and more nobly built. He was a small man, but he was given height by the rightness of his proportions, his carriage, his long-tailed shirt and the loose trousers that tapered down to his well-made feet. He was a brooder. His regular features were tormented by nervousness and irritability. He often came out of the kitchen and stood for minutes on the veranda of the hut, gazing at the lake, his bare feet beating the floorboards.

Our first meal was all ritual. The concrete floor of the dining-room had been spread with old matting; and on the table two small plastic buckets sprouted long-stemmed red, blue, green and yellow plastic daisies. 'Mr Butt he buy,' Aziz said. 'Six rupees.' He went out for the soup; and presently we saw him and Ali Mohammed, each holding a plate of soup, coming out of the hut and walking carefully, concentrating on the soup, down the garden path.

'Hot box coming next week,' Aziz said.

'Hot box?'

'*Next* week.' His voice was low; he was like a sweet-tempered nurse humouring a spoilt and irascible infant. He took a napkin off his shoulder and flicked away tiny flies. 'This is *nothing*. Get little hot, little flies dead. Big flies come chase little flies. Then mosquito come bite big flies and *they* go away.'

And we believed him. He withdrew and stood

outside below the projecting sitting-room; and almost immediately we heard him shouting to the kitchen or to some passing lake-dweller in a voice that was entirely altered. Through the windows at our back we had a view of reeds, mountains, snow and sky; before us from time to time we had a glimpse of Aziz's night-capped head as he peered through the as yet glassless window-frame. We were in the middle of the unknown, but on our little island we were in good hands; we were being looked after; no harm could come to us; and with every dish that came out of the hut at the end of the garden our sense of security grew.

Aziz, his delight matching ours, shouted for the *khansamah*. It seemed an impertinent thing to do. A grumble, a silence, a delay showed that it was so taken. When at last the *khansamah* appeared he was without his apron; he was nervous and bashful. What would we like for dinner? What would we like for dinner? 'You want scones for tea? And pudding, what you want for pudding? Tipsy pudding? Trifle? Apple tart?'

Snow White had gone, but her imparted skills remained.

It was only early spring, and on some mornings there was fresh snow on the mountains. The lake was cold and clear; you could see the fish feeding like land animals on the weeds and on the lake bed, and when the sun came out every fish cast a shadow. It could be hot then, with the sun out, and woollen clothes were uncomfortable. But heat presently led to rain, and then the temperature dropped sharply. The clouds fell low over the mountains, sometimes in a level bank, sometimes shredding far into the valleys. The temple at the top of Shankaracharya Hill, one thousand feet above fish, so numerous in the clear water that they could be seen just below the steps of the busy *ghat*. On some days the lake was dotted with fishermen who seemed to be walking on water: they stood erect and still on the edge of their barely moving *shikaras*, their tridents raised, their eyes as sharp as those of the kingfishers on the willows.

The hot box, promised by Aziz, came. It was a large wooden crate, grey with age and exposure. It occupied one corner of the dining-room, standing on its end at a slight angle on the uneven concrete floor. It was lined on the inside with the flattened metal of various tins, one side was hinged to make a door, and it was fitted with shelves. At mealtimes a charcoal brazier stood at the bottom. So the soup no longer came in steaming plates from the kitchen; and every morning we found Ali Mohammed squatting before the brazier, his back to us, utterly absorbed, turning over slices of bread with his fingers. A dedicated toastmaker he appeared, but he was in reality listening to the fifteen-minute programme of Kashmiri devotional songs that followed the news in English on Radio Kashmir. In the curve of his back there could be sensed a small but distinct anxiety: the toast might be required too soon, we might turn to another station, or he might be called away to other duties. Already at this time he was in his official suit; and I doubt whether, if otherwise dressed, he would have turned abruptly from his toast one morning and asked, 'You want see Kashmiri dancing girl?' His top dentures projected in a sad attempt at a smile. 'I bring here.'

Something had startled where I thought I was safest. The tourist's terror of extortion gripped me. 'No, Ali. You take me see first. I like, I bring here.'

130

He turned to face the hot box and the toast again. It had been a momentary impulse; he never mentioned dancing girls again.

And after the hot box, improvements came fast. Two strips of torn matting were laid down the narrow, pansy-lined path that connected the kitchen with the dining-room. The strips lay at a slight angle to one another; when it rained they looked black against the lawn. And presently – the lake giving up more of its treasures – uneven lengths of old board appeared on this matting. The polisher, a silent boy, came. He polished the 'sofa-set' in the sitting-room, and the old writing-table (stuffed with Russian propaganda: Ali brought back armfuls from the Russians he met at the Tourist Reception Centre). He polished the chairs and the bed and the dining-table; he polished day after day, saying nothing, ate platefuls of rice in the kitchen, and at last went away, leaving the furniture almost exactly as it had been. The turf-layer came; he tore and rammed and tamped on one bare bank.

It was all activity now. But there were periods of repose, especially in the afternoons. Then Aziz squatted on the kitchen veranda before the hookah and pulled; he had changed his woollen nightcap for a fur cap and had become a workaday Kashmiri, with a gift for instantaneous repose. Visitors called, boatmen, vendors; and from the hut came sounds of romping and chatter. After one outburst of gaiety we had a glimpse of Aziz running out to the veranda without his cap, and he had changed again: he was quite bald. On sunny afternoons Mr Butt and the *khansamah* wrapped themselves in blankets from head to toe and slept on the lawn.

The painters came, to give that second coat. One was

even acknowledged. Aziz knew the forms. So when, not long after, I complained about the weakness of the bulbs and asked for one to be replaced, and he said, 'Two-three rupees. You buy, I buy – what difference?' I didn't really feel I could object. I bought.

The season had begun. The hotel was not recognized, but accommodation was limited in Srinagar, our prices were reasonable, and soon we began to get guests. I had been full of plans for publicizing the hotel. I had put some of these plans to Aziz and, through him, to Mr Butt. They smiled, grateful for my interest; but all they wanted me to do was to talk to those tourists in jacket and tie whom Ali brought back from the Reception Centre. When I failed I felt humiliated. When I succeeded I was miserable. I was jealous; I wanted the hotel to myself. Aziz understood, and he was like a parent comforting a child. 'You will eat first. You will eat by yourself. We give you special. This is not Mr Butt hotel. This is your hotel.' When he announced new guests he would say, 'Is good, sahib. Good for hotel. Good for Mr Butt.' Sometimes he would raise one hand and say, 'God send customer.'

I remained unhappy. Being an unorthodox hotel, we attracted the orthodox. There had been the brahmin family, the first of many, who had insisted on cooking for themselves. They shelled peas, sifted rice and cut carrots in the doorway of their room; they cooked in the broom cupboard below the steps and washed their pots and pans at the garden tap; they turned part of the new turf to mud. Others threw their rubbish on the lawn; others spread their washing on the lawn. And I believed that the idyll was at an end when Aziz announced one day, with a well-managed mixture of enthusiasm and condolence, that twenty orthodox Indians were coming to the hotel for four days. Some would sleep in the dining-room; we would eat in the sitting-room. I was beyond condolence. Aziz recognized this and offered none. We waited. Aziz became morose, almost offended, in our presence. But the twenty did not turn up; and then for a day or two Aziz looked genuinely offended.

There were other difficulties. I had had it established that the radio in the dining-room was to be turned on just before eight. As soon as we heard the pips we went down to breakfast and the news in English. One morning no pips came, only Hindi film songs and Hindi commercials for Aspro and Horlicks: the radio was tuned to Radio Ceylon. I shouted through the window for Aziz. He came up and said he had explained to the boy from Bombay about the eight o'clock news from Delhi, but the boy had paid no attention.

I had loathed the boy from Bombay on sight. He wore tight trousers and a black imitation-leather jacket; his hair was thick and carefully combed; he carried his shoulders with something of the left-hander's elegant crookedness; he had the boxer's light walk and his movements were swift and abrupt. I thought of him as the Bombay Brando; I set him against a background of swarming Bombay slum. We had not spoken. But now, leather jacket or no leather jacket, this was war.

I ran downstairs. The radio was on full blast, and Brando was sitting in a derelict wicker chair on the lawn. I lowered the volume, almost to silence at first, in my haste; and turned to Radio Kashmir. Ali was making toast; the curve of his back signalled that he wasn't going to interfere. Nothing happened during the news. As soon as it was over, however, Brando pushed violently through the curtained doorway, went to the radio, wiped out Radio Kashmir for Radio Ceylon, and pushed out again violently through the curtain.

And so now it went on, morning and evening. Aziz I knew to be neutral. Ali I thought to be on my side. He crouched silently before the hot box, deprived now of his Kashmiri devotional songs. The conflict had reached stalemate. I longed for some development and one morning I suggested to Ali that Kashmiri songs were better than the commercials from Radio Ceylon. He looked up from his toast with alarm. Then I discovered that in the few short weeks of the tourist season, of tourist transistors tuned to Radio Ceylon, his taste had changed. He liked the commercial jingles, he liked the film songs. They were modern, an accessible part of that world beyond the mountains from which the advanced, money-laden Indian tourists came. Kashmiri music belonged to the lake and the valley; it was rude. So fragile are our fairylands.

Then I went down with a stomach upset and had to stay in bed. The next morning there was a knock on the door. It was Brando.

'I didn't see you yesterday,' he said. 'They told me you were not well. How are you today?'

I said I was better and thanked him for coming. There was a pause. I tried to think of something more to say. He wasn't trying at all. He stood unembarrassed beside the bed.

'Where do you come from?' I asked.

'I come from Bombay.'

'Bombay. What part of Bombay?'

'Dadar. You know Dadar?'

It was what I had imagined. 'What do you do? Are you a medical student?'

He barely raised his left foot off the floor, and his shoulders went crooked. 'I am *guest* in the hotel.'

'Yes, I know that,' I said.

'*You* are guest in the hotel.'

'I am a guest in the hotel.'

'So *why* you say I am *medical* student? *Why?* You are guest in the hotel. I am guest in the hotel. You get sick. I come to see you. Why you say I am *medical* student?'

'I am sorry. I know that you have come to see me only because we are both guests in the hotel. But I didn't mean to offend you. I just wanted to find out what you did.'

'I work for an insurance company.'

'Thank you very much for coming to see me.'

'You are welcome, mister.'

And, leading with the left shoulder, he pushed through the curtains and left.

Thereafter courtesy was imposed on both of us. I offered him Radio Ceylon; he offered me Radio Kashmir.

'Huzoor!' the *khansamah* called one afternoon, knocking and coming into the room at the same time. 'Today my day off, and I going home *now*, huzoor.' He spoke rapidly, like a man with little time. Normally Aziz came with him to our room; but this afternoon he had managed to elude Aziz, whom I saw, through the window, reclining on a string bed in the kitchen veranda.

'My son is sick, huzoor.' He gave a crooked bashful smile and shifted about on his elegant feet.

It was not necessary. My hand was already in my pocket, detaching notes from a stapled wad of a hundred. It was all that the local State Bank of India had that week. It encouraged this type of protracted furtive

This was something; it removed one doubt. 'Aziz, get the tailor to make you a suit. I will pay.'

He became stern and preoccupied, a man worn down by duties; this was a sign of pleasure.

'How much do you think it will cost, Aziz?'

'Twelve rupees, sahib.'

And in this mood, catching sight of Ali Mohammed about to go off to the Tourist Reception Centre in his shabby striped blue suit, his waistcoat and watch-chain, I surrendered to the pathos of his appearance.

'Ali, get the tailor to make you a new waistcoat. I will pay.'

'Very good, sir.'

It was hard to tell with Ali. He always looked slightly stunned whenever he was addressed directly.

'How much will it cost?'

'Twelve rupees, sir.'

It appeared to be a popular price. I went up to my room. I had hardly settled down at the blue table when the door was roughly pushed open and I turned to see the *khansamah*, blue apron on, advancing upon me. He seemed to be in an uncontrollable rage. He put a hand on the jacket that was hanging on the back of my chair and said, 'I want a coat.' Then, as if alarmed by his own violence, he stepped back two paces. 'You give Ali Mohammed jacket and you give that man Aziz suit.'

Had they been taunting him in the kitchen? I thought of Aziz's tight-lipped smile, his stern look of a moment before: suppressions of triumph that had inevitably to be released. Ali had been about to go off to the Tourist Reception Centre; he must have gone back to the kitchen to break the news.

'I am a poor man.' The *khansamah* made a sweeping gesture with both hands down his elegant clothes.

'How much will it cost?'

'Fifteen rupees. No, twenty.'

It was too much. 'When I leave I will give you coat. When I leave.'

He dropped to the floor and tried to seize my feet in mark of gratitude, but the legs and rungs of the chair were in the way.

He was a tormented man; and I knew, from what I heard and saw, that there were rows in the kitchen. He was careful of his honour. He was a cook. He was not a general servant; he had not learned the art of pleasing and probably despised those, like Aziz, who prospered by pleasing. I could see that he would provoke situations with which he could not cope; and after every defeat he would suffer.

It must have been a week later. For dinner he sent across meat stew and vegetable stew. The stews were identical, apart from the shreds and cubes of meat in one. I was not a meat-eater, and I was irrationally upset. I could not touch the vegetable stew. Aziz was wounded; this gave me pleasure. He went out with the stew to the kitchen, from where the *khansamah*'s voice was presently heard, angrily raised. Aziz returned alone, walking carefully, as though his feet were sore. After some time there was a call from behind the curtained doorway. It was the *khansamah*. In one hand he held a frying-pan, in another a fish-slice. His face was flushed from the fire and ugly with anger and insult.

'Why you don't eat my vegetable stew?'

As soon as he began to speak he lost control of himself. He stood over me and was almost screaming. 'Why you don't eat my vegetable stew?' I feared he was about to hit me with the frying-pan, which he had raised, and in which I saw an omelette. Immediately after his

'But permits are no longer required. Your friend, I imagine, has a British passport.'

I could not blame him for misunderstanding. Ali was not a tourist, I said. He wanted to meet tourists. He was a Kashmiri, a hotel servant; he wanted to get inside the Tourist Reception Centre. I knew that tourists had to be protected. Still. My trivialities burdened me. I became more and more earnest, anxious to get out of the encounter with dignity.

Mr Madan behaved well. If Ali applied, he said, he would consider the application.

I bade him good morning and walked briskly out with the news to Mr Butt.

'You see head clerk now,' Mr Butt said, and I allowed myself to be led into a room of desks and clerks.

The head clerk was not at his desk. We found him later in the corridor, a smiling well-built young man in a pale grey suit. He knew my letter; he understood my request. Let the hotel apply tomorrow; he would see what he could do.

'Tomorrow,' I said to Mr Butt. 'You come tomorrow.'

Hurriedly, I left him and made my way through the grounds of the Government Emporium, once the British Residency, to the Bund along the muddy Jhelum River. The elaborate Kashmiri woodwork of the Residency had decayed here and there; next to it a dingy little shack – very English, very Indian – proclaimed itself as the Emporium Café. But the chenar-shaded grounds remained grandiloquent, carefully irregular patches of daisies dramatizing the vast lawn. The Residency stood at one end of the Bund, on which, I had often been told, no Indian was allowed in the old days. Now the turnstiles were broken. Signs forbade cycling and walking on the grass bank; but there was constant cycling, and a deep path had been worn into the bank. Cows nibbled at the front gardens of buildings which, though in reality no more than an adoption of the Kashmiri style, at first sight appeared a type of mock mock-Tudor. Some old-fashioned shops survived, roomy, dark, with many glass cases; they still seemed to hold the anticipations of a thousand Anglo-Indian 'leaves'. Faded advertisements for things like water biscuits, no longer obtainable, could be still seen; boards and walls still carried the names of British patrons, viceroys and commanders-in-chief. In a taxidermist's shop there was a framed photograph of an English cavalry officer with his polished boot on a dead tiger.

One type of glory had gone. The other brightness, of the bazaar, had not yet come. But it was on the way. 'You needn't tell me, sir. I can see from your dress and your speech that your taste is English. Step inside and let me show you my English-taste rugs. Observe. This is English taste. I *know*. Now on the other hand observe this. It is heavy, Indian and of course inferior . . .'

Kashmirs Most Extraordinary Entertaining Rendezvous
YAP – LET'S GO TO PREMIERS
RESTAURANT
Hey-Fellers-Tony is At the Mike
With All the Five Bops
Fellers enjoy the 36 Varieties of Icecreams
DRINK DRINKS
IN OUR STARLIT GOLDEN BAR

That was what the leaflets said. Now the rendezvous itself, new, contemporary – 'most gayest', according to another leaflet, 'most delicious in tours' – was before

6

THE MEDIEVAL CITY

The level of the lake dropped to the last step of the landing-stage; the water became muddier and swarmed with black colonies of summer fish. The snow on the mountains to the north melted and the exposed rock looked bleached and eroded. On the cool parkland of the foothills the firs became darker blobs of green. The poplars on the lake lost their fresh greenness and the willows scattered spinning leaves in high wind. The reeds became so tall they curved, and when the wind blew they swayed and tossed like waves. The lotus leaves rose crinkled and disordered out of the water, thrust up on thick stalks. Then, like blind tulips, the lotus buds appeared, and a week later opened in explosions of dying pink. In the garden the Californian poppies and the clarkia grew straggly and were pulled out; the French marigolds, which had taken the place of the pansies, thickened and put out buds. The petunias in the shade of the dining-room wall were failing; they, like the geraniums, had been discoloured and weighted down with distemper from the painters' brushes. The godetias were at their peak: a mass of whipped colour, white and pink and pale violet. The sunflowers, seedlings when we arrived, were so tall, their leaves so broad, I could no longer look down into their hearts to examine the progress of the star-shaped buds. The dahlias put out one small red bloom, a touch of vivid colour against the green of reeds and willows and poplars.

We still had the kingfisher. But other birds appeared less frequently in the garden. We missed the hoopoe, with his long busy bill, his curved black and white wing stripes, his crest fanning out as he landed. With the heat the little flies died, as Aziz had said; and their place was taken by the house-fly. The flies I had known so far were shy of man; these settled on my face and hands even while I worked, and for several mornings in succession I was awakened before six by the buzzing of a single, Flit-surviving fly. Aziz promised mosquitoes; they would rout the flies. To him a fly was an act of God; one afternoon I saw him happily asleep in the kitchen, his cap on, his face black with still, contented flies.

I had asked for Flit, and more Flit. Now I asked for ice.

'Anybody don't like ice,' Aziz said. 'Ice is heating.'

And this reply led to one of our silences.

On very hot days the mountains to the north were hidden by haze from morning till evening. When the sun began to go down an amber light filled the valley and the mist rose slowly between the poplars on the lake. Each tree was distinct; and from Shankaracharya Hill Srinagar, smoking, appeared to be a vast industrial town, the poplars as erect as chimneys. Against this the fort of Akbar, standing on its reddish hill in the centre of the lake, was silhouetted: the sun to the left, a white disc slowly turning pale yellow, the mountains fading from grey to nothing as they receded.

Beyond the Bund it was a medieval town, and it might have been of medieval Europe. It was a town, damp or here, moored there for the night. A doonga party could last for days; people might get off at some point to attend to their affairs on land and might rejoin the boat later at another point. A dull, strenuous entertainment it seemed to me; but my winters were full. The fair in the grove at Ganderbal, a few miles to the northwest, climaxed the season. All the doongas and shikaras made their way there and moored for the night: movement for the sake of movement, crowd for the sake of crowd, noise for the sake of noise.

And in this medieval town, as in all medieval towns, the people were surrounded by wonders. About them in Srinagar were the gardens of the Mogul emperors. The pavilions were neglected but they were still whole. On Sundays the fountains of Shalimar still played, with here and there a bent or broken nozzle. But the builders had receded beyond history into legend: fabulous personages of whom little was known except that they were *very* handsome or *very* brave or *very* wise, with wives who were *very* beautiful. 'That?' said the Kashmiri engineer, waving towards Akbar's late-sixteenth-century fort in the Dal Lake. 'That is five thousand years old.' In the Hazratbal mosque on the lake there was a hair from the beard of the Prophet Mohammed. It had been brought through untold dangers to Kashmir, the medical student told me, by 'a man'. Who was this man? What did he do? Where did he come from? My student couldn't say; he knew only that once, when this man was in an especially dangerous situation, he had gashed himself in the arm and in the gash had concealed the holy hair. It was an authentic relic, there could be no doubt of that. It was so potent that birds never flew over the chapel in which it was kept and cows, sacred to Hindus, never sat with their backs to the chapel.

God watched over them all, and they responded with enthusiasm. Mohurram was the month in which for ten days they mourned Hussain, the Prophet's descendant, murdered at Kerbala. The wails and songs of the Shias came to us over the water at night. Aziz, of the Sunni sect, said with a smile, 'Shia not Muslim.' Yet on the seventh morning, when on the radio the well-known story of Kerbala was being told, tears came to Aziz's eyes, his face grew small, and he hurried out of the dining-room, saying, 'I can't stop. I don't like listen.'

There was to be a Shia procession at Hasanbad; there would be people whipping themselves with chains. Aziz, recovered from the morning's emotion, insisted that we should go, and made the arrangements. We went by *shikara*, quickly penetrating into the green-scummed, willow-hung water highways of the lake town, past the dirty yards terminating in broken concrete steps, gutters running down their sides, on which men and women and children were washing clothes, our own washerman, I was sorry to see, among them. The highways were altogether foul, smelling of the sewer; but at every yard children, miniature adults, rushed out to greet us: 'Salaam!'

At Hasanbad we moored among dozens of *shikaras*, many brilliantly canopied, walked past the foundations of a ruin of which we had never heard, and found ourselves in the middle of a dusty summer fair. The streets had been swept; water-carts laid the dust. There were awnings and stalls. The well-to-do among the women in the crowd were veiled in black or brown from head to well-shod feet; they were in groups of two or three, and through the grilled netting over their eyes we felt ourselves scrutinized. It was the poor who were unveiled; here, as everywhere else, to be conservative and correct had licence. He had earned it by his bloody back. He had turned dull virtue into spectacle.

Religious enthusiasm derived, in performance and admiration, from simplicity, from a knowledge of religion only as ritual and form. 'Shia not Muslim,' Aziz had said. The Shia, he added, demonstrating, bowed in this way when he said his prayers; the Muslim, now, bowed in this. Christians were closer to Muslims than to Hindus because Christians and Muslims buried their dead. 'But, Aziz, many Christians are cremated.' 'They not Christian.' The medical student, explaining the difference between Islam and Sikhism, which he particularly detested, said that Muslims slaughtered their animals by bleeding them slowly to death, uttering prayers the while. Sikhs struck off an animal's head at one blow, without prayers. He sketched out the gesture, involuntarily shook his head with repulsion, and put his hand over his face. On the day of Id Mr Butt gave us a cake iced *Id Mubarak*, Id Greetings. The day took us by surprise; *shikara*-loads of Kashmiris, men, women and children, were ferried about the lake all morning, subdued and stiff and startling in clean clothes of white and blue. It was a day of visits and gifts and feasting; but, too, for the Kashmiri, the year's solitary day of cleanliness, a penitential debauch of soap and water and itching new cloth. Yet neither the medical student nor the engineer nor the merchant, all of whom came to visit us and offered gifts, could explain the significance of the day. It was only what we had seen; it was a day when Muslims had to eat meat.

Religion was a spectacle, and festivals, women veiled ('so that men wouldn't get excited and think bad things,' the merchant said), women bred and breeding like battery hens; it was the ceremonial washing of the genitals in public before prayers; it was ten thousand simultaneous prostrations. It was this complete day-filling, season-filling mixture of the gay, the penitential, the hysterical and, importantly, the absurd. It answered every simple mood. It was life and the Law, and its forms could admit of no change or query, since change and query would throw the whole system, would throw life itself, in danger. 'I am a bad Muslim,' the medical student had said at our first meeting. 'How can I believe that the world was made in six days? I believe in evolution. My mother would grow mad if I said these things to her.' But he rejected none of the forms, no particle of the Law; and was more of a religious fanatic than Aziz who, secure in his system, inspected other systems with tolerant interest. The sputniks had momentarily shaken some in their faith, for the upper atmosphere had been decreed closed to all but Mohammed and his white horse. But doctrine could be made to accommodate this – what the Russians had done was to send up their sputniks on the white horse – and the faith could survive because doctrine was not as important as the forms it had bred. The abandoning of the veil was more to be feared and resisted than the theory of evolution.

These forms had not developed over the centuries. They had been imposed whole and suddenly by a for-eign conqueror, displacing another set of forms, once no doubt thought equally unalterable, of which no trace remained. The medieval mind could assess a building as five thousand years old, and do so casually; with like facility it buried events three and four hundred years old. And it was because it was without a sense of history that it was capable of so complete a conversion. Many Kashmiri clan names – like that of Mr Butt of my blood will grow another Sheikh Abdullah." When the Maharaja heard this he was *very* frightened, and he gave up the throne. That was how Sheikh Abdullah won the freedom for the people of Kashmir.'

I objected. I said that people didn't behave like that in real life.

'But it's true. Ask any Kashmiri.'

It was an account of the events of 1947 that ignored Congress, Gandhi, the British, the Pakistan invasion. And this was at the high level of literacy in English. Below this there were people like Aziz, who almost daily regretted the Maharaja's repressive rule because things were so much cheaper then. Recent history was already sinking into medieval legend. Aziz and the *khansamah* had served the British; they knew them as people of certain tastes, skills and language ('padre' for priest, and to Aziz 'bugger' was an affectionate word for a dog) who had departed as unaccountably as they had come. But there had grown up a generation of students who had learned of the British only from their history books, and to them the British intervention was as remote as the Mogul glory.

Bashir told me one day that the 'East India Company went away in 1947'; and this, in our political discussions, was his sole reference to the British. Bashir was nineteen, college-educated. 'I am *best* sportsman,' he had said, introducing himself to me. 'I am *best* swimmer. I know *all* chemistry and *all* physics.' He detested the Kashmiri and Indian habit of wearing pyjamas in public; and he told me he never spat in the street. He regarded himself as educated and emancipated: he 'inter-dined' (one of the English locutions of the sub-continent) with everyone, regardless of religion or sect. He wore western-style suits, and he spoke English as

well as he did because 'I come from an unusually intelligent family'.

It might be that Bashir's ignorance of history was due
to his stupidity, or to his education in a language he did
not fully understand (when he said *best* he only meant
'very good'), or to bad teachers and bad textbooks. (I
examined one of his history books later. It was a typical
Indian textbook; it was in question-and-answer form
and gave the preservation of purity as one of the virtues
of the caste system and gave miscegenation as one of
the reasons for the decline of Portuguese power in
India.) Or it might simply have been that Bashir and
his friends took no interest in politics; and indeed, without newspapers and the radio, it was possible to be in
Kashmir for weeks without realizing that there was a
Kashmir problem. But Kashmir was being talked about
on every side. All-India Radio was carrying detailed
reports of the annual United Nations debate; Radio
Pakistan tirelessly warned that in Kashmir as in the rest
of India Islam was in danger, and Radio Kashmir as
tirelessly retaliated. Mr Nehru came to Srinagar, and
Radio Pakistan reported that a public meeting he addressed broke up in disorder. (He was in fact convales-
cing after an illness.) Whatever might be said, Bashir's
ignorance of the recent history and situation of his
country was startling. And he was privileged. Below him
were the grimy, barefooted, undernourished primary-
school boys in blue shirts who had no chance of going
to college; below them were those who didn't go to
school at all.

I was in bed one afternoon with an inflamed throat
when Bashir brought Kadir to see me. Kadir was seventeen, small, with soft brown eyes in a square gentle face;
he was studying engineering but wanted to be a writer.

Post Office was the post office on the Bund, a type of super-shop, doing brisk business every day, which the Indian Government wanted to steal from Kashmir. He was an educated man; and doubtless the fact of a demand for greater autonomy had undergone further distortion and simplification before it had passed down to the peasants. Propaganda needs to find its level; and medieval propaganda was as simple-clever and as fearful as any technique of hidden persuasion. Radio Pakistan could claim that the large sums of money being spent on education in Kashmir were a means of undermining Islam and the Law; and it was more effective propaganda than the Kashmir Government's boards giving development facts and figures.

'But Sheikh Abdullah was Prime Minister for more than five years. What did he do?'

'Ah, that is the beauty. He did nothing. He wouldn't take help from anyone. He wanted the people of Kashmir to learn to stand on their own feet.'

'But if he did nothing in five years, why do you think he is great? Give me an example of his greatness.'

'I will give you an example. One year, you know, the rice crop failed and the people were starving. They went to Sheikh Abdullah and said to him, "Sheikh Abdullah, we have no rice and we are starving. Give us rice." And you know what he said to them? He said, "Eat potatoes."'

Humour was not intended, and the advice was sound. Indians are willing to eat only what they have always eaten; and staples vary from province to province. In the Punjab they ate wheat. In Kashmir, as in the South, they ate rice. It was rice alone, enormous platefuls of it, moistened perhaps with a little tomato sauce, which energized Aziz's active little body. When there was no rice the Kashmiris starved; they might have potatoes, but potatoes were not food. In this lay the point of Sheikh Abdullah's advice. Needless to say, it had gone unheeded and had instead been transformed into a piece of almost prophetic wisdom, to be relished and passed on as such. *Once there was no food in the land, and the people went to the leader and said, 'We have no food. We are starving.' The leader said, 'You might think you have no food. But you have. You have potatoes. And potatoes are food.'*

Regularly white jeeps and station-wagons raced along the roads. In the afternoons they appeared to carry picnic parties of women and children in straw hats; in the evenings, bridge parties. The jeeps and station-wagons were marked U.N. in thin, square letters; they watched over the ceasefire line. In Kashmir they seemed as anachronistic as the clock in *Julius Caesar.*

But there was money in Kashmir, more than there had ever been. In 1947, I was told, there were fifty-two private cars in the entire state; now there were nearly eight thousand. In 1947 a carpenter earned two or three rupees a day; now he could get eleven rupees. The new wealth showed in the increased number of veiled women: for people like tonga-wallahs and fuel-vendors a new, veiled wife was a symbol of status. It is estimated that in Kashmir, as in the rest of India, one-third of development funds drains away in corruption and the exchanging of gifts. No disgrace attaches to this. The Kashmiri tailor spoke with envious admiration of his *patwari* friend, a surveyor and type of records-keeper, who in one day might collect as much as a hundred rupees; a lorry-driver had a similar admiration for a dangerously low from many of the telegraph poles in Srinagar.

We seemed to be in danger of losing the hotel garden altogether. First there had come the digging for the ugly telegraph pole to carry the electric wires. And now there came the digging for the poles of the awning, which was put up like lightning with the rough-and-ready carpentry of the lake, and the irruption into the hotel garden of dozens of the lake folk, variously clad in pyjamas or flapping trousers, offering advice, help or simply interest. The awning was an appanage of the houseboat; this was the reason for its appearance in the garden, where it served no purpose. It provided little shade and much heat when the sun was out, and it was taken down whenever rain threatened. It had scalloped edges, trimmed with black, and was exactly like every other houseboat awning in the area. These awnings were all made in the single-roomed tailor's shack on the water highway, where everyone, flower-sellers, grocers, red-turbanned policemen, appeared to stop for a chat and a pull at the hookah.

A day or so later Mr Butt was painting the poles of the awning a light green, and I went down to watch him. He looked up and smiled, and went on with his painting. When he looked up again he wasn't smiling.

'Sir, you ask Mr Madan to tea?'

'Mr Butt, no.'

The summer had seemed endless. We had put off the ruins: the Palace of the Fairies, which we could see low on the hills beyond the lake; Akbar's lake fort, Hari Parbat; the temple at Pandrethan; the sun temple at

Martand; the temple at Awantipur. Now we did them all at once.

It was a cool day when we went to Awantipur, the dry fields a warm brown against the dark grey-blue mountains. We could make little of the ruins, the massive central platform, the anvil-shaped fonts of solid stone that lay among the rubble, the carvings; and the villager who attached himself to us didn't help. 'It *all* fell down,' he said in Hindustani, waving a hand. '*All?*' '*All.*' It was a type of North Indian dialogue, made possible by the stresses of the language, which I had grown to enjoy. He showed the base of a column and indicated by gestures that it was the bottom stone of a quern. That was the limit of his knowledge. No tip for him; and we walked down to the village to wait for the bus.

The blue-shirted boys had just been released from school; down a side lane we saw the young Sikh teacher organizing a ball game in the schoolyard. The boys gathered around us; they all carried enormous bundles of books wrapped in grubby, inky cloths. We made one boy take out his English book. He opened it at a page headed 'Our Pets', read out: 'Our Body', and began reeling off a text which, after a search, we found on another page. And what book was this? Urdu? They became helpless with laughter: it was Pharsi, Persian, as any child could tell. The crowd had now grown. We broke out of it, saying we wanted to get back to Srinagar; and they all then began waving down buses for us. Many buses passed, full; then one shot past, hesitated, stopped. A Kashmiri attempted to get on but was repelled by the conductor, who made room for us.

We sat in the back among some sensationally unwashed people, their cotton dhotis brown with dirt, and many Dalda tins. The man next to me was stretched out on the seat, clearly unwell, his eyes without expression, the pestilential Indian flies undisturbed on his lips and cheeks; from time to time he gave a theatrical groan, to which no one in the chattering bus paid the slightest attention. We saw that we were in a bus of 'lower-income' tourists and that we were sitting with their servants.

At the ruins the bus stopped and the khaki-clad moustached driver turned around and tried to persuade his passengers to go out and have a look. No one moved. The driver spoke again, and at length one elderly man, whom we had already recognized as the wit and leader of the bus, heaved himself up with a sigh and went out. He wore a black Indian jacket, and his topknot proclaimed him a brahmin. The others followed.

From nowhere children appeared: '*Paisa, sahib, paisa.*' 'Oh,' said the leader in Hindi. 'You want money? Now what does a little child like you want money for?' '*Roti, roti,*' they chanted. 'Bread, bread.' 'Bread, eh?' He was only teasing. He gave; the others gave.

The leader climbed to the top of the stone steps and regarded the ruins with patronage. He made a witticism; he lectured. The others idled about dutifully, looking without interest where he looked.

A sixteen-year-old boy in white flannel trousers hurried over to me and said, 'This is Pandavas' fort.'

I said, 'This is not a fort.'

'It is Pandavas' fort.'

'No.'

He waved hesitantly towards the leader. 'He says it's Pandavas' fort.'

'You tell him no. He doesn't know what he's talking about.'

The boy looked shocked, as though I had offered

him violence. He edged away from me, turned and fled to the group around the leader.

We were all back in the bus and about to start when the leader suggested food. The conductor threw open the door again and an especially grimy manservant, old and toothless, came to life. Briskly, proprietorially, he shoved the Dalda tins along the dusty floor and lifted them out on to the verge. I began to protest at the delay; the boy in white flannels looked at me in terror; and I realized that we had fallen among a family, that the bus was chartered, that we had been offered a lift out of charity. The bus again emptied. We remained helpless in our seats, while Srinagar-bound passenger buses, visibly holding spare seats, went past.

They were a brahmin family and their vegetarian food was served according to established form. No one was allowed to touch it except the dirty old servant who, at the mention of food, had been kindled into such important activity. With the very fingers that a moment before had been rolling a crinkled cigarette and had then seized the dusty Dalda tins from off the dusty bus floor, he now – using only the right hand, of course – distributed puris from one tin, scooped out curried potatoes from another, and from a third secured dripping fingerfuls of chutney. He was of the right caste; nothing served by the fingers of his right hand could be unclean; and the eaters ate with relish. The verge had been deserted; now, in the twinkling of an eye, the eaters were surrounded by villagers and long-haired Kashmiri dogs. The dogs kept their distance; they stood still, their tails low and alert, the fields stretching out behind them to the mountains. The villagers, men and children, stood right over the squatting eaters who, like celebrities in the midst of an admiring

It was above all a respect for the forms, for the way things had always been done.

Yet three generations and a lost language lay between us. This is Pandavas' fort, the boy had said. The Pandavas were the heroes of the *Mahabharata*, one of the two Hindu epics which are universally known and have something of the sanctity of holy books; the Gita is embedded in the *Mahabharata*. The *Mahabharata* is placed by some in the fourth century B.C.; the events it describes are put at 1500 B.C. Yet the ruins of what was so obviously a four-walled building, exposed on all

that the man of fashion 'should reside where he has a good chance of earning riches but should for preference select a city, a metropolis or a big or small town', prescribes the furnishings of a drawing-room: 'This outer room should contain a bed, richly mattressed, and somewhat depressed in the middle. It should have pillows at the head and the bottom and should be covered with a perfectly white clean sheet. Near this bed there should be a small couch on which the sexual act should be performed so as not to soil the bed. Over the head of the bed there should be fixed on the wall a lotus-shaped bracket on which a coloured portrait or an image of one's favourite deity should be placed. Beneath this bracket should be placed a small table, one cubit in breadth, set against the wall. On this table the following articles, required for the night's enjoyments, should be arranged: balms and perfumed unguents, garlands, coloured waxen vessels, pots for holding perfumes, pomegranate rinds and prepared betels. There should be a spittoon on the floor near the bed; a lute, a drawing slab, a pot with colours and brushes, a few books and wreaths of flowers, too, hung from elephants' tusks let into the wall. Near the bed upon the floor should be placed a circular chair with a back for resting the head on. Boards for the games of dice and chess should be placed against the wall. In a gallery outside the room cages for pet birds should be hung from ivory tusks fixed into the wall.' (Translated by B. N. Basu.)

sides, that could by no stretch of the imagination be the
fort of five warrior princes, were the ruins of the fort of
the Pandavas. It was not that forts were unknown; in
Srinagar itself there was one which nobody could miss.
The tourists in the bus went against the evidence of
their eyes not because they were eager for marvels but
because, living with marvels, they had no sense of the
marvellous. It was with reluctance that they had got out
of the bus. They had known and accepted the story of
the *Mahabharata* from childhood. It was part of them.
They were indifferent to its confirmation in rocks and
stones, fallen into ruin and become material common-
places which could only be viewed literally. So this was
the fort of the Pandavas, this rubble, no longer of use
to anyone. Well, it was time to eat, time for the puris
and the potatoes. The true wonder of the Pandavas and
the *Mahabharata* they carried in their hearts.

Some miles nearer Srinagar, at Pandrethan, in the
middle of the army camp, a tiny, single-chambered
temple, set in a hollow and shaded by a great tree,
stood a little crookedly in the centre of a small artificial
pool. The water was stale, leaf-littered; and the heavy,
inelegant stonework of the temple was roughly patched
with new concrete. The temple was in the style of the
Awantipur ruin, the 'fort of the Pandavas'; but it was
still in use, and it was this, rather than its age, which
gave it greater meaning. Romance arose out of a sense
of more than physical loss; and here, for Muslim as well
as Hindu, nothing had been lost. A building might collapse or be destroyed or cease to be of use; another
would take its place, of lesser or greater size or beauty.
On the eastern side of Akbar's lake fort an exquisite
building lay in ruin. It might have been a mausoleum.
Two towers stood at one end of a small cool quadrangle

'Sahib, you come have tea.'

I had just had coffee.

'Sahib, you come have tea.' He was panting. 'Mr Butt he say. Not your tea.'

I went down to the young man. I had often been called upon to handle difficult 'customers' and some-times to encourage acceptance of a price more realistic than that mentioned by Ali Mohammed at the Tourist Reception Centre.

The young man put down his cup with some awk-wardness, stood up and looked at me uncertainly. I sat down in one of the hotel's weatherbeaten, shredding wicker chairs and invited him to resume his tea. Aziz, seconds before the urgent administrator, now the self-effacing, characterless servitor, deferentially poured for me and withdrew, never looking back, yet somehow – in spite of his loose flapping trousers, his tilted fur cap, the serving rag thrown rakishly over one shoulder, the soles of his bare feet flapping hard, black and cracked – communicating total alertness.

It was hot, I said to the young man; and he agreed. But it would soon cool down, I said; you had these changes of temperature in Srinagar. The lake was cer-tainly cooler than the city, and the hotel was cooler than any houseboat.

'So you are enjoying?'

'Yes,' I said, 'I am enjoying very much.'

He had given me an opening and I made use of it. But he was not with me; he did not lose his look of embarrassment. I decided he was one of my failures.

'Where do you come from?' I put the Indian question.

'Oh, I come from Srinagar. I work in the Tourist Office. I have been seeing you around for *months*.'

Where I and my typewriter had failed, Mr Butt and Aziz had succeeded. But Aziz did not behave as though I had failed. He said that the kitchen was pleased with my handling of the young man, and a few days later he announced, as though I alone was responsible for it, that Mr Kak, Mr Madan's deputy, was coming soon to the hotel, to inspect and possibly to have tea.

Mr Kak came. I saw his *shikara* glide up to the landing-stage and I decided to hide. I locked myself in the bathroom. But no feet came tripping up the steps. No summons came. No mention of Mr Kak's visit was made that day or on subsequent days; and I learned of the outcome of his visit only when Mr Butt, accompanied by the secretary of the All Shikara Workers Union, came into my room one morning to ask me to type out the 'particulars' of the hotel for inclusion in the Tourist Office's register of hotels. I had failed; even my final cowardice was irrelevant. Mr Butt was smiling; he was a happy man. Dutifully, I began to type.

'Hotel,' said the secretary, looking over my shoulder, 'is Western style.'

'Yes, yes,' Mr Butt said. 'Western style.'

'I can't type that,' I said. 'Hotel is not Western style.'

'Flush system,' Mr Butt said. 'English food. Western style.'

I got up and pointed through the open window to a little roofed box next to the kitchen hut.

The box was perhaps six feet long, four feet wide and five feet high. And it was inhabited. By a thin, sour middle-aged couple whom we had christened the Borrowers. They were Jains. They had brought their pots and pans to Kashmir; they cooked for themselves; they washed up for themselves, scouring their vessels with mud, of which there was now a plentiful supply

This was Ali Mohammed's story.

'But they say,' he told us at breakfast, '"We don't want houseboat, we want here."'

It was the hotel's biggest kill, and Ali Mohammed was pleased. He was not Aziz; he could not sympathize with us. Nor could Aziz. He, as if recognizing the hopelessness of the situation, stayed away from us altogether.

They had come equipped for holiness. In their limousines, the wonder of the lake folk, they had brought bundles of especially holy leaves, off which they were to eat, like the sages in the days before plates were plentiful. They did not trust tap-water; they had brought special containers and early in the morning they went off to Chasmashahi, the Royal Spring, to get pure spring water. They had of course to cook for themselves; and the cooking was done, on stones placed on the lawn, by four epicene saffron-robed young men who, when their duties were done, simply idled: they had a fantastic capacity for inactivity. Holiness meant simplicity of this sort: cooking on stones, eating off leaves, fetching water from the spring. It also meant casualness and disorder. Rugs were rolled up in the hotel rooms, curtains hooked up high, furniture disarranged. Simplicity and the possession of a holy man induced arrogance. The men among the pilgrims strutted about the lawn, reducing Ali and Aziz and even Mr Butt to tiptoeing insignificance. They spoke loudly. They hawked loudly and spat with noisy repeated relish everywhere but more especially on the water-lilies, plants which had been introduced to Kashmir from England by the last maharaja and were without the religious associations of the lotus. After their meal, eaten off leaves on the very lawn on which they had been spitting, they belched. They belched thunderously but always with control: it was possible to tell, from the belches alone, who was the leader of the party. He was about forty, tall and fat; a singular element of his holy dress was the multicoloured towel he wore wrapped around his head. The young men did press-ups and other exercises. They had all lived well; this was a pious boy-scout interlude; and the Liward was their camp.

It seemed that no definite message had come from the holy man about the time of his arrival. The pilgrims took no chances. They drove off to meet every aeroplane from Delhi, leaving behind the epicene young men in saffron robes who, fatigued at last by their idleness, began to indulge in what I at first regarded as a type of child's play. Gathering whatever material they could find they constructed, with slow, silent intensity, a rough barricade around the cooking stones on the lawn. But they were not playing: they were protecting their food from the gaze of the unclean. This was not all. The turf had been trodden on by numberless unclean people: the turf had therefore to be torn up. And it was this that the squatting saffron-robed vandals were now silently doing.

I sent for Aziz. Since the arrival of the pilgrims we had not had a confrontation. His face was small. He had seen. He had done more: he had provided a plank which the saffron robes, following a logic of their own, had laid over the mud they had instantly created. What could he do? He spoke of Mr Butt's need for money; he said that God sent customers. He said that they were a holy group and that the holy man, who was expected any day, was almost a saint.

The pilgrims brought the holy man back that afternoon; and the atmosphere of arrogant, belching disorder was replaced by one of silent, self-important

'O no, sahib. *Too* much bus.'

We got to the bus station just after eight. Aziz, unfamiliar in big brown shoes (Mr Butt's), went to buy the tickets.

'We miss eight o'clock bus,' he said, coming back.

'When is the next one?'

'Twelve o'clock.'

'What are we going to do, Aziz?'

'What we do? We wait.'

It was a new bus station. Kashmiris, emerging from the gentlemen's lavatory, wiped their hands on the curtains, which were of a contemporary fabric. A well-dressed beggar woman distributed printed leaflets which told of her tragedy. We waited.

What was it about Gulmarg that attracted Aziz? It was a holiday settlement of unpainted wooden huts about a small green meadow set in the mountains some three thousand feet above the Valley. On one side the meadow fell away to the Valley through pine forests; on the other it was bounded by higher mountains in the interstices of which, even in August, snow lay in brown drifts. We arrived in rain. At the bungalow of the friends with whom we were going to stay Aziz was at once sent off to the servants' quarters, and we saw him again only when the rain was over. He was walking back down the muddy road from such centre as the settlement had. His gait was made unusual by the weight of Mr Butt's shoes. (Mr Butt later reported, almost with emotion, that Aziz had ruined his shoes on this visit.) His smile and greeting were of pure friendliness. 'How you liking Gulmarg, sir?'

So far we had seen little. We had seen the mountains lost in black cloud; we had seen the purple flowers on the wet green meadow. We had seen the buildings and foundations of buildings looted and burned by the Pakistanis in 1947: one grand wooden building cracked open from the roof, like a toy, and left derelict, still, with its broken coloured panes and all its noises, a setting for nightmare.

Had Aziz seen more? Was there an especial friend in Gulmarg? Was there a woman? His moods had been so varied that day. In the morning he had been the efficient hotel servant. At the bus station, settling down for the long wait, he had wiped anticipation off his face, which had grown blank, almost stupefied. In the bus at last, clutching the sandwich basket, he had shown a subdued sociability. Then, as soon as he had got on to the pony for the ride through the pines up to Gulmarg, he had become animated and mischievous, bobbing up and down in his saddle, twirling the reins, making clucking noises, racing ahead, riding back, surprising the other ponies into trots. I think it was the ponies of Gulmarg he looked forward to; somewhere in him there must have been the blood of horsemen. On a pony, and even with his shoes on, he ceased to be comic; the loose tapering trousers were right; they were the trousers of a horseman. On our excursions on the following days he never walked when he could ride, even on the steepest, rockiest, nastiest paths; and as long as he was on the back of a pony he remained animated, crying out delightedly when the pony slipped, 'Oash! Oash! Easy, easy.' He became talkative. He spoke of the events of 1947 and told of raiders who were so ignorant they took brass for gold. And he told us why he was reluctant to walk. One winter, he said, he had left the service of an employer beyond the Valley; he was without money and had had to cross the snow-covered Banihal Pass on

7

PILGRIMAGE

It was Karan Singh, the young Maharaja of Kashmir, now the elected Head of the Jammu and Kashmir State, who encouraged us to join the pilgrimage to the Cave of Amarnath, the Eternal Lord. The cave lies thirteen thousand feet up the eighteen-thousand-foot Amarnath Mountain, some ninety miles north-east of Srinagar, and is made holy by the five-foot ice *lingam*, symbol of Shiva, which forms there during the summer months. The *lingam*, it is believed, waxes and wanes with the moon and reaches its greatest height on the day of the August full moon: on this day the pilgrimage arrives. It was a mystery, like Delphi, of the older world. It had survived because it was of India and Hinduism which, without beginning, without end, scarcely a religion, continued as a repository and living record of man's religious consciousness.

Karan Singh had gone to the cave some years before, though not with the traditional pilgrimage, and he had published a vivid account of the journey I could not share his religious fervour, but I relished his exact descriptions of snowclad mountains, icy green lakes and changing weather. To me the true mystery of the cave lay in its situation. It was at the end of a twenty-mile track, a journey of two days, from Chandanwari, which was as far as the jeep-road went. For many months of the year this track disappeared under

Himalayan snow and the cave was inaccessible; and in summer, in spite of the annual efforts of the Public Works Department, the track was difficult and in bad weather dangerous. It zigzagged up a two-thousand-foot drop; it led over a pass fifteen thousand feet high; it was a narrow ledge on a bare, curving mountainside. Beyond the tree-line breathing was not easy, and the nights were very cold. The snow never completely melted. It remained hard in sheltered gullies and canyons; it formed solid bridges over summer-slackened streams, bridges which on the surface were as brown and gritty as the surrounding land but which several feet below, just above the water, were scooped out into low, ice-blue caverns.

How had the cave been discovered? How had its mystery been established? The land was bare; it offered no fuel or food. The Himalayan summer was short, its weather treacherous. Every exploration, like every pilgrimage even today, had to be swift. And how had this mystery, so much of ice and snow, so briefly glimpsed each year, penetrated to every corner of ancient India? Himalayas, 'abode of snow': how could they be related to the burning North Indian plain and the palm-fringed beaches of the South? But they had been charted, their mysteries unearthed. Beyond the Amarnath Cave was the mountain of Kailas and beyond that the lake of Manasarovar. And legends attached to every stage of the Amarnath pilgrimage. These rocks were what remained of defeated demons; out of that lake Lord Vishnu arose on the back of a thousand-headed serpent; on this plain Lord Shiva once did the cosmic dance of destruction and his locks, becoming undone, created these five streams: wonders revealed only for a

Tabel a chare Bed	15.0.0.
one colie	30.0.0.
	350.0.0.
Sweeper	20.0.0.
Extre loding and Noey Loding colie	20.0.0.
	390.0.0.
From 11 august up to 17 august	
7 day conteri Food	161.0.0.
	Rs551.0.0.

If you going Bus for Imri Nath then is last 100 Rs.

It was a remarkable document: an unfamiliar language, an unfamiliar script, and most of its approximations understandable. Too understandable: I was being over-charged. I was bitterly disappointed. I had known them for four months; I had declared my affection for them; I had done what I could for the hotel; I had given them a party. It must have been the depth of this disappoint-ment; or it might have been my two days in bed. I jumped up, pushed Aziz aside, ran to the window, threw it open and heard myself shouting to Mr Butt in a strange insincere-sincere voice, the result perhaps of remembering, even while I shouted, that I had to speak clearly, as to a child, and to use words which he would understand: 'This is not *good*, Mr Butt. Butt Sahib, this is not *honest*. Mr Butt, do you know what you have done? You have *hurt* me.'

He was standing in the garden with some boatmen. He looked up, startled and uncomprehending. Then his face, still turned up to me, went blank. He said nothing.

In the silence that followed my words I felt foolish

and not a little uneasy. I closed the window and quietly got back into bed. India, it was said, brought out concealed elements of the personality. Was this me? Was this the effect of India?

Whatever it was, it alarmed them at the hotel; and when, after giving me time to cool down, they gathered around my bed to discuss the estimate, they were solicitous, as though I was ill with more than a cold. Their manner also held reproach: it was as if, during all the weeks I had been with them, I had concealed my emotionalism, thereby encouraging an approach for which they could not, with justice, be blamed.

In the end many rupees were knocked off the estimate and we became friends again. Mr Butt seemed happy; he came with us to Pahalgam to see us off. Aziz was happy. He was wearing his fur cap, Ali Mohammed's striped blue suit, sandals (Mr Butt had refused to lend his shoes again), and a pair of my socks. He did not have the retinue he would have liked, but no one else on the pilgrimage appeared to be travelling in comparable style. We did, after all, have a staff; and we had a second tent for the staff. And when, at sunset, we halted at the crowded camp in the smoking woods of Chandanwari, he not only managed by his swift, intelligent arrangements to create something like luxury in the midst of restrictions, but he also managed, by his mixture of bustle, of orders sharply given to the pony man and his assistant, and of reverential exaggerated attentions to us, to hedge us around with dignity. The camp was a chaos of tents and guy-ropes and cooking stones and pilgrims defecating behind every bush. The woods were already littered with uncovered excrement; hanks and twists of excrement crowned every accessible boulder of the Lidder River, beside which we had it was: 'You go see Government. They take away *ghora-wallah* permit.' He was out for blood; I had never seen him so determined.

In front and behind the pilgrimage stretched in a thin irrelevant line of movement which appeared to have no beginning or end, which gave scale to the mountains and emphasized their stillness. The path had been trampled into dust, inches thick, that rose at every step. It was important not to overtake or be overtaken. Dust overcame the dampness below wet rock; dust powdered the hard snow in gullies. Over one such gully a skull-capped Kashmiri had made himself the harassed master. He had a spade and feverishly dug up snow, which he offered, for a few coins, to pilgrims. The pilgrims, continually pressed from behind, could not stop. Nor could the Kashmiri: he frantically dug, ran with extended spade after the pilgrims already departing, did a lightning haggle, took his coins, ran back, dug again. He was all motion: it was a one-day-a-year trade.

We had passed the tree-line and now we came into sight of the milky green lake of Sheshnag and the glacier that fed it. From Karan Singh's essay I had learned that the icy waters of Sheshnag were auspicious. Some members of his party had gone down the half a mile or so to the lake, to have a lucky dip. But he had made a compromise: 'I have to admit that I used the less ortho-dox, though certainly more convenient, method of getting water from the lake carried up and warming it for my bath.' It would have been pleasant to dawdle here, to go down to the lake. But the pilgrimage pressed us on, and Aziz was anxious to camp.

He was right to be anxious. The camping ground, when we got to it, was crowded; the rocky banks of the turbulent mountain river were already lined with

defecating pilgrims, and soon it would have been difficult to find an accessible washing spot that was
unsullied. Hundreds of ponies, freed of their burdens,
had been hobbled and turned loose on the mountainside, browsing on what they could find; some were to
die on this journey. The evening light fell golden on the
three snowy peaks above Sheshnag; it shot through
the smoke which, rising above the camp, converted the
tents into an extensive miniature mountain range, peak
beyond white peak dissolving in evening mist; it fell on
the two long rows of sadhus, more brilliant splashes of
saffron and scarlet, who were being fed, at the Kashmir
Government's expense, in an open area that had been
spared impurity. These sadhus had been gathered from
every corner of India, and their feeding, I believe, was
part of the Tourist Department's public relations: offi-
cially we were all 'tourists-cum-pilgrims'.

Aziz did not cease to complain about the runaway
ghora-wallah. I knew that he had chosen me as the
instrument of his vengeance and I cannot understand
why I did not rebel. His complaints and pleas wore me
down; and after dinner I allowed myself to be led
through the dark, cold camp, past ropes and glinting
rivulets and heaven knows what other dangers, to the
tent of one of the government officials accompanying
the pilgrimage. I had met him the previous evening at
Chandanwari, and now he greeted me warmly. I was
glad for Aziz's sake and my own at this proof of my
influence. Aziz behaved like a man already satisfied. He
was no longer the leader; he was only my deferential
servant. By his behaviour, his interruptions, he presented me as the aggrieved party, a duped tourist; then
he withdrew, leaving me to get out of the situation as
best I could. My complaint was half-hearted. The

official made notes. We talked about the difficulties of organizing such a pilgrimage, and he offered me a cup of coffee with the compliments of the Indian Coffee Board.

I was in the Coffee Board's tent, sipping coffee, when a tall white girl of striking appearance came in.

'Hi,' she said, sitting beside me. 'I'm Laraine.'

She was American; she was thrilled by the *yatra*, the pilgrimage. Her speech abounded in Hindi words.

She attracted me. But I had grown tired of meeting young Americans in unlikely places. It was amusing, and charitable, to think that some of them were spies for the CIA or whatever it was. But there were too many of them. It seemed more likely that they were a new type of American whose privilege it was to go slumming about the world and sometimes scrounging, exacting a personal repayment for a national generosity. I had met the type in Egypt, looking for Lawrence Durrell's Alexandria, living on a few piastres a day, eating *foul* and willing to accept any Eastern hospitality that was going. In Greece for one day I had had to feed an unashamed beggar, a 'teacher', who said he never went to restaurants or hotels: 'As long as there are doors to knack on, I knack.' (He was almost certainly a spy, and he thought I was one too. 'Why is it,' he said, 'that every goddam outa-the-way place I go, I meet Indians?') In New Delhi I had met the type in its most developed form: this was a 'research student', of ineradicable grossness, who had billeted himself for six weeks in the house of a stranger, casually encountered at a wedding party. India, the world's largest slum, had an added attraction: 'cultural' humility was sweet, but 'spiritual' humility was sweeter.

So: No, I said, I wasn't thrilled by the *yatra*. I thought

the *yatris* had no idea of sanitation; they polluted every river we came to; I wished they would follow Gandhi's advice about the need for a little spade.

'Then you shouldn't have come.'

It was the only reply, and it was unanswerable. My resentment had made me speak foolishly. I sought to work the conversation back to a more normal give-and-take and tried to get her to tell me about herself.

She had come to India, she said, for two weeks, and had already stayed six months. She was attracted to Hindu philosophy; when she left the *yatra* she was going to spend some time in an ashram. She was a seeker.

Her cheekbones were high; her neck was slender. But her leanness was of the sort which holds fleshy surprises; her breasts were good and full. I did not think it was the body of someone who would be allowed to remain a seeker for long. Yet in the light of the pressure lamp her eyes conveyed uncertainty. I thought they hinted at family problems and childhood distress. This, and a certain coarseness of her skin, added a disturbing edge to her good looks.

I would have liked to see more of her. But though we promised to look out for one another, we never met again during the pilgrimage.

That, however, was not the last of Laraine.

Ridiculously, the next morning I allowed Aziz to persuade me to complain to the government official again about the missing *ghora-wallah*. Aziz wanted blood, and his faith in the power of officials was boundless. He was almost triumphant when we started out. We had gone less than a mile, however, Aziz serene on his pony, when our bedding bundle rolled off the untended pony and have formed a line ten to fifteen miles long. For hours, then, the line must have moved, unbroken, from camp to camp. Even as the sun was going down over the grey, whistling plain where a pony had died, where ponies every year died, the pilgrims continued to come down the mountains and across the plain, a thin wriggling line of colour rapidly merging into the darkness there, here in the lights of the camp revealed as a slow, silent march of Kashmiri pony men, skullcapped, with dusty feet in disintegrating straw sandals, Gujjars whose studded leather shoes, curiously small and elegant, curling back at the tips, matched the sharpness of their fine features, and ladies riding side-saddle muffled against the dust during the day, now muffled against the cold.

They came into a camp where the tension of adventure, so high only that morning, had already slackened. The adventure was nearly over; the restlessness was the restlessness of anticipated breaking-up and return. Many of the pilgrims had turned in early; they wished to be up for the four o'clock dash to the cave the next morning. The posters in the tent of the Indian Coffee Board were tarnished: they would be needed for only a few hours more. There were fewer wanderers about the camp than at Sheshnag or Chandanwari. No one gazed at the silver rods which for a century had been sent on the pilgrimage by the Kashmir royal house and were displayed in a lighted tent at the head of the camp; that wonder had been seen before. The crowd around the pundit in the second tent was small and settled, a sifting of the crowds of the two previous nights. From Karan Singh's essay, I imagine that during our night halts he had been reciting from the *Amarkatha*, a Sanskrit account of the pilgrimage 'believed to have been related by Lord Shiva himself to his consort Parvati in the Amarnath Cave'. He was a man of ferocious, magazine-illustration handsomeness, exactly filling his role: he had a wavy black beard, long hair, large bright eyes, and remained bare-shouldered even in the bitter cold. Tonight in his windy tent he was chanting, his eyes closed, his fingers delicately bunched on his knees. Just beyond the yellow of his pressure lamp, light was silver: the moon, almost full. Rock was as white as raging water; the wind blew; the camp went stiller.

The path to the cave was a narrow ledge cut diagonally, ever rising, ever curving, into the mountains beyond Panchtarni. Pilgrims were already returned from the cave when we started in bright sunlight the next morning; and men with red Public Works Department armbands stood at dangerous corners, controlling the two-way traffic. The foreheads of the returning pilgrims were marked with sandalwood paste. Their faces were bright with ecstasy. They had seen the god; they were exuberant and aggressive. They were unwilling to give way. They shouted, *'Jai Shiva Shankar!'* and the cave-bound pilgrims, as subdued as a cinema queue when the earlier, fulfilled audience streams out, replied softly, *'Jai Shiva Shankar!'*

'You!' a sandalwood-smeared young man shouted to me in English. 'You say, "*Jai Shiva Shankar!*"'

'Jai Shiva Shankar!'

My promptness confused him. 'All right. Good.' And he passed on. *'Jai Shiva Shankar!'*

Down the steep mountainside yellow flowers presently appeared in profusion, and everyone was reminded that fresh flowers were an acceptable offering to the god. Since four o'clock that morning, though, pilgrims had been passing this way: few flowers remained within easy reach, and it seemed that for

We would experience their weather – that morning in the camp at Sheshnag mist had suddenly swirled down the snowcapped mountains, adding ominousness to beauty, and had as suddenly lifted, revealing the bright sky. And in the afternoons we would have the streams to ourselves. But 'later' is always part of these moments. Already, in fact, the desolate camp at Panchtarni had affected me. The pilgrimage was over, our path was known; the journey had grown stale.

Some time in the afternoon a Kashmiri in a green cap joined our party, and a quarrel instantly blew up between him and Aziz. I was on foot; from afar I could see the gesticulating figures; and when I drew near I recognized the man in the green cap as the missing *ghora-wallah*. He was attempting to take charge of the pony he had abandoned two days before; there was nothing to stop him, but at every shout from Aziz he behaved like a man who was being restrained by physical force. Vengeance was now Aziz's; this was the moment he had been waiting for; and his anger and contempt were frightening, except perhaps to another Kashmiri. For all its passion, in fact, the exchange had something of play. The *ghora-wallah* pleaded, but he seemed untouched by Aziz's abuse. He wept. Aziz, astride his shabby little pony, his socked, sandalled feet hanging very low, refused to be mollified. Suddenly, no longer weeping, the *ghora-wallah* ran to the abandoned pony and made as if to seize the reins. Aziz screamed; the *ghora-wallah* stopped short, as though he had been surprised in a furtive act and struck a heavy blow on the head. Finally he ceased to weep or plead; he blustered; he became abusive; and Aziz replied. He hung back; he ran forward; he hung back again. Then he didn't run forward, and gradually dwindled in the distance, a still, standing figure occasionally roused to frenzy, shaking a fist against the Himalayan skyline.

'When we reach Pahalgam you report Tourism Office,' Aziz, perfectly calm, said to me. 'They take away his permit.'

Sheshnag camp was almost deserted; it looked trampled over and unsavoury. We passed it by and at dusk pitched our tents at a small encampment a few miles on. For hours afterwards lights came twinkling down the mountain, and went past: pilgrims hastening back to Chandanwari, puffs of dust in the light of the full moon.

The journey that remained was easy. We ourselves were in the woods of Chandanwari early next morning and by midday we were in sight of Pahalgam, back in a green world of fields and trees and earth. It was all downhill now. I got off my pony and scrambled down, avoiding the lengthy twists and turns of the jeep-track, and soon was far ahead of Aziz and the others. Aziz made no attempt to catch up with me; and even when, together again, we were on the metalled road and passing the bus station and the Tourist Office, he said not a word about the missing *ghora-wallah*. I did not remind him. He jumped off his pony to take an uninvited, and unresented, pull at someone's hookah: he had abandoned the role of the aloof majordomo. Momentarily we lost him, and when he reappeared he was carrying a quantity of peas in his shirt, the front of which was knotted to form something like a tray, which he did not need to support. The transformation from major domo to hotel servant was complete. He was even without the vacuum flask; that, like Mr Butt's shoes, he had destroyed.

At our base, a tent in the shade of a tree, the *ghora-wallah* in the green cap was waiting for us. As soon as he caught sight of me he began to wail and weep: a formal self-abasement, a formal weeping, dry and scraping, without a hint of real distress. He ran to me, dropped to his knees and grabbed my legs with his powerful hands. The pony men gathered round with looks of satisfaction. Aziz, his shirtful of peas before him, was openly smiling down at the *ghora-wallah*.

'He is poor man, sahib.'

What was this? After all that I had heard from him about the *ghora-wallah*, could this be Aziz?

The *ghora-wallah* wept more loudly.

'He have wife,' Aziz said. 'He have children. You not report Touriasm, sahib.'

The *ghora-wallah* ran his hands down my legs and banged his forehead on my shoes.

'He very poor man, sahib. You not dock his pay. You not take away his permit.'

Holding my knees firmly, the *ghora-wallah* rubbed his forehead against them.

'He not honest man, sahib. He bloody swine. But he poor. You not report Touriasm.'

The ritual went on, without any reference, it seemed, to me.

'All right, all right,' I said, 'I not report.'

Instantly the *ghora-wallah* was up, not a trace of anxiety or relief on his broad peasant's face: he had simply been working. He dusted the knees of his trousers in a businesslike way, took out some rupee notes from a pocket, counted five and, even as I looked, gave them to Aziz.

This was the price of Aziz's intercession. Had they come to some arrangement the previous afternoon? Had it been planned days before? Had Aziz intended all his groans and complaints to lead to this, an extra five rupees? It seemed unlikely – that labour up Pissu Ghati had been real – but with Aziz I could no longer be sure. He seemed surer of me: he had taken a gift – in the long run my money – in my presence. Throughout the journey he had promoted my dignity; he must have frightened the *ghora-wallah* with my importance. But his true assessment was plain. I was harmless. Faced with this assessment, I felt my will weaken. No, I wouldn't, simply for the sake of my pride, make a scene; when all was said and done, Aziz was my servant. It would be less troublesome to preserve my character, as he had read it, until we got back to Srinagar.

The five rupees, checked, disappeared into one of Aziz's pockets. The moment for reprimand passed. I said nothing. His assessment had, after all, proved correct.

Then the *ghora-wallah*, leading his pony by the reins, came up to me again.

'*Bakshish?*' he said, and stretched out one hand.

The sunflowers in the garden faded and were like emblems of dying suns, their tongues of fire limp and shrivelled. My work was almost done; it would soon be time to go. Farewell visits had to be made. We went first to our friends at Gulmarg.

'We've been having our adventures too,' Ishmael said.

They always had. They attracted drama. They were interested in the arts and their house was always full of writers and musicians.

'You didn't by any chance meet a girl called Laraine on your pilgrimage?'

'An American girl?'

'She said she was going to Amarnath.'

'But how extraordinary! Was she staying here too?'

'She and Rafiq nearly drove us mad.'

This adventure (Ishmael said) had begun in Srinagar, in the Indian Coffee House on Residency Road. There one morning Ishmael met Rafiq. Rafiq was a musician. He played the sitar. The apprenticeship of a musician in India is long and severe. And though Rafiq was nearly thirty and though, according to Ishmael, he was very good, he had not yet made a name; he was just beginning to give recitals on local radio stations. It was in order to relax before one such recital that Rafiq had come to Kashmir for a fortnight. He had little money. Ishmael, generous and impulsive as always, invited Rafiq, whom he had met that morning for the first time, to stay at his bungalow in Gulmarg. Rafiq took his sitar and went.

The arrangement worked well. Rafiq found himself with a couple who understood the artistic temperament. His music delighted them; he could never practise enough. The routine of the house was also congenial. Dinner was at midnight, after music, talk and drink. Breakfast was at midday. Then perhaps the masseur called, carrying his equipment in a small black box marked with his name. Afterwards, if it was not raining, there was a walk through the pines. Sometimes they collected mushrooms; sometimes they collected cones for the fire, to give a quick aromatic blaze.

Then one afternoon all this changed.

They were having coffee on the sunlit lawn when on the path below there appeared a white girl. She was arguing with a Kashmiri *ghora-wallah*: she had no companion and was clearly in some trouble. Ishmael sent Rafiq down to see what he could do. In that moment Rafiq's holiday was ruined; in that moment he was lost. When, a minute or so later, he returned, his hosts could scarcely recognize him as the mild, courteous sitar-player they had picked mushrooms with. He was like a man possessed. In that short time, during which he had also settled with the *ghora-wallah*, he had conquered and had surrendered: a relationship had been decided and had become explosive. Rafiq did not return alone. He had the girl, Laraine, with him. She was going to stay with them, he said. Did they mind? Could they make the necessary arrangements?

Stunned, they agreed. Later that afternoon they suggested a walk: they would show their new guest the peak of Nanga Parbat, forty miles away, on which the snow glistened like oil paint. Rafiq and Laraine soon fell behind, then disappeared. Ishmael and his wife were a little aggrieved. Self-consciously and silently, like guests rather than hosts, they continued on their walk, pausing here and there to admire the view. In time they were rejoined by Rafiq and Laraine. No fulfilment on their faces, no fatigue: they were both hysterical. They were quarrelling and their rage was real. Presently they exchanged blows. The faces of both were already marked. She kicked him. He groaned, and slapped her. She cried out, swung her bag at him, kicked him again, and he tumbled down the brambly slope. Torn, bleeding, he came bellowing up, snatched her bag and threw it far down into a valley, where it would remain until the snows came and washed it away. At this she sat down and wept like a child. His rage vanished; he went to her; she yielded to him.

He took it out on the sitar when they got back to the bungalow. He practised like a man gone mad; the sitar whined and whined. That night they had another fight. Their shouts and screams brought the police, ever on the alert for Pakistani raiders, who had made a swift

'No!'

'Mr Butt and Ali Mohammed take them Mufti. She turn Muslim, get Muslim name. They get married. They mealing at *one* o'clock last night.' The lateness of the meal had impressed him almost as much as the marriage.

And now from the bridal chamber, silence: not even the sitar. No wedding breakfast, no coming out to look at the view. All morning the room remained closed, as though they were both hiding inside, awed at what had happened. After lunch they slipped out. I did not see them go.

It was not until the late afternoon, when I was having tea on the lawn, that I saw Laraine returning alone across the lake to the hotel. She was wearing a blue cotton frock; she looked cool; and she was carrying a paperback. She might have been a simple tourist.

'Hi!'

'Is it true what I hear? That you're married?'

'You know me. Impulsive.'

'Congratulations.'

'Thank you.'

She sat down; she was a little frightened; she wanted to talk.

'But isn't it crazy? Me with all this interest in Hinduism' – she showed the paperback she was carrying: it was Mr Rajagopalachari's retelling of the *Mahabharata* – 'and now overnight I'm a Muslim and everything.'

'What is your new name?'

'Zenobia. Don't you think it's pretty?'

It was a pretty name, but it had brought problems. She didn't know whether she had lost her American nationality as a result of her marriage, and she wasn't sure whether she would be allowed to work in India.

She had some idea that she was now very poor and would have to live in straitened circumstances – not, I felt, fully visualized – in some Indian town. But already she was speaking of 'my husband' as though she had used the words all her life; already she was concerned about 'my husband's career' and 'my husband's recital'.

They were poorer than she had perhaps imagined. Even the Liward was too expensive for them. They were to move elsewhere the following day, and trouble about their hotel bill blew up in the morning.

Aziz reported, 'He say I overcharge. He say, "Why you tell other sahib I married?" I say, "Why you want secret? Man get married. This is for good. He give party. He invite. He not hide. And why I not tell? You wake up my sahib and he complain."'

'Are you sure you are not overcharging them, Aziz?'

'O no, sahib.'

'But he doesn't have a lot of money, Aziz. He wasn't expecting to get married when he came to Kashmir. How much did they spend on their marriage?'

'O sahib, how much they spend? Some people give Mufti five, some give fifteen, some give fifty.'

'How much did they give?'

'A hundred.'

'You are a brute. You shouldn't have let him. He couldn't afford a hundred rupees. No wonder he can't pay you now.'

'But this is for good, sahib. You get married American memsahib, you give big party. You give Parsi *khana*, *bangola* fireworks. You not hide. They not give party, they not give nothing.'

'The memsahib is American, but they don't have money.'

'No, sahib. They hide. Lotta people come Kashmir,

entertainment. We ate sitting on the floor of an upper room that had been cleared of all furniture and people, whose presence we could yet detect in close whispers and the sounds of movement; and Aziz knelt before us, talking, no longer a hotel servant but our host, grave, independent, a man of substance, a man of views and, when the women and the babies flooded in, a responsible family man. The walls were thick, comfortingly grimed, full of arched recesses; windows were small. The room promised idleness and the warmth of charcoal braziers in winter, when the lake would freeze so hard a jeep could be driven over it: we would follow the weather in Srinagar.

After our last dinner in the hotel Mr Butt assembled the servants for the tipping ceremony: Aziz, Ali Mohammed, the cook, the gardener, the odd-job boy. They had been disappointed in a wedding; I hoped I wasn't going to disappoint them further: their smiling faces carried the conviction that the age of style was not yet over. They acknowledged my gifts and typewritten testimonials with graceful Muslim gestures; they continued to smile. Perhaps they were merely being courteous; perhaps they had learned to accommodate themselves to the lesser age. But Aziz was pleased. I could tell that from the indifferent manner with which, after a lightning assessment, he thrust the money into his pocket. He became morose, active, a man harassed by duties that were never done: money was not as important to him at that moment as setting the dining-room to rights. He would relax as soon as he left the room; they would all relax. And going to the kitchen later that evening for a last pull at the hookah, I surprised them giggling over the testimonial I had written, with some care, for the odd-job boy.

We left early in the morning. Mr Butt paddled u
over to the lake boulevard. It was not yet light. The
water was still; on the boulevard the tonga waited. We
went past the closed houseboats, the lotus beds. On
the balustrade of the boulevard a man was exercising.
The tonga roof sloped low: we had to lean forward to
see the lake and the mountains. The town was awakening from minute to minute, and the Tourist Reception
Centre, when we got to it, was infernally alive.

'Three rupees,' the tonga-wallah said.

In four months I had established among the lakeside
tongas that I never paid more than one and a quarter
rupees for the ride into town. But the circumstances
were extraordinary. I offered two. The tonga-wallah
refused to touch the notes. I offered no more. He
threatened me with his whip; and I found, to my
surprise – it must have been the earliness of the hour –
that I had seized him by the throat.

Aziz intervened. 'He not tourist.'

'Oh,' the tonga-wallah said.

He dropped his whip hand, and I released him.

Our seats on the bus had been booked, but it was
necessary to scramble, to fight, to shout. Aziz and Ali
Mohammed scrambled and shouted for us, and we
withdrew to the edge of the crowd.

Then we saw Laraine, Zenobia.

She was alone, and was peering short-sightedly at
buses. She wore a chocolate skirt and a cream-coloured
blouse. She looked thinner. She was not happy to meet
us and had little news to give. She was off to her Hindu
ashram after all; later she would be joining her husband. Now she was busy: she had to find her bus. It was
a bus of the Radhakishun service. She turned this name
to the more familiar 'Radha Krishna'; her mind still ran

the Hindu legends. Krishna was the dark god, dha the fair milkmaid with whom he sported.

And, asking for Radha Krishna, peering at the number plates on buses, she disappeared into the crowd.

Our own seats had now been secured, our bags placed below the tarpaulin on the roof of the bus. We shook hands with Aziz and Ali and went inside.

'You don't worry about tonga-wallah,' Aziz said. 'I settle.' There were tears in his eyes.

The engine started.

'Tonga-wallah?'

'You don't worry, sahib. Correct fare three rupees. I pay.'

The driver was blowing his horn.

'Correct fare?'

'Morning fare, sahib.'

He was right; I knew that.

'Two rupees, three rupees, what different? Good-bye, good-bye. You don't worry.'

I dug into my pockets.

'Don't worry, sahib. Good-bye.'

Through the window I pushed out some rupee notes.

He took them. Tears were running down his cheeks. Even at that moment I could not be sure that he had ever been mine.

She wore a chocolate skirt and a cream-coloured blouse. Rafiq would remember those garments; perhaps he had seen her lay them out the previous evening. He never saw her after that morning. She went to her ashram; and then she left India. He wrote; she replied; then his letters were returned unopened. Her parents had been separated and lived in different countries. He was supported by one, rejected by the other. Still he wrote; and months later he was still grieving.

But I heard this in another season. And in the Poste Restante of another town this letter awaited me:

HOTEL LIWARD
Advance Arrangements for
Trecking, Shooting, Fishing,
Gulmarg Hut & Pahalgam Experienced Guide
Prop: M. S. Butt

My dear Sir,

I beg to acknowledge your kind favour of the 7th inst. and find that you had to face a lot of trouble en route to your destination, since the bus in which were you travelling broke. However I am pleased to find that you have reached safely your destination by His Grace.

I quite realize how the Kashmir view and other things of this place don't go out of your memory. I wish you to be here again and thus give me a chance to serve you.

In your room there was one client from Bombay and other from Delhi.

The whole family of ours send their best compliments to you.

Hoping this would find you in the best of health and cheerful spirits.

> Thanking you in anticipation,
> Yours sincerely,
> M. S. Butt
> (Mohd. Sidiq Butt).

PART THREE

grandmother's house, there was no alien presence. How could such a thing be conceived? Our own world, though clearly fading, was still separate; and an involvement with the English, of whom on the island we knew little, would have seemed a more unlikely violation than an involvement with the Chinese or the Africans, of whom we knew more. Into this alienness we daily ventured, and at length we were absorbed into it. But we knew there had been change, gain, loss. We knew that something which was once whole had been washed away. What was whole was the idea of India.

To preserve this conception of India as a country still whole, historical facts had not been suppressed. They had been acknowledged and ignored; and it was only in India that I was able to see this as part of the Indian ability to retreat, the ability genuinely not to see what was obvious: with others a foundation of neurosis, but with Indians only part of a greater philosophy of despair, leading to passivity, detachment, acceptance. It is only now, as the impatience of the observer is dissipated in the process of writing and self-inquiry, that I see how much this philosophy had also been mine. It had enabled me, through the stresses of a long residence in England, to withdraw completely from nationality and loyalties except to persons; it had made me content to be myself alone, my work, my name (the last two so different from the first); it had convinced me that every man was an island, and taught me to shield all that I knew to be good and pure within myself from the corruption of causes.

Before the reminders of this England of India, then, I ought to have been calm. But they revealed one type of self-deception as self-deception; and though this was lodged in that part of the mind where fantasy was permissible, the revelation was painful. It was an encounter with a humiliation I had never before experienced, and perhaps more so to me than to those Indians who hurried about streets with unlikely English names, in the shadow of imperial-grand houses, as others might have felt for me the colonial humiliation I did not feel in Trinidad.

Colonial India I could not link with colonial Trinidad. Trinidad was a British colony; but every child knew that we were only a dot on the map of the world, and it was therefore important to be British: that at least anchored us within a wider system. It was a system which we did not feel to be oppressive; and though British, in institutions and education as well as in political fact, we were in the New World, our population was greatly mixed, English people were few and kept themselves to themselves, and England was as a result only one of the countries of which we were aware.

It was a country to a large extent unknown; a taste for English things was something a cultivated islander might affect. To the majority America was more important. The English made good tiny cars for careful drivers. The Americans made the real automobiles, as they made the real films and produced the best singers and the best bands. Their films spoke universal sentiments and their humour was immediately comprehensible. American radio was modern and marvellous and at least you could understand the accent; you could listen to fifteen minutes of news on the BBC and not understand a word. The American soldiers loved a fat backstreet whore, the blacker the better; they packed them into their jeeps and raced from club to club, throwing their money about; and they could always be enticed into unequal brawls. They were people with whom communication was possible. Beside them the British soldiers were like foreigners. In Trinidad they were incapable of hitting the right note. They were either too loud or too withdrawn; they spoke this strange English; they referred to themselves as 'blokes' (this was once the subject of a news-item in the *Trinidad Guardian*), not knowing that in Trinidad a bloke was a term of abuse; their uniforms, their shorts in particular, were ugly. They had little money and little sense of propriety: they could be seen in the Syrian shops buying cheap women's underwear. This was the England of popular conception. There was of course the other England – the source of governors and senior civil servants – but this was too remote to be real.

We were colonials in a special position. The British Empire in the West Indies was old. It was an empire of the sea and apart from a square here and a harbour there it had left few monuments; and because we were in the New World – Trinidad was virtually without a population in 1800 – these monuments appeared to belong to our prehistory. By its very age the Empire had ceased to be incongruous. It required some detachment to see that our institutions and our language were the results of empire.

The England of India was totally different. It remained an incongruous imposition. Fort St George, grey and massive and of an eighteenth-century English taste known from day trips, could not be related to the Madras landscape; in Calcutta the wide-fronted, pillared house, pointed out as Clive's, on the choked road to Dum Dum airport, appeared to require a less exotic setting. And because it was incongruous, its age, which was less than the age of the empire in the West Indies, came as a surprise: these eighteenth-century monuments ought to have appeared superficial, but now one saw that they had become part of this country of alien ruins. This was one aspect of Indian England; it belonged to the history of India; it was dead.

Distinct from this was the England of the Raj. This still lived. It lived in the division of country towns into 'cantonments', 'civil lines' and bazaars. It lived in army officers' messes, in the silver so frequently given, so reverentially polished and displayed, in uniforms and moustaches and swagger sticks and mannerisms and jargon. It lived in the collectorates, in the neat fading handwriting of those settlements which add up to a Domesday book of a continent: suggesting endless days in the sun on horseback, with many servants but few real comforts, and evenings of patient effort. ('The effort exhausted them,' a young IAS officer said to me. After this they just couldn't move on to anything else.') It lived in the clubs, the Sunday morning bingo, the yellow-covered overseas edition of the *Daily Mirror* in the manicured hands of middle-class Indian ladies; it lived in the dance-floors of city restaurants. It was an England more full-blooded than anyone coming from Trinidad might have thought possible. It was grander, more creative and more vulgar.

Yet it did not ring true. It had never rung true to me in Kipling and other writers; and it did not ring true now. Was it the mixture of England and India? Was it my colonial, Trinidad-American, English-speaking prejudice which could not quite accept as real this imposition, without apparent competition, of one culture on another? With one part of myself I felt the coming together of England and India as a violation; with the other I saw it as ridiculous, resulting in a comic

To say that Kipling is a club writer is of course to use a loaded word. The club is one of the symbols of Anglo-India. In *Something of Myself* Kipling tells how every evening in Lahore he went to dine at the club and there met people who had just been reading what he had written the day before. He regarded this as a valuable discipline. The approbation of the club was important to him: he wrote about the club for the club. In this lies his peculiar honesty, his value as a poetic chronicler of Anglo-India. But in this also lies his special vulnerability, for by applying to the club only the values of the club he has exposed both the club and himself.

His work is of a piece with the architecture of the Raj; and within the imperial shell we find, not billiard-room cartoons or a suburban taste in novels, as in the district clubs, but Mrs Hauksbee, the wit, the queen, the manipulator and card of Simla. How she suffers from the very generosity which sought to bestow on her the attributes she desired! Her wit is no wit; and to us today the susceptibility of her admirers is a little provincial, a little sad. Yet the circle – queen, courtiers, jester – is so complete; something, whether we approve of it or not, has been created by which men can live in special circumstances; and it seems an intolerable cruelty to point to its falseness. A response to Kipling cannot but be personal and on this level. He is too honest and generous; he is too simple; he is too gifted. His vulnerability is an embarrassment; the criticism he invites can only seem a type of brutality. Mr Somerset Maugham has already disposed of the pretensions of Mrs Hauksbee. She once said of the voice of another woman that it was like the screech of the brakes of an underground train as it came into Earl's Court station. If Mrs Hauksbee were what she claimed to be, Mr

Maugham commented, she had no business to be in
Earl's Court; and she certainly oughtn't to have gone
there by underground. There is much in Kipling that
can be dealt with in this way. He genuinely saw people
bigger than they were; they, perhaps less securely, saw
themselves bigger than they were. They reacted one
on the other; fantasy hardened into conviction. And to
us they are now all betrayed.

There is a night train from Delhi to Kalka; from Kalka
you continue to Simla by road or by the narrow-gauge,
toy railroad that winds up the mountains. I went by
road, in the company of a young IAS officer, encountered on the train to Kalka. He spoke sadly of the decay
of the town since 1947. To him, as to all Indians, the
myth was real. The glory of Simla was part of the
Indian inheritance, which was being squandered: there
were now *pan*-shops in the town. While we talked rustles came from the back of the van from the officer's pet
weaver-birds. They were in a large covered cage, and
when the rustles appeared to be reaching a pitch of
frenzy the officer clucked and cooed and spoke sooth-
ingly to the cage. From time to time we had a glimpse
of the toy train going into or coming out of a toy tunnel.
It was mid-January, the air frosty, but the shirtsleeved
passengers leaned passively out of open windows as
though, this being India, it was always summer.

And at first it seemed that the officer was right, that
Kipling's city had altogether decayed. It was wet and
cold; the narrow streets were muddy; barefooted
stunted men stamped uphill with heavy loads strapped
to their backs; their caps recalled Kashmir and those
ragged porters who ran shouting after every arriving
bus at village resorts. Could glamour ever have been

found here? But so it was with every Indian landscape known from books. Deception, one thought; and then, decay. But it was only that the figures in the foreground had to make their impact before fading from a vision grown as selective as when, in a dark room full of familiar objects, one's eyes have grown accustomed to the dark.

Vision contracted: Simla outlined itself: a town built on a series of ridges, a network of switchback lanes in which it was easy to get lost. In my imagination the Mall was broad and straight; it turned out to be narrow and winding. Every few yards notices warned against spitting; but the *pan*-shops were there, as the IAS man had said, and the streets were stained red with betel-juice. The photographers' windows carried faded photographs of Englishwomen in styles of the thirties. They were not relics; the shops were busy. But in India everything is inherited, nothing is abolished; everything grows out of something else, and now the Mall was given over to the offices, clamantly labelled, of the Himachal Pradesh administration, whose officers drove about the narrow lanes in green Chevrolets of the late nineteen-forties: decay upon decay. The sun sank behind the mountains; the cold grew intense. The unsettling figures disappeared, the bazaar impression faded. The ridge sparkled with electric light, and in the lamplit darkness the town centre defined itself more clearly: an English country town of fairyland, of mock mock-styles, the great ecclesiastical building asserting the alien faith, the mean-fronted shops, ornately gabled, out of which nightcapped, nightgowned men might have appeared, holding lanterns or candles: a grandiloquent assertion of a smallness and cosiness that never were. A fabulous creation, of fantasy supported by a confidence which it was impossible not to admire. But it was not what I had expected. My disappointment was the disappointment we momentarily feel when, after reading of the house at Combray, we see the photograph of the house at Illiers. The vision is correct; but it is a child's myth-creating vision. No city or landscape is truly real unless it has been given the quality of myth by writer, painter or by its association with great events. Simla will never cease to be Kipling's city: a child's vision of Home, doubly a fairyland. India distorts and enlarges; with the Raj it enlarged upon what was already a fantasy. This is what Kipling caught; this is his uniqueness.

During the night it snowed, the first snow of the winter. In the morning the hotel servant, like a magician, announced: '*Barf!* Snow.' He pulled the curtains to one side and I saw the valley white and wet with mist. After breakfast the mist cleared. The roofs dripped; the crows cawed, flapping from pine to pine, shaking down snow; the dogs barked far below and there was a sound as of revelry. On the government boards marked 'Himachal Pradesh' – sweet name: the Snow State – snow lay emblematically, as in a Christmas poster. The Mall was busy with holidaymakers, doing the morning promenade. For a long way down the snow was still thick. As we left Simla farther and farther behind, high up in the sky, the snow thinned, became like scattered cakings of salt on hard ground, then disappeared; and it was through a thick and very white Punjab fog, which delayed trains and grounded aircraft, that we crawled all the way to Delhi.

To understand the eighteenth-century England that one saw in India, it was necessary to see it as part of India. Warren Hastings can only with difficulty be read as an Englishman; as an Indian, he fits. But the Raj, though so completely of India, is part of nineteenth-century England.

Consider Adela and Ronny in *A Passage to India*. The sun is going down over the Chandrapore *maidan*; and they, turning their backs on the polo game, walk to a distant seat, to talk. He apologizes for his bad temper earlier in the day. She cuts into his apologies and says: 'I've finally decided we are not going to be married, my dear boy.' They are both disturbed. But they remain controlled; nothing passionate or profound is said; and the moment passes. Then Adela says:

> 'We've been awfully British over it, but I
> suppose that's all right.'
> 'As we are British, I suppose it is.'

It is an amusing exchange, still fresh after forty years. It might be said that 'British', as Adela uses it, is given point by the imperial Indian background; but the word might have been used by many of Forster's characters and its intention would have been the same. To Forster's characters their Englishness is like an extra quality which challenges, and is challenged by, all that is alien. It is a formulated ideal; it needs no elucidation. The word British, as used by Adela, can almost be spelt with a small *b*. It is difficult to imagine the word being so used in Jane Austen. In *Pride and Prejudice* it occurs once, when Mr Collins, on his first visit to Longbourn, is speaking of the virtues of his patroness's daughter, Miss de Bourgh:

> 'Her indifferent state of health unhappily prevents
> her being in town; and by that means, as I told

Lady Catherine myself one day, has deprived the British court of its brightest ornament.'

For Jane Austen and Mr Collins the word is geographical; it is entirely different from Adela's 'British'.

Between the two uses of the word lie a hundred years of industrial and imperial power. In the beginning of this period we can sense the swiftness of change, from stagecoach to railway, from the essays of Hazlitt to those of Macaulay, from the *Pickwick Papers* to *Our Mutual Friend*. In painting it is like a second spring-time: Constable discovering the sky, Bonington discovering the glory of light, of sand and sea: youth and delight that can communicate themselves to us even today. It is a period of newness and self-discovery: Dickens discovering England, London discovering the novel; newness even in Keats and Shelley. It is a period of vigour and expectation. And then, abruptly, there come fulfilment and middle-age. The process of self-discovery is over; the English national myth appears, complete. The reasons are well known: the narcissism was justifiable. But with this there was loss. A way of looking was weakened. What was English was settled; by this the world was to be assessed, and in the travel-writing of the century we can observe a progressive deterioration, from Darwin (1832) to Trollope (1859) to Kingsley (1870) to Froude (1887). More and more these writers are reporting not on themselves but on their Englishness.

At the beginning of this period Hazlitt can dismiss the English writings of Washington Irving with scorn because Irving insisted on finding Sir Roger de Coverleys and Will Wimbles in a country that had moved on since the days of *The Spectator*. Hazlitt's myth-rejecting characters begin to appear in Dickens! There is Mr Podsnap of *Our Mutual Friend*, he knows foreigners and is proud to be British. John Halifax is only a gentleman; Rider Haggard dedicates one of his books to his son in the hope that he will become an Englishman and a gentleman; it was with a similar hope that Tom Brown was sent off by his father to Rugby. By the time we get to *Howards End* even Leonard Bast can be found saying 'I am an Englishman', and meaning by this more than de Quincey ever meant; now the word is loaded indeed.

Writers cannot be blamed for being of their society; and in the novel, then, interest shifts from human behaviour to the Englishness of behaviour, Englishness held up for approval or dissection: a shift of interest reflected in the difference between the inns of the early Dickens and Simpson's Restaurant in the Strand just seventy-five years later, of which Forster in *Howards End* (1910) says:

> Her eyes surveyed the restaurant, and admired its well-calculated tributes to the solidity of our past. Though no more Old English than the works of Kipling, it had selected its reminiscences so adroitly that her criticism was lulled, and the guests whom it was nourishing for imperial purposes bore the outer semblance of Parson Adams and Tom Jones. Scraps of talk jarred oddly on the ear.
>
> 'Right you are! I'll cable out to Uganda this evening . . .'

Forster has made his point exactly. He has pointed at the contradiction in the myth of a people overtaken by industrial and imperial power. Between the possession of Uganda and the conscious possession of Tom Jones there is as little connexion as there is between the stories of Kipling and the novels of his contemporary, Hardy. So, at the height of their power, the British gave the impression of a people at play, a people playing at being English, playing at being English of a certain class. The reality conceals the play; the play conceals the reality.

This endears them to some and exposes them to the charge of hypocrisy from others. And in this imperialist period, when the pink spreads like a rash on the map of the world, the English myth is like a developing language. Quantities alter; new elements are added; codification, repeatedly attempted, cannot keep pace with change; and always between the projected, adjustable myth – Parson Adams in Simpson's, the harassed empire-builder in Uganda or India – and the reality there is some distance. It is long after Waterloo, in a period which begins with the disasters of the Crimea and ends with the humiliations of South Africa, that we have a period of jingoistic militarism. It is after the empire has been built that the concept arises of the merchant and administrator as an empire-builder; and, sternly, Kipling summons the rulers of the world to their pleasant duties. It is the play of puritans. At Home it creates Simpson's in the Strand. In India it creates Simla, the summer seat of the Raj where, as Philip Woodruff tells us in *The Guardians*, the 'affectation' existed among officials, at about the same time, 'of being very English, of knowing nothing at all about India, of eschewing Indian words and customs'.

Half-way across the world was Trinidad, a truly imperial creation. There people of many races accepted

English rule, English institutions and the English language without questioning; yet England and Englishness, as displayed in India, were absent. And to me this remained the peculiar quality of the Raj: this affectation of being very English, this sense of a nation at play, acting out a fantasy. It was there in all the architecture of the Raj and especially in its faintly ridiculous monuments: the Victoria Memorial in Calcutta, the India Gate in New Delhi. They were not monuments worthy of the power they celebrated; they were without the integrity of the earlier British buildings and the even earlier Portuguese cathedrals in Goa.

In *The Men Who Ruled India* Philip Woodruff has written with sad, Roman piety of the British achievement. It was a tremendous achievement; it deserved this piety. But Woodruff's Raj is far from the Raj of the popular English imagination: the sun-helmet (which Gandhi thought sensible but which, for reasons of national pride, he could not wear), the innumerable salaaming, sahib-ing and memsahib-ing servants, and English man as superman, the native as wog and servant and clerk, specimens of whose imperfect English can be gathered into little books (still found in second-hand bookstalls) for the amusement of those who know the language well: a Raj that can be found in a thousand English books on India, particularly in children's books with an Indian setting, and can be found even in Vincent Smith's annotations, for the Oxford University Press, on the writings of the great Sleeman.

To Woodruff this side of the Raj, however established and real, is an embarrassment; it does not represent the truth of the British endeavour. But so it is with all who wish to see purpose, creative or negative, in the Raj, be it Woodruff or be it an Indian like K. M. Munshi, author of a 1946 pamphlet whose title, *The Ruin That Britain Wrought*, makes description unnecessary. There is always an embarrassment, of racial arrogance on the one hand and of genuine endeavour on the other. Which is the reality? They both are; and there is no contradiction. Racial arrogance was part of the Simpson's-in-the-Strand fantasy, inevitably heightened in the puniness of the Indian setting, the completeness of the Indian subjection. Equally heightened, and part of the same fantasy, was the spirit of service. They both issued out of people who knew their roles and knew what was expected of their Englishness. As Woodruff himself says, there is something un-English, something too premeditated about the administration of the Raj. It could not have been otherwise. To be English in India was to be larger than life.

The newspaperman in Madras presses me to attend his lecture on 'The Shakespearean Hero in Crisis'. The business executive in Calcutta, explaining why he feels he must join the army to fight the Chinese, begins solemnly, 'I feel I am defending my right – my right to –' and ends hurriedly with a self-deprecating laugh, 'play a game of golf when I want to.' Almost the last true Englishmen, Malcolm Muggeridge wrote some time ago, are Indians. It is a statement that has point only because it recognizes the English 'character' as a creation of fantasy. In India the Moguls were also foreigners, with fantasies as heady; they ruled as foreigners; but they were finally absorbed into India. The English, as Indians say again and again, did not become part of India; and in the end they escaped back to England. They left no noble monuments behind and no religion save a concept of Englishness as a desirable code of behaviour – of chivalry, it might be described, tempered by legalism – which in Indian minds can be dissociated from the fact of English rule, the vulgarities of racial arrogance or the position of England today. The Madras brahmin was reading O'Hara's *From the Terrace* and loathing it: 'You wouldn't get a well-bred Englishman writing this sort of tosh.' It is a remarkable distinction for a former subject people to make; it is a remarkable thing for a ruling nation to have left behind. This concept of Englishness will survive because it was the product of fantasy, a work of national art; it will outlast England. It explains why withdrawal was easy, why there is no nostalgia such as the Dutch still have for Java, why there was no Algeria, and why after less than twenty years India has almost faded out of the British consciousness: the Raj was an expression of the English involvement with themselves rather than with the country they ruled. It is not, properly, an imperialist attitude. It points, not to the good or evil of British rule in India, but to its failure.

It is well that Indians are unable to look at their country directly, for the distress they would see would drive them mad. And it is well that they have no sense of history, for how then would they be able to continue to squat amid their ruins, and which Indian would be able to read the history of his country for the last thousand years without anger and pain? It is better to retreat into fantasy and fatalism, to trust to the stars in which the fortunes of all are written – there are lecturers in astrology in some universities – and to regard the progress of the rest of the world with the tired tolerance of one who has been through it all before. The aeroplane was known to ancient India, and the telephone, and the atom bomb: there is evidence in the Indian epics.

Surgery was highly developed in ancient India; here, in an important national newspaper, is the text of a lecture proving it. Indian shipbuilding was the wonder of the world. And democracy flourished in ancient India. Every village was a republic, self-sufficient, ordered, controlling its own affairs; the village council could hang an offending villager or chop off his hand. This is what must be recreated, this idyllic ancient India; and when *panchayati raj*, a type of village self-rule, is introduced in 1962 there will be so much talk of the glories of ancient India, so much talk by enthusiastic politicians of hands anciently chopped off, that in some villages of the Madhya Pradesh state hands will be chopped off and people will be hanged by village councils.

Eighteenth-century India was squalid. It invited conquest. But not in Indian eyes: before the British came, as every Indian will tell you, India was rich, on the brink of an industrial breakthrough; and K. M. Munshi says that every village had a school. Indian interpretations of their history are almost as painful as the history itself; and it is especially painful to see the earlier squalor being repeated today, as it has been in the creation of Pakistan and the reawakening within India of disputes about language, religion, caste and region. India, it seems, will never cease to require the arbitration of a conqueror. A people with a sense of history might have ordered matters differently. But this is precisely the saddening element in Indian history: this absence of growth and development. It is a history whose only lesson is that life goes on. There is only a series of beginnings, no final creation.

the road from Kampli goes straight through some of the old buildings and leads to the main street, very wide, very long, still impressive, a flight of stone steps at one end, the towering *gopuram* of the temple, alive with sculpture, at the other. The square-pillared lower storeys of the stone buildings still stand; in the doorways are carvings of dancers with raised legs. And, inside, the inheritors of this greatness: men and women and children, thin as crickets, like lizards among the stones.

A child was squatting in the mud of the street; the hairless, pink-skinned dog waited for the excrement. The child, big-bellied, rose; the dog ate. Outside the temple there were two wooden juggernauts decorated with erotic carvings: couples engaged in copulation and fellatio: passionless, stylized. They were my first glimpse of Indian erotic carving, which I had been longing to see; but after the first excitement came depression. Sex as pain, creation its own decay; Shiva, god of the phallus, performing the dance of life and the dance of death: what a concept he is, how entirely of India! The ruins were inhabited. Set among the buildings of the main street was a brand-new whitewashed temple, pennants flying; and at the end of the street the old temple was still in use, still marked with the alternating vertical stripes of white and rust. One noticeboard about six feet high gave a list of fees for various services. Another, of the same size, gave the history of Vijayanagar: once, after the Raja had prayed, there was 'rain of gold'; this, in India, was history.

Rain, not of gold, swept suddenly across the Tungabhadra River and over the city. We took shelter up a rock slope behind the main street, in the recesses of an unfinished gateway of rough hewn stone. A very thin man followed us there. He was wrapped in a thin white cotton sheet, dappled with wet. He let the sheet fall off his chest to show us that he was all skin and bones, and he made the gestures of eating. I paid no attention. He looked away. He coughed; it was the cough of a sick man. His staff slipped from his hand and fell with a clatter on the stone floor down which water was now streaming. He hoisted himself on to a stone platform and let his staff lie where it had fallen. He withdrew into the angle of platform and wall and was unwilling to make any motion, to do anything that might draw attention to himself. The dark gateway framed light: rain was grey over the pagoda-ed city of stone. On the grey hillside, shining with water, there were the marks of quarryings. When the rain was over the man climbed down, picked up his wet staff, wrapped his sheet about him and made as if to go. I had converted fear and distaste into anger and contempt; it plagued me like a wound. I went to him and gave him some money. How easy it was to feel power in India! He, earning his money, took us out into the open, led us up the washed rock slope and pointed silently to buildings. Here was the hill of rock. Here were the buildings. Here the five-hundred-year-old marks of chisels. An abandoned, unfinished labour, like some of the rock caves at Ellora, which remain as the workmen left them one particular day.

All creation in India hints at the imminence of interruption and destruction. Building is like an elemental urge, like the act of sex among the starved. It is building for the sake of building, creation for the sake of creation; and each creation is separate, a beginning and an end in itself. 'Castles built on the waste sand of the seashore': not quite exact, but at Mahabalipuram near Madras, on the waste sand of the sea shore, stands the about the zoological gardens of Lucknow, in the mock-Vijayanagar stone brackets of the Gandhi Mandap in Madras.

The architecture of nationalist India comes close in spirit to the architecture of the Raj: they are both the work of people consciously seeking to express ideas of themselves. It is comic and it is also sad. It is not of India, this reverence for the past, this attempt to proclaim it. It does not speak of vigour. It speaks as much as any ruin of exhaustion and people who have lost their way. It is as though, after all these endless separate creations, the vital sap has at last failed. Since the schools of Kangra and Basohli, Indian art has been all confusion. There is an idea of the behaviour required in the new world, but the new world is still bewildering. At Amritsar the monument honouring those who fell in the massacre is a pathetic affair of flames cut into heavy red stone. At Lucknow the British memorial of the Mutiny is the ruined Residency, preserved by Indians with a love the visitor must find strange; and just across the road is the rival Indian memorial, a white marble pillar of inelegant proportions capped by a comic little dome which might, again, represent a flame. It is like seeing Indians on a dance floor: they are attempting attitudes which do not become them. I did not see a Buddhist site that had not been disfigured by attempts to recreate India's ancient culture. Near Gorakhpur, for instance, there now stands amid the ruins of an old monastery a reconstructed temple of the period. On the flat wasteland of Kurukshetra, the scene of the Gita dialogue between Arjuna and Krishna, his charioteer, there is a new temple, and in its garden there is a representation in marble of the scene. It is less than bazaar art. That chariot will never move; the horses are dead, to its limit – and blamed it on the British intervention. The British pillaged the country thoroughly; during their rule manufactures and crafts declined. This has to be accepted, and set against the achievements listed by Woodruff: a biscuit factory is a poor exchange for gold embroidery. The country had been pillaged before. But continuity had been maintained. With the British, continuity was broken. And perhaps the British are responsible for this Indian artistic failure, which is part of the general Indian bewilderment, in the way that the Spaniards were responsible for the stupefaction of the Mexicans and the Peruvians. It was a clash between a positive principle and a negative; and nothing more negative can be imagined than the conjunction in the eighteenth century of a static Islam and a decadent Hinduism. In any clash between post-Renaissance Europe and India, India was bound to lose.*

* If I had read Camus's *The Rebel* before writing this chapter, I might have used his terminology. Where Camus might have said 'capable of rebellion' I have said 'positive' and 'capable of self-assessment'; and it is interesting that Camus gives, as examples of people incapable of rebellion, the Hindus and the Incas. 'The problem of rebellion . . . has no meaning except within our Western society . . . Thanks to the theory of political freedom, there is, in the very heart of our society, an increasing awareness in man of the idea of man and, thanks to the application of this theory of freedom, a corresponding dissatisfaction . . . What is at stake is humanity's gradually increasing self-awareness as it pursues its course. In fact, for the Inca and the [Hindu] pariah the problem never arises, because for them it had been solved by a tradition, even before they had had time to raise it – the answer being that tradition is sacred. If in a world where things are held sacred the problem of rebellion does not arise, it is because no real problems are to be found in such a world, all the answers having

stiff, heavy. And this is the work of people whose sculpture is worth all the sculpture of the rest of the world, who in the South, at Vijayanagar, could create a whole 'Horse Court' of horses rampant.

Somewhere something has snapped. Where does one begin to look for this failure? One begins with that Kurukshetra temple. On it there is a plaque which says this exactly:

THIS TEMPAL HAS BEEN BUILT THROUGH THE CHARITY OF RAJA SETH BALDEO DAS BIRLA AND HAS BEEN DEDICATED OF SHREE ARYA DHARMA SEVA SANGH IN NEW DELHI. HINDU PILGRIMS OF ALL SECTS E.G. SANATANISTS, ARYA SAMAJISTS, JAINS, SIKHS AND BUDDHISTS ETC WILL BE ENTERTAINED PROVIDED THEY ARE MORALLY AND PHYSICALLY PURE AND CLEAN

NOTE PERSONS SUFFERING FROM INFECTIOUS OR CONTAGIOUS DISEASES WILL NOT BE ADMITTED

The crudity of the language is matched by the crudity of the self-appraisal. India may be poor, the plaque says in effect, but spiritually she is rich; and her people are morally and physically pure and clean. Self-appraisal, the crudity of the stonework and marblework, the imperfect use of the foreign language: they are all related.

Some Indians denied that the Indian plastic sense had decayed. Those who thought it had, rejected the view that the Moguls were partly responsible – for the quantity and extravagance of their building: Akbar exhausting experimentation, his successors taking decoration

The stupefaction of peoples is one of our mysteries. At school in Trinidad we were taught that the aboriginal inhabitants of the West Indies 'sickened and died' when the Spaniards came. In Grenada, the spice island, there is a cliff with the terrible name of Sauteurs: here the Amerindians committed mass suicide, leaping down into the sea. Stupefied communities of other, later races survive. There are the degraded Hindus of Martinique and Jamaica, swamped by Africa; and it is hard to associate the dispirited Javanese of Surinam in South America, objects of local ridicule, with the rioters and embassy-burners of Djakarta. India did not wither, like Peru and Mexico, at the touch of Europe. If she were wholly Muslim she might have done. But her Hindu experience of conquerors was great; Hindu India met conquerors half-way and had always been able to absorb them. And it is interesting, and now a little sad, to see Indians, above all in Bengal, reacting to the British as they might have done to any other conqueror, Indian or Asiatic.

The attempt at a half-way meeting is there in an early English-inspired reformer like Ram Mohun Roy, who is buried in Bristol. It is there, generations later, in the upbringing of Sri Aurobindo, the revolutionary turned mystic, whose father, sending him as a boy of seven to be educated in England, required his English guardians to shield him from all Indian contacts. It is there, a little later still, but now pathetically, in the Mullick Palace in Calcutta. Decaying already, since this is India, with servants cooking in the marble galleries, the Palace is like

---

been given simultaneously. Metaphysic is replaced by myth. There are no more questions, only eternal answers and commentaries, which may be metaphysical.' (Translated by Anthony Bower.)

a film set. As we go through the tall gateway we feel that this is how a film might begin; the camera will advance with us, will pause here on this broken masonry, there on this faded decoration; there will be silence, and then the voices will come through the echo chamber, the sound of carriages on the crescent-shaped drive: for Mullick's entertainments were fabulous. Great columns of the Calcutta Corinthian style dominate the façade; fountains imported from Europe still play in its grounds; statues representing the four continents stand in the corners of the marble patio where the family now keep birds in cages; on the lower floor a large room is made small by a colossal statue of Queen Victoria; and elsewhere, below excessively chandeliered ceilings, dust has gathered on what looks like the jumble of a hundred English antique shops: a collector's zeal turned to mania: the Bengali landowner displaying his appreciation of European culture to the supercilious European. Nothing here is Indian, save perhaps the portrait of the owner; but already we can sense the Anglo-Bengali encounter going sour.

Englishness, unlike the faith of other conquerors, required no converts; and for the Bengali, who was most susceptible to Englishness, the English in India reserved a special scorn. An imperial ideal, well on the way to a necessarily delayed realization, was foundering on the imperialist myth, equally delayed, of the empire-builder, on the English fantasy of Englishness, 'the cherished conviction', as one English official wrote in 1883, 'which was shared by every Englishman in India, from the highest to the lowest, by the planter's assistant in his lowly bungalow ... to the Viceroy on his throne ... that he belongs to a race whom God has destined to govern and subdue'. The mock-imperial rhetoric of the dedication of Nirad Chaudhuri's *Auto-biography of an Unknown Indian* might serve as an epitaph on this unfulfilled imperial encounter. Translated into Latin, it might be carved in Trajan lettering on the India Gate in New Delhi: 'To the memory of the British Empire in India, which conferred subjecthood on us but withheld citizenship, to which yet every one of us threw out the challenge *Civis Britannicus sum*, because all that was good and living within us was made, shaped, and quickened by the same British rule.'

No other country was more fitted to welcome a conqueror; no other conqueror was more welcome than the British. What went wrong? Some say the Mutiny; some say the arrival in India afterwards of white women. It is possible. But the French, with or without their women, might have reacted differently to the francophile Bengali. The cause, I believe, has to be looked for not in India but in England where, at a time we cannot precisely fix, occurred that break in English sensibility as radical and as seemingly abrupt as that which we have witnessed in our time. The civilization to which the Indians were attracted had been replaced by another. It was confusing – the guests whom Simpson's Restaurant in the Strand was nourishing for imperial purposes continued to bear the outer semblance of Parson Adams and Tom Jones – and many Indians, from Aurobindo to Tagore to Nehru to Chaudhuri, have recorded their bewilderment.

It is perhaps only now that we can see what a clean break with the past the Raj was. The British refused to be absorbed into India; they did not proclaim, like the Mogul, that if there was a paradise on earth, it was this, and it was this, and it was this. While dominating India they expressed their contempt for it, and projected

England; and Indians were forced into a nationalism which in the beginning was like a mimicry of the British. To look at themselves, to measure themselves against the new, positive standards of the conqueror, Indians had to step out of themselves. It was an immense self-violation; and in the beginning, in fact, a flattering self-assessment could only be achieved with the help of Europeans like Max Muller and those others who are quoted so profusely in nationalist writings.

It resulted in the conscious possession of spirituality, proclaimed as in the plaque of the Kurukshetra temple. *Spiritualise Science, Says Prasad* is a newspaper headline over a report of one of the late President's almost daily speeches in retirement. It results in this, from the *Times of India*:

A 'RETAILER' OF SPIRITUALITY
Santiniketan, January 16

Acharya Vinoba Bhave yesterday described himself as a 'retailer' with regard to the wealth of spirituality.

He made this remark at a reception here saying that the Buddha, Jesus, Krishna, Tagore, Ramakrishna and Vivekananda were 'wholesalers of spirituality while I myself am a retailer, drawing from that inexhaustible storehouse to supply to the villagers.' – PTI

It resulted in the conscious possession of an ancient culture. At an official reception for the former governor of a state someone called across to me, as we sat silently in deep chairs set against the walls of the room, 'How is Indian culture getting on in your part of the world?'

rickshaw-men; innumerable pretty young girls either simply and suddenly died, or shared the landlord's bed, paid the family's medical bills and then committed suicide; and many of the 'modern' short stories were only refurbished folk tales. In Andhra I was given a brochure of a Telugu writers' conference. The brochure spoke of the heroic struggle of the people to establish a Telugu state, to me an endeavour of pure frivolity, listed martyrs, and then gave a brief history of the Telugu novel. It seems that the Telugu novel began with Telugu adaptations of *The Vicar of Wakefield* and *East Lynne*. A little farther south I was told of a writer greatly influenced by Ernest Hemingway.

The Vicar of Wakefield and *The Old Man and the Sea*: it is difficult to relate them to the Indian landscape or to Indian attitudes. The Japanese novel also began as part of the mimicry of the West. Tanizaki has, I believe, confessed that in his early work he was too greatly influenced by the Europeans. Even through the mimicry, however, it can be seen that the Japanese are possessed of a way of looking. It flavours the early work of Tanizaki as it flavours the recent novels of Yukio Mishima: that curious literalness which adds up to a detachment formidable enough to make the writing seem pointless. However odd, this derives from a hunger for the seen and is an expression of concern with men. The sweetness and sadness which can be found in Indian writing and Indian films are a turning away from a too overwhelming reality; they reduce the horror to a warm, virtuous emotion. Indian sentimentality is the opposite of concern.

The virtues of R. K. Narayan are Indian failings magically transmuted. I say this without disrespect: he is a writer whose work I admire and enjoy. He seems forever headed for that *aimlessness* of Indian fiction – which comes from a profound doubt about the purpose and value of fiction – but he is forever rescued by his honesty, his sense of humour and above all by his attitude of total acceptance. He operates from deep within his society. Some years ago he told me in London that, whatever happened, India would go on. He said it casually; it was a conviction so deep it required no stressing. It is a negative attitude, part of that older India which was incapable of self-assessment. It has this result: the India of Narayan's novels is not the India the visitor sees. He tells an Indian truth. Too much that is overwhelming has been left out; too much has been taken for granted. There is a contradiction in Narayan, between his form, which implies concern, and his attitude, which denies it; and in this calm contradiction lies his magic which some have called Chekovian. He is inimitable, and it cannot be supposed that his is the synthesis at which Indian writing will arrive. The younger writers in English have moved far from Narayan. In those novels which tell of the difficulties of the Europe-returned student they are still only expressing a personal bewilderment; the novels themselves are documents of the Indian confusion. The only writer who, while working from within the society, is yet able to impose on it a vision which is an acceptable type of comment, is R. Prawer Jhabvala. And she is European.*

---

* 'It is possible to separate the literature of consent, which coincides, by and large, with ancient history and the classical period, from the literature of rebellion, which begins in modern times. We note the scarcity of fiction in the former. When it exists, with very few exceptions, it is not concerned with a story but with fantasy . . . These are fairy tales, not novels. In the latter period, on the contrary, the

The Indo-British encounter was abortive; it ended in a double fantasy. Their new self-awareness makes it impossible for Indians to go back; their cherishing of Indianness makes it difficult for them to go ahead. It is possible to find the India that appears not to have changed since Mogul times but has, profoundly; it is possible to find the India whose mimicry of the West is convincing until, sometimes with dismay, sometimes with impatience, one realizes that complete communication is not possible, that a gift of vision cannot be shared, that there still survive inaccessible areas of Indian retreat. Both the negative and the positive principles have been diluted; one balances the other. The penetration was not complete; the attempt at conversion was abandoned. India's strength, her ability to endure, came from the negative principle, her unexamined sense of continuity. It is a principle which, once diluted, loses its virtue. In the concept of Indianness the sense of continuity was bound to be lost. The creative urge failed. Instead of continuity we have the static. It is there in the 'ancient culture' architecture; it is there in the much bewailed loss of drive, which is psychological more than political and economic. It is there in the political gossip of Bunty. It is there in the dead horses and immobile chariot of the Kurukshetra temple. Shiva has ceased to dance.

---

novel form is really developed – a form that has not ceased to thrive and extend its field of activity up to the present day . . . The novel is born at the same time as the spirit of rebellion and expresses, on the aesthetic plane, the same ambition.' Camus: *The Rebel*.

9

THE GARLAND ON MY PILLOW

'I am sure you will never guess what my duties are.'

He was middle-aged, thin, sharp-featured, with spectacles. His eyes were running and there was a drop of moisture on the tip of his nose. It was a winter's morning and our second-class railway compartment was unheated.

'I will give you a little assistance. I work for the Railways. This is my pass. Have you ever seen one?'

'You are a ticket inspector!'

A smile revealed his missing teeth. 'No, no, my dear sir. They wear a uniform.'

'You are from the Police.'

His smile cracked into a wet laugh. 'I see that you will never guess. Well, I will tell you. I am an Inspector of Forms and Stationery, Northern Railway.'

'Forms and Stationery!'

'Indeed. I travel about, night and day, winter and summer, from railway station to railway station, inspecting forms and stationery.'

'But how did this begin, Mr Inspector?'

'Why do you ask, sir? My life has been a failure.'

'Please don't say that, Mr Inspector.'

'I might have done so much better, sir. You have no doubt observed my English. My teacher was Mr Harding. I was a Bachelor of Arts, you know. When I joined the Service I expected to go far. I was put in Stores. In those days I would take down bundles of forms and

'We'll go there.'

'Sir?'

'Two coffees.'

'No coffee.'

'Oh. Well, bring a pot of tea for two. And bring the Complaints Book.'

'Sir?'

'Complaints Book.'

'Let me talk to the manager, sir.'

'No, no. You just bring a pot of tea and the Book.'

'I am sorry about this. But we don't do the catering here. That's in the hand of a local contractor. We give him coffee and tea of a certain quality. He just sells it to somebody else. We can't do anything about it. Our contractor knows a minister. It's the Indian story. But look. Our friend is coming back.'

'Is he bringing the Complaints Book?'

'No. He's bringing two cups of coffee.'

Indian Railways! They are part of the memory of every traveller, in the north, east, west or south. Yet few have written of the romance of this stupendous organization which makes the Indian distances shrink and which, out of an immense assurance, proclaims in a faded notice in every railway station: *Trains running late are likely to make up lost time.* And the trains usually do. But does the romance exist? A service so complex and fine deserves a richer country, with shining cities organized for adventure. But it is only distance, or the knowledge of distance, that gives romance to the place-names on the yellow boards of Indian coaches. The locomotive will consume distance and will seem to convert it into waste. And it will do so with a speed that will presently appear as pointless as the poor, repetitive vastness of the pigmy land which, supine below a high sky, will abruptly at railway stations burst into shrill life, as though all energy had been spared for this spot and this moment: the shouts of stunted, sweating porters, over-eager in red turbans and tunics, the cries of tea-vendors with their urns and clay cups (the cups to be broken after use), the cries of *pan*-vendors and the vendors of fried or curried messes (the leaf-plates, pinned together by thin dried twigs, to be thrown afterwards on to the platform or on the tracks, where the pariah dogs, fierce only with their fellows, will fight over them – and one defeated dog will howl and howl), the whole scene – yet animated only in the foreground, for these stations are havens as well as social centres, and the smooth, cool concrete platforms are places where the futile can sleep – the whole scene ceilinged by low fans which spin in empty frenzy. The sun will rise and set, and the racing train, caught in the golden light of dawn or dusk, will throw a perfect elongated shadow from the tops of the coaches to the very rails; and distance will still not have been consumed. The land has become distance. Will the metal not ignite? Will there be no release into a land which is fruitful, where the men grow straight? There is only another station, more shouting, the magenta coaches coated with hot dust, more prostrate bodies, more dogs, the fraudulent comfort of a shower in the first-class waiting-room and a meal poisoned by one's own distress and cautiousness. And indeed people are less important to Indian Railways than freight; and less revenue comes from the first-class than from the third, the sub-standard for whom there is never enough room, even in their rudimentary coaches. The railway administrator, who knows this, can be forgiven if he fails to see the romance of his service or its brilliance.

poorer; he showed me that tenderness which physically big men can show to the small.

It was nearly midnight when we came to the junction where I had to leave the train. The platforms were like mortuaries. In the dim light prostrate men showed as shrunken white bundles out of which protruded bony Indian arms, shining stringy legs, collapsed grey-stubbled faces. Men slept; dogs slept; and among them, like emanations risen from the senseless bodies, over which they appeared to trample, other men and other dogs moved. Silent third-class carriages turned out to be packed with dark, waiting, sweating faces; the yellow boards above the grilled windows showed that they were going somewhere. The engines hissed. *Trains running late are likely to make up lost time*. The fans spun urgently. From everywhere dogs howled. One hobbled off into the darkness at the end of the platform; its fore-leg had been freshly torn off; a raw bloody stump remained.

The Sikh helped me with my luggage. I was grateful to him for his presence, his wholeness. We had already exchanged addresses and arranged when and where we were to meet again. Now we repeated our promises. We would travel over the South. India yet had its pleasures. We would go hunting. He would show me: it was easy, and I would enjoy the elephants. Then he returned to his air-conditioned coach, behind the double glass. Whistles blew; the train moved mightily off. Yet the station remained so little changed: so many bodies remained, awaiting transportation.

My own train was due to leave in about two hours; the coaches were waiting. I changed my third-class ticket for a first-class one, picked my way down dim platforms past the bodies of dogs and men, past third-class carriages which were already full and hot. The conductor opened the door of my compartment and I climbed in. I bolted the door, pulled down all the blinds, trying to shut out the howls of dogs, shutting out intruders, all those staring faces and skeletal bodies. I put on no lights. I required darkness.

I did not expect it, but we met again as we planned. It was in a town where the only other person I knew was a prosperous sweetshop-owner. I had learned to fear his hospitality. At every meeting it was necessary to eat a selection of his sweets. They were corrosively sweet; they killed appetite for a day. The Sikh's hospitality was easier. He sought to revive my appetite with drink and he gave me food. He also gave me much of his time. I felt he was offering more than hospitality: he was offering his friendship, and it embarrassed me that I couldn't respond. But I was calmer now than I had been on the train, and his moods no longer always answered mine.

'They've let this cantonment area go down,' he said. 'In the old days they didn't allow niggers here. Now the blackies are all over the place.'

The anger was plain, and was not tempered by the humour or self-satire I had seen, or made myself see, in his outbursts on the train.

'These people! You have to shout "Boy!" Otherwise they just don't hear you.'

I had noted this. At the hotel I was shouting 'Boy!' with everybody else, but I couldn't manage the correct tone. Both boys and guests wore South Indian dress, and I had already more than once shouted at the wrong man. My shouts therefore always held muted enquiry and apology.

and again, when we tilted to one of these possibilities, one of us applied a corrective pressure. There still existed concern between us. We drank coffee; our conversation see-sawed more and more falsely; and in the end even this concern had been talked away.

'We were going to go hunting,' the Sikh said, as he left. 'I had *plans* for you.'

It was a good Hollywood exit line. Perhaps it was meant. I couldn't say. The English language in India could be so misleading. Exhaustion overcame me: for all our coffee and play-acting talk, the break had been violent. It brought relief and regret. There had been so much goodwill and generosity there; my misunderstanding had been so great.

In the morning horror was uppermost. I had seen photographs of the Punjab massacres of 1947 and of the Great Calcutta Killing; I had heard of trains – those Indian trains! – ferrying dead bodies across the border; I had seen the burial mounds beside the Punjab roads. Yet until now I had never thought of India as a land of violence. Now violence was something I could smell in the air; the city seemed tainted by the threat of violence and self-torment of the sort I had seen. I wanted to get away at once. But the trains and buses were booked for days ahead.

I went to the sweetshop-owner. He was soft and welcoming. He sat me at a table; one of his waiters brought me a plate of the sweetest sweets; and master and servant watched me eat. Those Indian sweets! 'Serves them in place of flesh': a Kipling phrase, perhaps altered by memory, came and stayed with me; and *flesh* seemed a raw and fearful word. For all that was soft and feeble and sweet-loving in that city I was grateful; and I feared for it.

In the sweetshop the next evening the owner introduced me to a relation of his, who was visiting. The relation started when he heard my name. Could it be true? He was reading one of my books; he had thought of me as someone thousands of miles away; he had never dreamed of finding me eating sweets in the bazaar of an out-of-the-way Indian town. But he had expected someone older. I was a *baccha*, a boy! However, he had met me, and he wished to show his appreciation. Could I tell him where I was staying?

Acrid white smoke billowed out of my hotel room when I opened the door that night. There was no fire. The smoke was incense. To enter, I had to cover my face with a handkerchief. I opened doors and windows, turned the ceiling fan on, and hurried out again to the corridor with streaming eyes. It was minutes before the incense-fog thinned. Great clumps of incense sticks burned like dying brands everywhere; on the floor the ash was like bird droppings. Flowers were strewn over my bed, and there was a garland on my pillow.

of the post office; then, behaving as one suddenly reminded of duty, he smiled and lifted the white cloth to reveal a monstrously deformed right arm. It was no arm at all; it was shaped like a woman's breast, ending not in a nipple but in a fingernail on a toy finger.

There was an audience of eight – not counting the secretary and the top-knotted watchman – for the lecture at the Triplicane Theosophical Society on 'Annie Besant, Our Leader'. The speaker was a middle-aged Canadian woman. She came from Vancouver. This was not as odd as it appeared, she said: according to Annie Besant, Vancouver had been a centre of the occult in far-off times. Annie Besant's Irish ancestry doubtless explained her psychic gifts, and much of her character could be explained by what she must have been in former lives. Annie Besant had been, above all, a great leader; and it was the duty of every Theosophist to be a leader, to keep Annie Besant's message alive and her books in circulation. The Theosophical Society was now encountering a certain indifference – the secretary had already said as much – and many people were no doubt asking why, if she was with us again, Annie Besant wasn't in the Theosophical Society. But there was no logic in the question. There was no reason why Annie Besant should be in the Society. Her work for the Society had been done in a previous life; she was now almost certainly, under what name we could not tell, doing equally important work in some other field. Two men in the audience were dozing.

Behind the high, clean walls of the Aurobindo Ashram in Pondicherry, one hundred miles to the south, they were perfectly calm. In 1950, the year of his death,

The Mother has certainly no idea of making people see it – it is of themselves that one after another, some 20 or 30 in the Ashram, I believe, have come to see. It is certainly one of the signs that the Higher Force (call it supramental or not) is beginning to influence Matter.

The Mother was also responsible for the organization of the Ashram; an occasional impatience in Aurobindo's replies to inmates hinted at early difficulties.

In the organization of work there was formerly a formidable waste due to the workers and *sadhaks* following their own fancy almost entirely without respect for the Mother's will; that was largely checked by reorganization.

It is a mistake to think that the Mother's not smiling means either displeasure or disapproval of something wrong in the *sadhak*. It is very often merely a sign of absorption or of inner concentration. On this occasion the Mother was putting a question to your soul.

Mother did not know at that time of your having spoken to T. So your conjecture of that being the cause of her fancied displeasure is quite groundless. Your idea about Mother's mysterious smile is your own imagination – Mother says that she smiled with the utmost kindness.

It is not because your French is full of mistakes that Mother does not correct it, but because I will not allow her to take more work on herself so far as I can help it. Already she has no time to rest sufficiently at night and most of the night she is working at the books, reports and letters that pour on her in masses. Even so she cannot finish in time in the morning. If she has to correct all the letters of the people who have just begun writing in French as well as the others, it means another hour or two of work – she will be able to finish only at nine in the morning and come down at 10.30. I am therefore trying to stop it.

All bad thoughts upon the Mother or throwing of impurities on her may affect her body, as she has taken the *sadhaks* into her consciousness; nor can she send these things back to them as it might hurt them.

Withdrawn though the Mother now was, her hand could still be seen in the running of the Ashram. The noticeboard carried notices about the cholera outbreak in Madras – inmates were warned against contact with people from that town – and about the annoyance of chatter at the Ashram gates; the notices were signed 'M', in a firm, stylish zigzag. And the Ashram was only part of the Aurobindo Society. Pondicherry had already melted into the rest of southern India; even the French language seemed to have disappeared. But the numerous, well-kept buildings of the Society still gave it the feel of a small French town that had been set down on a tropical coast. Walls were shuttered and blank against the light, which was intense above the raging surf; and the Society's walls were painted in the Society's colours. The Society seemed to be the only flourishing thing in Pondicherry. It had its estates outside the town;

and culture. It's driving me mad. What do you think of the hotel? I think it's *creepy*.' He hunched his shoulders. 'It's the food.' Mouth working, he struck his palm against his dark glasses. 'It's sending me *blind*. It's these people. They're *crazy*. They don't accept you. Help me. You have people running in and out of your room all day. You know some English people here. Talk to them about me. Introduce me to them. They might take me in. You must help me.'

I promised to try.

The first person I spoke to said, 'Well, I don't know. Experience tells me that when people are doing inward things like answering the call of the East it is better to stay away.'

I did not try again. And now I feared to meet the young American. I did not meet him. The trains between Madras and Calcutta were running again, after the long dislocation caused by floods and the movement of troops.

Ladies, painted in yellow on some carriages. *Military*, marked in chalk on many more. It was so unlikely, this train-load of soldiers moving north through all the distress of India to the calamity on the frontiers. With their olive-green uniforms, their good looks and good manners, and their moustached, swagger-sticked officers, they transformed the railway platforms at which we stopped: they lent drama and order, and to them how comforting the familiar, receding squalor must have been! The plump little major in my compartment, carrying his water in a champagne bottle, had been so quiet after leaving his wife and daughter at Madras Central station – the three had simply sat silently side by side. Now, as the journey lengthened, he brightened;

he asked me the Indian questions: where did I come from, what did I do? And the soldiers became playful. Once the train stopped beside a field of sugarcane. A soldier jumped out and began to cut stalks of cane with his knife. More soldiers jumped out, more cane was cut. The angry farmer appeared. Money passed, anger turned to smiles and waves as we moved off again.

Afternoon now, and the train's shadow racing beside us. Sunset, evening, night; station after dimly-lit station. It was an Indian railway journey, but everything that had before seemed pointless was now threatened and seemed worth cherishing; and as in the mild sunshine of a winter morning we drew near to green Bengal, which I had longed to see, my mood towards India and her people became soft. I had taken so much for granted. There, among the Bengali passengers who had come on, was a man who wore a long woollen scarf and a brown tweed jacket above his Bengali dhoti. The casual elegance of his dress was matched by his fine features and relaxed posture. Out of all its squalor and human decay, its eruptions of butchery, India produced so many people of grace and beauty, ruled by elaborate courtesy. Producing too much life, it denied the value of life; yet it permitted a unique human development to so many. Nowhere were people so heightened, rounded and individualistic; nowhere did they offer themselves so fully and with such assurance. To know Indians was to take a delight in people as people; every encounter was an adventure. I did not want India to sink; the mere thought was painful.

And it was in this mood that I walked about Calcutta, the 'nightmare experience' of Mr Nehru, 'the world's most miserable city', according to an American magazine, 'the pestilential behemoth' of another

American writer, the world's last stronghold of Asiatic cholera, according to the World Health Organization: a city which, built for two million, now accommodated six million on its pavements and in its *bastees*.

'*Chuha*,' the waiter at Howrah station restaurant said affectionately, pointing. 'Look, a rat.' And the pink, depilated creature, barely noticed by the Assamese soldier and his wife, both sucking away at rice and curried fish, sluggishly made its way across the tiled floor and up a pipe. This promised horror. But nothing I had read or heard had prepared me for the red-brick city on the other side of Howrah Bridge which, if one could ignore the stalls and rickshaws and white-clad hurrying crowds, was at first like another Birmingham; and then, in the centre, at dusk, was like London, with the misty, tree-blobbed Maidan as Hyde Park, Chownringhee as a mixture of Oxford Street, Park Lane and Bayswater Road, with neon invitations, fuzzy in the mist, to bars, coffee-houses and air travel, and the Hooghly a muddier, grander Thames, not far away. On a high floodlit platform in the Maidan General Cariappa, the former commander-in-chief, erect, dark-suited, was addressing a small, relaxed crowd in Sandhurst-accented Hindustani on the Chinese attack. Around and about the prowed, battleship-grey Calcutta trams, bulging at exits and entrances with men in white, tanked away at less than ten miles an hour. Here, unexpectedly and for the first time in India, one was in a big city, the recognizable metropolis, with street names – Elgin, Lindsay, Allenby – oddly unrelated to the people who thronged them: incongruity that deepened as the mist thickened to smog and as, driving out to the suburbs, one saw the chimneys smoking among the palm trees.

This was the city which, according to bazaar rumour,

Chou En-lai had promised the Chinese people as a Christmas present. The Indian Marwari merchants, it was said, were already making enquiries about business prospects under Chinese rule; the same rumour had it that in the South the Madrasis, despite their objection to Hindi, were already learning Chinese. Morale was low; the administration in Assam had collapsed and there were tales of flight and panic. But it was not in this alone that the sadness of the city lay. With or without the Chinese, Calcutta was dead. Partition had deprived it of half its hinterland and burdened it with a vast dispirited refugee population. Even Nature had turned: the Hooghly was silting up. But Calcutta's death was also of the heart. With its thin glitter, its filth and overpopulation, its tainted money, its exhaustion, it held the total Indian tragedy and the terrible British failure. Here the Indo-British encounter had at one time promised to be fruitful. Here the Indian renaissance had begun: so many of the great names of Indian reform are Bengali. But it was here, too, that the encounter had ended in mutual recoil. The cross-fertilization had not occurred, and Indian energy had turned sour. Once Bengal led India, in ideas and idealism; now, just forty years later, Calcutta, even to Indians, was a word of terror, conveying crowds, cholera and corruption. Its aesthetic impulses had not faded – there was an appealing sensibility in every Bengali souvenir, every over-exploited refugee 'craft' – but they, pathetically, threw into relief the greater decay. Calcutta had no leaders now, and apart from Ray, the film director, and Janah, the photographer, had no great names. It had withdrawn from the Indian experiment, as area after area of India was withdrawing, individual after individual. The British, who had built

Calcutta, had ever been withdrawn from their creation; and they survived. Their business houses still flourished in Chownringhee; and to the Indians, products of the dead Indian renaissance, who now sat in some of the air-conditioned offices, Independence had meant no more than this: the opportunity to withdraw, British-like, from India. What then was the India that was left, for which one felt such concern? Was it no more than a word, an idea?

From the train Durgapur, the new steel town, was a spreading pattern of lights. I went out to the corridor and watched them until they disappeared. Such a small hope, and it was easy to imagine the lights extinguished. Bomdi-la fell that night. Assam lay open; Mr Nehru offered the people of the state comfort which was already like helpless condolence. Tibetan refugees got off the train at Banaras. There was smiling bewilderment on their broad, ruddy faces; no one spoke their language and they stood uncertainly beside their boxes, outlandish in their bulky wrappings, grimed to khaki, their long hair, their boots and hats. The hotel was deserted: internal air services had been cancelled. The young dark-suited manager and the uniformed servants stood silent and idle in the veranda. Something of the bazaar spirit and the spirit of wartime opportunism stirred within me. I stood on the steps and haggled. Success went to my head. 'And that is to include morning coffee,' I said. 'Yes,' the manager said sadly. 'That is to include coffee.'

Here in the cantonment area Banaras felt abandoned, and it was easy to imagine oneself a squatter. But in the town nothing hinted at tragedy. Wood was piled high on the *ghats*. Brightly shrouded bodies lay on flower-strewn litters at the water's edge, unimportantly awaiting their pyres; and above occasional blazes, oddly casual and not too visible in the reflected glare of the Ganges, family groups smiled and chattered. The steep *ghats*, platformed and stepped, their names marked in large letters, were as thronged as a holiday beach. The pious stood in the water, relaxed below beach umbrellas or gathered round an expounding pundit; young men did exercises. Above, behind the high white river front, in the twisting alleys, dark between solid masonry and enchanting but for the cowdung, hawkers offered Banaras toys, silk and brass; and in the temples the guide-priests, young, washed and combed, chewed *pan* and cursed those who refused them alms.

I went to the Nepalese Temple, 'disfigured', Murray's *Handbook* said, 'by erotic carvings; they do not catch the eye, provided that the attendant can be discouraged from pointing them out'. The attendant was a youth with a long switch; I begged him to point them out. 'Here man and woman,' he began unexcitedly. 'Here other man. He Mr Hurry-up because he say, "Hurry up, hurry up."' Tourist lore: the gloss did not please me. The pleasures of erotic art are fragile; I wished I had followed Murray's advice.

At dinner I asked the sad young manager to put on the radio for the news. It was as bad as could be expected. The manager held his hands behind his back and looked down, correct even in his growing distress. Then a reference to 'Chinese Frontier Guards' alerted me.

'But we are listening to Peking, Mr Manager.'

'It is All-India Radio. It's the station I always listen to.'

'Only the Chinese and Radio Pakistan talk of the Chinese Frontier Guards.'

'But it is in English. And the accent . . . And it sounds so close.'

It did indeed; it was coming over loud and clear. We tried to get New Delhi; we got squawks and static and a feeble, disappearing voice.

And the next day it was all over. The Chinese declared a ceasefire and promised a withdrawal. And, as if by magic, the hotel began to fill up.

The fighting was over but the Emergency continued, and it was the duty of this Commissioner to make tours through his Division, keeping up morale and raising funds. He had just finished one tour and had been presented with an album of photographs, mainly of himself receiving and being received. I sat in the back of his station-wagon now with some junior officers and looked through the photographs. We were travelling along an Indian road: a thin metalled strip between two lanes of earth that had been ground to fine, thick dust by the wheels of bullock-carts. This was Indian dust: it disfigured the trees that lined the road, it discoloured the fields for a hundred yards on either side. And regularly, at stations in the dust, there were reception committees, garlands, displays of calisthenics and rough exhibitions of rough local manufactures.

The Commissioner was keen on soap and shoes, and everywhere we stopped the bearded Muslim shoemakers stood beside their shoes and the soapmakers stood beside their heavy, imperfectly moulded cubes of soap. At dinner one evening the Commissioner, dressed in a dark suit, explained his interest in soap and shoes. His voice dropped to tenderness. His daughter, he said, was at school in England. Through television or some other educational medium her companions had learned that there were no towns in India, that no one wore shoes or lived in houses or washed. 'Is it true, Daddy?' the distressed child had asked. So now the craftsmen of the Division made soap and shoes. Sometimes, when he was being received, the Commissioner broke through the circle of local dignitaries to greet the children of the very poor who were on the other side of the road. Sometimes, exercising the Commissioner's prerogative, he took cakes of soap from the display and distributed them to these children, while the photographers, another album in mind, took pictures.

It was a swift tour. To me it was remarkable that an area so large and nondescript and comfortless should be capable of such organization, and that behind the clouds of dust there should be people who, with so little encouragement and such poor materials, should yet be exercising craftsman's skills. I would have liked to linger, to draw hope. But there was no time. The displays were too many. I was sitting in the back of the station-wagon and was the last to get out whenever we stopped; and it frequently happened that before I had had time to inspect the first exhibit the Commissioner and his officials were back at the station-wagon and waiting for me: since I was the last to get out I was the first to get in.

We spent more time at the meetings. Here the thin-limbed boys in white shorts and vests had been assembled in the sun, ready to go through their gymnastic exercises. Here there were arches marked welcome in Hindi. Here the Commissioner was garlanded. The Indian politician, when garlanded, at once removes the garland and hands it to an attendant; this acceptance and instant rejection of dignity is the stylish Indian form. The Commissioner did not remove his garlands. Hoop after hoop of marigold was hung on his bowed head, until the marigolds rose to his ears and, from the back, he looked like an idol incongruously armed: in one hand he carried his lighted cigar, in the other his sun-helmet. His attendant was not far away. He carried his master's cigar box and was dressed like a Mogul courtier: so the British had sought to degrade their predecessors.

In the decorated tent the peasants sat on mats. For the officials there were chairs and a table. Names were read out and peasants rose, came to the Commissioner, bowed and presented rupee notes for the National Defence Fund. (As the Fund rose in the area, an IAS man told me, National Savings dropped.) Some women shyly presented jewellery. Sometimes there was no response to a name, and then from all corners of the tent came explanations: a death, of man or beast, an illness, a sudden journey. The money rose in a shaky pile on the plate and was handled casually by all.

Then the Commissioner spoke. The Emergency was not over, not at all; the Chinese were still on India's sacred soil. The people of India had been preached at for too long about peace and nonviolence. Now they had to be roused. The Commissioner sought to do so first by appealing to the patriotism of the peasants and then by analysing the nature of the Chinese threat. By any Indian standard the Chinese were unclean. They ate beef: this was for the Hindus in the audience. They ate pork: this was for the Muslims. They ate dogs: this was for everyone. They ate cats, rats, snakes. The peasants remained passive, and were only roused when the Commissioner, playing his last card, invoked the Hindu goddesses of destruction.

The Commissioner had a cheer-leader, a tall elderly

man in an old double-breasted grey suit. He wore spectacles and carried a sun-helmet which was the fellow of the Commissioner's. He chewed *pan* constantly; his mouth was large, with flapping red-stained lips. His face was without expression; he seemed to be doing sums in his head all the time. Clerk-like, adjusting his spectacles, he went to the microphone and stood silently before it. Suddenly he opened his enormous red mouth, revealing fillings and pieces of mangled betel-nut, and screamed: '*Kali Mata ki –*'

'*Jai!*' the peasants shouted, their eyes brightening, the smiles staying on their faces. 'Long live Mother Kali!'

'But what is this?' the Commissioner's assistant said. 'I heard nothing.' It was his line; at every meeting he used it. 'We will try again, and this time I want to hear you. *Kali Mata ki –*'

'*Jai! Jai! Jai!*'

Once, twice, three times the goddesses were invoked, to growing enthusiasm. Then abruptly the assistant turned, walked back to his seat, sat on it decisively, slapped his sun-helmet on his knees, stared straight ahead and, teeth and lips working over the *pan*, seemed immediately absorbed in mental arithmetic.

When the audience was too small, the Commissioner showed his displeasure by refusing to speak or to leave. Then officials and policemen bustled penitentially about; they summoned peasants from the fields and their homes and marched children out from the schools. But there was never any trouble in finding an audience for the evening concerts. Singers of local renown chewed *pan* and sang songs of their own about the Chinese invasion into microphones shrouded with cloth to protect them from *pan*-splutterings. There were sketches about the need to save, to grow more food, to contribute to the National Defence Fund, to give blood. Once or twice an ambitious playwright showed a local hero dying in battle against the Chinese; and it was clear that no one in the village knew what the Chinese looked like.

From the railway train and from the dusty roads India appeared to require only pity. It was an easy emotion, and perhaps the Indians were right: it was compassion like mine, so strenuously maintained, that denied humanity to many. It separated; it permitted the surprise and emotion I felt at these concerts, simple exhibitions of humanity. Anger, compassion and contempt were aspects of the same emotion; they were without value because they could not endure. Achievement could begin only with acceptance.

We were now in a region which, though physically no different from the surrounding areas, was famous for its soldiers. Was this due to some ancient mixing of bloods preserved by caste rules? To some pertinacious Rajput strain? India was full of such puzzles. The crowd here was too large for the tent. Some had put on their uniforms and decorations. The cheer-leader picked them out and seated them on a bench at the edge of the tent. But one or two preferred to walk slowly up and down the road while the Commissioner spoke. So far the Commissioner had been speaking to people who were a little irritated and resentful at having to leave their fields or the idleness of their homes. But this crowd was attentive from the first. The old soldiers gazed steadily at the Commissioner and every point he made was registered on their faces. The Chinese ate pork. Brows puckered. The Chinese ate dogs. Brows puckered more deeply. The Chinese ate rats. Eyes popped, heads lifted as struck.

The Commissioner had scarcely finished speaking when a man ran out from the crowd and threw himself at his feet, weeping.

The crowd relaxed and smiled.

'Get up, get up,' the Commissioner said, 'and tell me what you have to say.'

'You ask me to fight, and I want to fight. But how can I fight when I have no food and my family has no food? How can I fight when I have lost my land?'

The crowd began to titter.

'You have lost your land?'

'In the resettlement.'

The Commissioner spoke to his cheer-leader.

'All my good land,' the man wept, 'they gave to somebody else. All the bad land they gave to me.'

There was laughter from the old soldiers.

'I will look into it,' the Commissioner said.

The crowd was breaking up. The weeping man disappeared; the jeers at his outburst died down; and we moved on to the tea which the headman, a man of few words, had prepared for us.

There was another concert that evening. It had been organized by the local teacher. He came on just before the end and said that he had written a new poem which he would recite to us if the Commissioner gave his permission. The Commissioner took his cigar out of his mouth and nodded. The teacher bowed; then, with passionate intonations and tormented gestures, he recited. The facile Hindi rhymes tumbled out as if newly discovered, and the teacher worked himself into a frenzy as he came to his climax, which was a plea for the settled reign on earth of

> . . . *satya ahimsa.*

He bowed again, anticipating applause.

'*Satya ahimsa!*' the Commissioner shouted, stilling hands about to clap. 'Are you mad? Truth and nonviolence, indeed. Is this what you are preaching with the Chinese about to rape your wife? Have I been wasting my breath all afternoon? This is a classical example of muddled thinking.'

The poet, holding his bow, cringed. The curtain fell unceremoniously on him.

Poor poet! He had devised a good evening's entertainment. He had written the anti-Chinese pieces and the songs about the Motherland; yet when it came to his own poem, the one he wished to recite himself, he had lost his head. For years he had recited, to official applause, poems about truth and nonviolence. Habit had been too strong, and had led to his public disgrace.

Some weeks later Mr Nehru went to Lucknow. Standing on the airport tarmac, he bowed his head forty-six times to receive forty-six garlands from the forty-six members of the State cabinet. This at any rate was the story I had from an IAS man in Lucknow, and he was a little peeved. The IAS, acting on instructions from Delhi, had taken civil defence seriously in Lucknow. They had practised blackouts and air-raid warnings; they had dug trenches; they had much to show Mr Nehru. But Mr Nehru only lost his temper. All this digging of trenches, he said, was a waste of time.

In a way, the Emergency was over.

11

THE VILLAGE OF THE DUBES

The emergency was over. And so was my year. The short winter was fading fast; it was no longer pleasant to sit out in the sun; the dust would not now be laid until the monsoon. One journey remained, and for this I had lost taste. India had not worked its magic on me. It remained the land of my childhood, an area of darkness; like the Himalayan passes, it was closing up again, as fast as I withdrew from it, into a land of myth; it seemed to exist in just the timelessness which I had imagined as a child, into which, for all that I walked on Indian earth, I knew I could not penetrate.

In a year I had not learned acceptance. I had learned my separateness from India, and was content to be a colonial, without a past, without ancestors. Duty alone had brought me to this town in eastern Uttar Pradesh, not even graced by a ruin, celebrated only for its connexions with the Buddha and its backwardness. And it was duty that, after a few days of indecision, idleness and reading, was taking me along this country road, infested with peasants indifferent to wheeled vehicles, to the village which my mother's father had left as an indentured labourer more than sixty years before.

When you drive through parts of western and central India you wonder about the teeming millions; settlements are so few, and the brown land looks so unfruitful and abandoned. Here wonder was of another sort. The land was flat. The sky was high, blue and stopped in front of a small thatched hut. Here resided Ramachandra, the present head of my grandfather's branch of the Dubes.

He was away. 'Oh,' exclaimed the men and boys who had joined us, 'why did he have to choose this day?' But the shrines, they would show me the shrines. They would show me how well they had been kept; they would show me my grandfather's name carved on the shrines. They unlocked the grilled doors and showed me the images, freshly washed, freshly dressed, marked with fresh sandalwood paste, the morning's offerings of flowers not yet faded. My mind leapt years, my sense of distance and time was shaken: before me were the very replicas of the images in the prayer-room of my grand-father's house.

An old woman was crying.

'Which son? Which one?'

And it was seconds before I realized that the old woman's words were in English.

'Jussodra!' the men said, and opened a way for her. She was on her haunches and in this posture was advancing towards me, weeping, screeching out words in English and Hindi. Her pale face was cracked like drying mud; her grey eyes were dim.

'Jussodra will tell you all about your grandfather,' the men said.

Jussodra had also been to Trinidad; she knew my grandfather. We were both led from the shrine to the hut. I was made to sit on a blanket on a string bed; and Jussodra, squatting at my feet, recited my grandfather's genealogy and recounted his adventures, weeping while the IAS officer translated. For thirty-six years Jussodra had lived in this village, and in that time she had pol-ished her story into a fluent Indian *khisa* or fairy tale.

It could not have been unknown, but everyone was solemn and attentive.

When he was a young man (Jussodra said) my grandfather left this village to go to Banaras to study, as brahmins had immemorially done. But my grandfather was poor, his family poor, and times were hard; there might even have been a famine. One day my grandfather met a man who told him of a country far away called Trinidad. There were Indians in Trinidad, labourers; they needed pundits and teachers. The wages were good, land was cheap and a free passage could be arranged. The man who spoke to my grandfather knew what he was talking about. He was an *arkatia*, a recruiter; when times were good he might be stoned out of a village, but now people were willing to listen to his stories. So my grandfather indentured himself for five years and went to Trinidad. He was not, of course, made a teacher; he worked in the sugar factory. He was given a room, he was given food; and in addition he received twelve annas, fourteen pence, a day. It was a lot of money, and even today it was a good wage in this part of India, twice as much as the government paid for relief work in distress areas. My grandfather added to this by doing his pundit's work in the evenings. Banaras-trained pundits were rare in Trinidad and my grandfather was in demand. Even the sahib at the factory respected him, and one day the sahib said, 'You are a pundit. Can you help me? I want a son.' 'All right,' my grandfather said. 'I'll see that you get a son.' And when the sahib's wife gave birth to a son, the sahib was so pleased he said to my grandfather, 'You see these thirty *bighas* of land? All the canes there are yours.' My grandfather had the canes cut and sold them for two thousand rupees, and with this he went into business.

Success attracted success. A well-to-do man, long settled in Trinidad, came to my grandfather one day and said, 'I've been keeping my eye on you for some time. I can see that you are going to go far. Now I have a daughter and would like her to be married to you. I will give you three acres of land.' My grandfather was not interested. Then the man said, 'I will give you a buggy. You can hire out the buggy and make a little extra money.' So my grandfather married. He prospered. He built two houses. Soon he was wealthy enough to come back to this village and redeem twenty-five acres of his family's land. Then he went back to Trinidad. But he was a restless man. He decided to make another trip to India. 'Come back quick,' his family said to him. (Jussodra spoke these words in English: 'buggy' had also been in English.) But my grandfather didn't see Trinidad again. On the train from Calcutta he fell ill, and he wrote to his family: 'The sun is setting.'

Her story finished, Jussodra wept and wept, and no one moved.

'What do I do?' I asked the IAS officer. 'She is very old. Will I offend her if I offer her some money?'

'It will be most welcome,' he said. 'Give her some money and tell her to arrange a *kattha*, a reading of the scriptures.'

I did so.

Photographs were then brought out, as old to me and as forgotten as the images; and it was again disturbing to my sense of place and time to handle them, to see, in the middle of a vast land where I was anchored to no familiar points and could so easily be lost, the purple stamp of the Trinidad photographer – his address so clearly pictured – still bright against the fading sepia figures, in my reawakened memory forever faded, belonging to imagination and never to reality like this.

I had come to them reluctantly. I had expected little, and I had been afraid. The ugliness was all mine.

Someone else wanted to see me. It was Ramachandra's wife and she was waiting in one of the inner rooms. I went in. A white-clad figure was bowed before me; she seized my feet, in all their Veldtschoen, and began to weep. She wept and would not let go.

'What do I do now?' I asked the IAS officer.

'Nothing. Soon someone will come in and tell her that this is no way to receive a relation, that she should be offering him food instead. It is the form.'

So it happened.

But food. Though they had overwhelmed me, my colonial prudence remained. It had prevented me emptying my pocket into Jussodra's sad, wrinkled hands. Now it reminded me of the Commissioner's advice: 'Once it's cooked, you can risk it. But never touch the water.' He, however, was of the country. So: no food, I said. I was not very well and had been put on a diet.

'Water,' Ramachandra's wife said. 'At least have water.'

The IAS officer said, 'You see that field? It is a field of peas. Ask for some of those.'

We ate a pod of peas each. I promised to come back again; the boys and men walked with us to the jeep; and I drove back along a road that had been robbed of all its terror.

In the hotel in the town that evening I wrote a letter. The day had provided such an unlikely adventure. It distorted time; again and again I came back, with wonder, to my presence in that town, in that hotel at that hour. There had been those images, those photographs, those scraps of Trinidad English in that Indian village. The letter did not exhaust my exaltation. The act of writing released not isolated memories but a whole forgotten mood. The letter finished, I went to sleep. Then there was a song, a duet, at first part of memory, it seemed, part of that recaptured mood. But I was not dreaming; I was lucid. The music was real.

> Tumhin ne mujhko prem sikhaya,
> Soté hué hirdaya ko jagaya.
> Tumhin ho roop singar balam.*

It was morning. The song came from a shop across the road. It was a song of the late thirties. I had ceased to hear it years before, and until this moment I had forgotten it. I did not even know the meaning of all the words; but then I never had. It was pure mood, and in that moment between waking and sleeping it had recreated a morning in another world, a recreation of this, which continued. And walking that day in the bazaar, I saw the harmoniums, one of which had lain broken and unused, part of the irrecoverable past, in my grandmother's house, the drums, the printing-blocks, the brass vessels. Again and again I had that sense of dissolving time, that alarming but exhilarating sense of wonder at my physical self.

At the barber shop, where I stopped for a shave and

---

* 'You gave my love meaning.

You awoke my sleeping heart.

My beauty is you, my lover,

my jewels are you.'

The translation is by my friend Aley Hasan of the BBC Indian Section.

begged in vain for hot water, exaltation died. I became again an impatient traveller. The sun was high; the faint morning chill had been burnt away.

I returned to the hotel and found a beggar outside my door.

'*Kya chahiye?*' I asked, in my poor Hindi. 'What do you want?'

He looked up. His head was shaved, except for the top-knot; his face was skeletal; his eyes blazed. My impatience momentarily turned to alarm. Monk, I thought, monk; I had been reading *Karamazov*.

'I am Ramachandra Dube,' he said. 'I did not see you yesterday.'

I had expected someone less ingratiating, less of a physical wreck. His effort at a smile did not make his expression warmer. Spittle, white and viscous, gathered at the corners of his mouth.

There were some IAS cadets in the hotel. Three of them came to act as interpreters.

'I have spent all day looking for you,' Ramachandra said.

'Tell him I thank him,' I said. 'But there was really no need. I told them at the village I was coming back. Ask him, though, how he found me. I left no address.'

He had walked for some miles; then he had taken a train to the town; then he had gone around the secretariat, asking for the IAS officer who had taken out a man from Trinidad.

While the cadets translated, Ramachandra smiled. His face, I now saw, was not the face of a monk but of someone grossly undernourished; his eyes were bright with illness; he was painfully thin. He was carrying a large white sack. This he now humped with difficulty on to my table.

'I have brought you some rice from your grandfather's land,' he said. 'I have also brought you *parsad*, offerings, from your grandfather's shrine.'

'What do I do?' I asked the cadets. 'I don't want thirty pounds of rice.'

'He doesn't want you to take it all. You just take a few grains. Take the *parsad*, though.'

I took a few grains of the poor rice, and took the *parsad*, grubby little grey beads of hard sugar, and placed them on the table.

'I have been looking for you all day,' Ramachandra said.

'I know.'

'I walked, then I took a train, then I walked around the town and asked for you.'

'It was good of you to take all that trouble.'

'I want to see you. I want to have you in my poor hut and to give you a meal.'

'I am coming back to the village in a few days.'

'I have been looking for you all day.'

'I know.'

'I want to have you in my hut. I want to talk to you.'

'We will talk when I come to the village.'

'I want to see you there. I want to talk to you. I have important things to say to you.'

'We will talk when the time comes.'

'Good. Now I will leave you. I have been looking for you all day. I have things to say to you. I want to have you in my hut.'

'I can't keep this up,' I said to the IAS cadets. 'Tell him to go away. Thank him and so on, but tell him to go.'

One of the cadets passed on my message, involving and extending it with expressions of courtesy.

'Now I must leave you,' Ramachandra replied. 'I must get back to the village before dark.'

'Yes, I can see that you must get back before dark.'

'But how can I talk to you in the village?'

'I will bring an interpreter.'

'I want to have you in my poor hut. I have spent all day looking for you. In the village there are too many people. How can I talk to you in the village?'

'Why can't you talk to me in the village? Can't we really get him out?'

They eased him towards the door.

'I have brought you rice from your grandfather's land.'

'Thank you. It will get dark soon.'

'I want to talk to you when you come.'

'We will talk.'

The door was closed. The cadets went away. I lay down on the bed below the fan. Then I had a shower. I was towelling myself when I heard a scratching on the barred window.

It was Ramachandra, in the veranda, attempting a smile. I summoned no interpreters. I needed none to understand what he was saying.

'I cannot talk in the village. There are too many people.'

'We will talk in the village,' I said in English. 'Now go home. You travel too much.' By signs I persuaded him to edge away from the window. Quickly, then, I drew the curtains.

Some days passed before I decided to go back to the village. The journey began badly. There was some trouble about transport and it was not until the middle of the afternoon that we were able to leave. Our progress was slow. It was market day at the junction settlement and the road was dangerous with carts, now occupying the right-hand lane, now changing without warning to the left, their manoeuvres obscured by clouds of dust. Dust was thick and constant; it obliterated trees, fields, villages. There were traffic jams, the carts inextricably snarled, the drivers then as passive as their bullocks.

At the junction it was simple chaos. I breathed dust. There was dust in my hair, dust down my shirt, dust, nauseatingly, on my fingernails. We halted and waited for the traffic to clear. Then our driver disappeared, taking the ignition key. It was useless to look for him: that would only have meant groping about in the dust. We sat in the jeep and occasionally sounded the horn. Half an hour later the driver returned. His eyelashes, moustache and oiled hair were blond with dust, but his smile was wet and triumphant: he had managed to buy some vegetables. It was late afternoon when we got on to the embankment; and the sun was setting, converting the dust into clouds of pure gold, so that each person walked in a golden aura, when we arrived at the village. No terror attached to the land now, no surprise. I felt I knew it well. Yet some anxiety remained: the village held Ramachandra.

He was waiting for me. He was without the cloak he had worn to the hotel. He wore only a dhoti and sacred thread, and I could scarcely bear to look at his emaciated, brittle body. As soon as he saw me he held himself in an attitude of ecstatic awe: shaved shining head thrown back, eyes staring, foam-flecked mouth resolutely closed, both sticks of arms raised. We already had an audience, and he was demonstrating his possession of me. It was seconds before he relaxed.

more dignified, presented me with a letter and withdrew; the ink on the envelope was still wet. A boy ran out to the jeep, tucking his shirt into his trousers, and asked for a lift into the town. While Ramachandra had been outlining his plans for litigation, while the letter was being written, this boy had hurriedly bathed, dressed and prepared his bundle; his clothes were fresh, his hair still wet. My visit had thrown the brahmins into a frenzy of activity. Too much had been assumed; I felt overwhelmed; I wished to extricate myself at once.

'Shall we take him on?' the IAS man asked, nodding towards the boy.

'No, let the idler walk.'

We drove off. I did not wave. The headlamps of the jeep shot two separate beams into the day's slowly settling dust which, made turbulent again by our passage, blotted out the scattered lights of the village.

So it ended, in futility and impatience, a gratuitous act of cruelty, self-reproach and flight.

FLIGHT

To be packed, after a year's journey, before dinner; to have dinner; to be at the airline office at ten, to see the decorative little fountain failed, the wing-shaped counter empty, the tiled turquoise basin of the fountain empty and wetly littered, the lights dim, the glossy magazines disarrayed and disregarded, the Punjabi emigrants sitting disconsolately with their bundles in a corner near the weighing machine; to be at the airport at eleven for an aircraft that leaves at midnight; and then to wait until after three in the morning, intermittently experiencing the horrors of an Indian public lavatory, is to know anxiety, exasperation and a creeping stupor. There comes a point at which the night is written off, and one waits for morning. The minutes lengthen; last night recedes far beyond last night. Lucidity grows intense but blinkered. The actions of minutes before are dim and isolated, and a cause of muted wonder when remembered. So even at the airport India faded; so during these hours its reality was wiped away, until more than space and time lay between it and me.

Paper fell into my lap in the aircraft. Long blond hair and a pair of big blue eyes appeared above the seat in front of me, and tiny feet pattered against the small of my back. 'Children!' cried the American next to me, awakening from middle-aged, safety-belted sleep.

332

'Where do they take on all these children? Why are all these children *travelling*? What's my crazy luck that every time I go to sleep on a plane and wake up I see children? Shall I tell you a funny thing a friend of mine said to a child on a plane? He said, "Sonny, why don't you go outside and play?" Little girl, why don't you take your pretty paper and go outside and play?' Eyes and hair sank below the dark blue seat. 'That child behind me is going to get hurt. The little bastard is kicking my kidneys in. Sir! Madam! Will you please *control* your child? *It* . . . is . . . annoying my *wife*.' She, the wife, lay relaxed beside him, her skirt riding up above a middle-aged slackly-stockinged knee. There was a smile on her face; she was asleep.

No sleep for me. Only a continuing stupor, heightened by the roar of the engines. I made frequent trips to the lavatory to refresh myself with the airline's eau-de-cologne. The Punjabis at the rear were wakeful, in a ripe smell: one or two had already been sick on the blue carpet. Lights were low. The night was long. We were flying against time, into a receding morning. Yet light was coming; and when at daybreak we reached Beirut it was like arriving, after a magical journey, with all its attendant torment, in a fresh, glittering world. Rain had fallen; the tarmac was glazed and cool. Beyond it was a city which one knew to be a city, full of men as whole as these who, in airport dungarees, now wheeled gangways and drove up in electric lorries to unload luggage: labourers, menials, yet arrogant in their gait, their big bodies and their skills. India was part of the night: a dead world, a long journey.

Rome, the airport, morning still. The Boeings and Caravelles lying this way and that, like toys. And within the airport building a uniformed girl paced up and down the concourse. She wore a jockey-cap hat, to me a new fashion; she wore boots, also new to me. She was extravagantly made up: she required to be noticed. How could I explain, how could I admit as reasonable, even to myself, my distaste, my sense of the insubstantiality and wrongness of the new world to which I had been so swiftly transported? This life confirmed that other death; yet that death rendered this fraudulent.

In the late afternoon I was in Madrid, most elegant of cities. Here I was to spend two or three days. I had been last in this city as a student, ten years before. Here I might have taken up my old life. I was a tourist, free, with money. But a whole experience had just occurred; India had ended only twenty-four hours before. It was a journey that ought not to have been made; it had broken my life in two. 'Write me as soon as you get to Europe,' an Indian friend had said. 'I want your freshest impressions.' I forget now what I wrote. It was violent and incoherent; but, like everything I wrote about India, it exorcized nothing.

In my last week in Delhi I had spent some time in the cloth shops, and I had arrived in Madrid with a jacket-length of material in an untied brown parcel printed with Hindi characters. This was the gift of an architect I had known for a short time. Two or three days after we met he had made a declaration of his affection and loyalty, and I had reciprocated. This was part of the sweetness of India; it went with everything else. He had driven me to the airport and had put up with my outbursts at news of the aircraft's delay. We had coffee; then, before he left, he gave me the parcel. 'Promise me you will have it stitched into a jacket as soon as you get to Europe,' he said.

I did so now; and above all the confused impressions

of a year, then, was this fresh memory of a friend and his gift of Indian cloth.

Some days later in London, facing as for the first time a culture whose point, going by the advertisements and shop-windows, appeared to be home-making, the creation of separate warm cells; walking down streets of such cells past gardens left derelict by the hard winter and trying, in vain, to summon up a positive response to this city where I had lived and worked; facing my own emptiness, my feeling of being physically lost, I had a dream.

An oblong of stiff new cloth lay before me, and I had the knowledge that if only out of this I could cut a smaller oblong of specific measurements, a specific section of this cloth, then the cloth would begin to unravel of itself, and the unravelling would spread from the cloth to the table to the house to all matter, *until the whole trick was undone.* Those were the words that were with me as I flattened the cloth and studied it for the clues which I knew existed, which I desired above everything else to find, but which I knew I never would.

The world is illusion, the Hindus say. We talk of despair, but true despair lies too deep for formulation. It was only now, as my experience of India defined itself more properly against my own homelessness, that I saw how close in the past year I had been to the total Indian negation, how much it had become the basis of thought and feeling. And already, with this awareness, in a world where illusion could only be a concept and not something felt in the bones, it was slipping away from me. I felt it as something true which I could never adequately express and never seize again.

February 1962–February 1964